LEAVING HOME

DUANE A. EIDE

LEAVING HOME

iUniverse books may be ordered through booksellers or by contacting:

iUniverse
1663 Liberty Drive
Bloomington, IN 47403
www.iuniverse.com
1-800-Authors (1-800-288-4677)

ISBN: 978-1-4917-2128-5 (sc)
ISBN: 978-1-4917-2129-2 (e)

Library of Congress Control Number: 2014901322

Print information available on the last page.

iUniverse rev. date: 04/22/2015

Dedication

To five important Eides:

Arthur, Thelma, Patricia, Tasha, and Patrick

Acknowledgement

Thank you to Wallace Wierson and to all my friends at Bay View Grand, Puerto Vallarta, Mexico, for their tireless editing of *Leaving Home*

Chapter 1

He leaned forward, grasping the neck of the Shetland pony, his closest friend. Though the pony definitely possessed a mind of his own, often deciding where he would run and where he would not, he still afforded Shane Stenlund constant companionship. Galloping through the recently plowed field, the pony, named First Mate since Shane considered himself the captain, responded with an increased rhythm. Familiar with the field, the pony skillfully stepped over small clumps of soil, some soft, some hard, turned up by curved plow shares which helped prepare the soil for the next spring seeding. Regardless of their size and texture, these scattered clumps of dirt could cause a pony to stumble.

Shane, ten years old, dreamed about riding out on the range, just like those cowboys in the movies. Fully aware of the unrealistic nature of this dream, he still gained from morning rides with his pony some sense of what roaming the range might entail. With the wind whipping back his long, black hair and a broad smile spreading his lips over slightly protruding teeth, and with his knees gently urging his pony to go faster, he could think of nothing that excited him more.

Without a saddle, Shane relied on his experience to sit securely on First Mate's back, his short legs spread over the pony's belly, his hands gripping the bridle intertwined with the long strands of the pony's mane. With all thoughts of the burdens of farm life forgotten, Shane sat up to yell "yippee" to the morning air.

Suddenly, First Mate dropped from beneath him. The pony stumbled, his head dropping, sending Shane sailing through the air. Hitting the plowed field hard, the boy rolled over several times before landing with his face pushed against the dirt. Behind him First Mate lay on his back, feet extended straight up into the air.

Shane rolled to his back, dazed by the abrupt end to his ride. He eased himself to his knees, nothing hurt except, perhaps, his pride. He turned to see his pony struggling to stand up on all four legs. Successful in the struggle, First Mate shook himself violently and moved unharmed closer to Shane, who reached to grab the pony's bridle, pulling himself to his feet. He patted his pony's neck, smoothing the disheveled mane. Reminded of his mother's advice, to avoid future insecurity always mount quickly after falling off, he jumped to swing his leg over First Mate's back. Apparently, nothing damaged for either pony or rider, Shane headed back to the barn to return his pony to the comfort of a clean stall.

"How was your ride?" Martin Stenlund, Shane's dad, leaned his six foot, slender frame on a pitch fork he used to spread hay to the five cattle confined to their stalls until after milking. It represented the hay Shane had pushed down from the loft earlier and which had delayed his pony ride.

At fifty-six, Shane's dad enjoyed excellent health, the demands of his farm keeping him in good physical condition. His once dark hair age now touched with gray around his temples. Bright blue eyes and an engaging smile, to Shane not used often enough, accentuated his tan Norwegian skin. The smooth contours of his narrow face sloped away from a distinct nose with nostrils that flared to show his anger. Again in Shane's mind he witnessed those flared nostrils much too often.

The owner of six hundred acres of Red River Valley farmland, a few miles west of Twin Pines and a few miles east of the North Dakota border, Martin Stenlund provided very well for his family producing tons of grain from the fertile land he acquired from his father. Essentially a grain farmer, Martin maintained a few cattle, pigs and chickens primarily for the family. His small herd of cattle supplied the family with dairy products; the chickens provided eggs and chicken dinners; the pigs offered pork chops and ham. To Shane fell the responsibility of feeding the chickens, picking their eggs, and cleaning their roosts. In addition, he took charge of feeding fifteen voracious pigs, whose eating habits reflected perfectly their name, and helped his dad milk the five cows.

Shane and his family shared the prosperity of the farm. Shane realized each family member had to assume a part of the responsibilities that comprised farm living. However, to Shane the distribution of those responsibilities was simply not fair. In his opinion, Danni, his sixteen year old sister, spent most of her time fixing her hair, smiling at herself in the mirror, or sitting on her ass playing with the computer. At the same time, his dad expected him to do all these jobs, milk the cows, feed the pigs, feed the chickens, pick the eggs and clean chicken shit off the roost.

"Okay." Shane answered, avoiding any hint of the mishap in the plowed field.

"Just okay?" His dad inquired.

"Yeah, I guess he wasn't very excited about running this morning." Shane kicked at pile of wet straw. "Maybe he's getting old." He led First Mate to his stall.

"Maybe, you push him too hard." Martin resumed his work.

Shane completed putting First Mate back in his small stall at the far end of the barn. Removing First Mate's bridle, Shane shook his head. Nothing pleased his dad, who always expressed some dissatisfaction with nearly everything Shane did. At least that was his impression.

Earlier in the morning Shane awakened with plans to ride his pony before anything else, to him a great way to start a Saturday, a day off from school. Shane had only opened his eyes when his mom, Iris, stood at the bottom of the stairs calling to wakeup her son. Both Shane and his sister enjoyed separate bedrooms located on the second floor of the Stenlund's modest but comfortable farm house. In the family for fifty years, the house gave the Stenlunds a spacious home with room for all to seek solitude if so desired. Often Shane so desired. He loved his family, harboring some reservations about his sister. Still he found delight in sometimes just being alone in his own world.

"Yeah," Shane grumbled.

"Hurry and get dressed. Your dad needs you in the barn."

"Shit!" Shane uttered to himself. "What does he want now?" He yelled back to his mom.

"I don't know. Just hurry and find out for yourself."

Shane pushed back the covers. Sitting on the edge of his bed, he ran his fingers through his long, black hair, stretched his arms to the side, then rubbed his eyes. He shared his father's bright blue eyes, naturally tan skin and delicate facial features. His small frame and, in his opinion, the accident of birth cursed him with delicate features often labeled as cute. When he used it, his smile could impress anyone, except, perhaps, his dad. His mom, on the other hand, occasionally pleaded with him to smile more often. His sister Danni typically considered any attention to her brother a waste of time. This morning's events did little to encourage any smiles.

He hung his legs over the side of his bed and stared at the opposite wall where hung a picture gallery of horses and baseball players. Though not a dedicated athlete, Shane liked to play baseball. Small for his age, he compensated for his size with an aggressive approach to whatever he did, including baseball. During the summer when demands of the farm didn't interfere, he played Little League baseball in Twin Pines. A left fielder with impressive speed, he could race down most fly balls hit his way.

Complying with his mom's command, Shane rushed through brushing his teeth and getting dressed. With steps heavy on the stairs, he reluctantly headed for yet another stupid job, one with obvious priority over that morning ride with First Mate.

His mother turned away from the kitchen sink, responding to the noise of her son's descent from up stairs. Still in her morning robe, she smiled at her petulant son. A slight woman, about five feet three with abundant, dark brown hair streaked with a touch of gray, she tugged on her robe which failed to conceal the few pounds age added to her small frame. Still the demands of a farm wife and mother left little time for lounging. At fifty-four years old she retained the appearance of a much younger woman. A dedicated mother, she always welcomed the morning with a smile, even for Shane, who greeted most mornings with a sneer.

"Can I get you anything, milk, juice?" She asked.

Shane paused briefly considering his mother's request. "Naw." He shook his head and stomped out the door.

Entering the barn, he faced his dad, not happy with his son's lethargy. "Well, you finally made it." With a gentle poke of his son's shoulder, Mr. Stenlund spread his lips into one of his rare smiles, not unlike the smiles of his son, "Do you think Saturday is a holiday?"

Shane stood firm, his eyes focused on the floor beneath him. He didn't find humor in much of what his dad said. Instead he saw his father as a task master without regard for his son's interests. After all, that son was only ten years old.

Martin squeezed his son's arm. "Come on. This will only take a short time. We need to push down hay from the loft and spread it in the mangers. You push it down; I'll spread it. Then you can do whatever you want."

Shane nodded, anticipating that morning ride on First Mate, then headed for the ladder to the loft attached to the wall behind him.

Chapter 2

Shane tolerated school. Generally, school reciprocated. He completed his homework reluctantly but regularly, his mom instrumental in his pseudo diligence. A precocious infant, Shane offered the promise of a productive student like his older sister. By the time he entered kindergarden, he had mastered the alphabet; he could count to a hundred; he could read Dr. Seuss books. His motivation derived more from a quest for independence than a taste for the thrill of learning. At home someone always hovered over him giving him directions, explaining why he was wrong, always telling him what to do. He often questioned why they couldn't leave him alone? Why his family couldn't treat him with a little more understanding of his quest for independence?

Early elementary grades found Shane exercising his independence, devoting more time to dreaming about what he would do after school each day rather than concentrating on his school work. Besides, most of what occurred in class he believed he already knew. His pony occupied a large chunk of his dreaming time. At a mere eight years old, he acquired his pony, a moment of parental generosity that both Mom and Dad frequently regretted. Shane's interest in his pony far exceeded his interest in school responsibilities. Nonetheless, he managed an average academic performance, his innate intelligence rendering work in the classroom much too easy.

Small for his age, Shane never sought leadership among his peers. Perhaps his size or simply his nature destined him to the edges of social interaction. Yes, when he wished to do so, he made friends easily with his warm, engaging smile that concealed a hint of insecurity. Consequently, social passivity suited him perfectly.

Often his mom worried about her son's reluctance to seek friends his own age. Time spent with his pony or with studying his baseball cards offered him sufficient satisfaction during idle hours.

After another weekend of time riding First Mate, including surviving the mishap in the plowed field, and completing the usual list of chores, Shane sat in the middle of the first row in Miss Elliot's sixth grade classroom. Starting in kindergarden, Shane attended school in Twin Pines, a northern Minnesota city of thirty-thousand people. Very likely he would eventually conclude his public education in Twin Pines. His sister Danni, already a sophomore, would do the same.

Oblivious to Miss Elliot's instructions, Shane let his mind stray with attention to the weekend incident in the plowed field. Resulting in no damage to either him or his pony, it certainly could have caused serious injury. In his mind Shane envisioned a range of crippling consequences for both of them. Seeing his pony on his back remained a stark memory. His thoughts brought on drowsiness, his eyes drooping, his head falling to his chest.

"Shane, oh Shane, are you tired today?" Miss Elliot's voice collided with the images floating through his mind.

His head popped up, eyes wide open. Shaking his head, Shane mumbled, "No."

"If you need to rest, I can send you to the nurse's office." Miss Elliot humored Shane to the enjoyment of the rest of the class.

Embarrassed by the attention he now suffered, Shane sat straight, hands folded on top his desk.

"Well," the teacher persisted with a smile, "do you want a pass to the nurse's office?"

Shane again shook his head, "No."

"Please, then, would you pay attention." Miss Elliot cautioned.

He fixed his eyes on the obscure name carved in the top of his desk as bits of laughter skipped around the classroom.

"Now that we have Shane's attention, let's continue with the questions on page thirty-seven of your history book."

Chapter 3

In the hall students deposited books in their lockers as they prepared for lunch. Having survived what Shane considered humiliation, he stood before his locker attempting to open the door while cradling three text books. Setting the books on the floor, he succeeded in unlocking the door. Narrow but tall, the locker presented another problem for smaller students, a group including Shane. With books in hand again, he strained reaching up as far as his slight body would allow, only to have one of the books tumble to the floor. Frustrated with events of the morning and now the wayward books, he kicked the fallen book across the hall.

A boy Shane knew only as Chuck stood before his locker a few feet away. Much bigger than Shane, he watched as the locker drama unfolded. After Shane kicked the book in disgust, Chuck intervened.

Standing in front of Shane, Chuck, at least a head taller, asked, "Need some help?"

Shane stepped back, looking up into Chuck's face, his answer couched in defiance, "No, I don't."

Extending his arm, Chuck volunteered, "Here, give me the books. I'll put em away for you."

Shane pushed Chuck's extended arm aside. "I don't need your damn help." He growled. "Leave me alone!"

"Okay." Chuck agreed. "Just keep your hands off me, kid." He gave Shane a gentle shove on the shoulder.

In a moment of senseless anger, Shane charged the much bigger Chuck, who caught Shane, pinning his arms to his side.

The hallway commotion caught the attention of a hall monitor who quickly moved in to stop the action before it developed into a serious fight.

In minutes the minor altercation found Chuck and Shane sitting morosely in Principal Dwight Littleton's office while they waited to explain the reason for the problem. Each attempted to give an account favorable to himself. Despite the reluctance to admit guilt and the insistence to place the blame on each other, the rules of the school demanded a two day suspension for fighting. The principal explained the rule then summoned the parents of each boy, insisting they come to school to take their sons home.

For only the second time Shane sat in Mr. Littleton's office, a small area with the usual desk, filing cabinets, and a book case covering one wall. Sullen, Shane sat between his mom and dad on plain chairs positioned in front of the principal's desk. Behind his desk, Mr. Littleton explained the school's policy on fighting. He then turned to Shane.

"Shane, can you explain what happened between you and Chuck in the hall?"

Shane studied the floor, his hands folded in his lap. He glanced up at the principal but said nothing. Sitting on his son's left, Mr. Stenlund faced him. With a firm voice he addressed his son. "Shane, Mr. Littleton has asked you a question. Now show some respect and answer him."

Shane turned to look, perhaps for support, at his mom sitting on his right. In his eyes she could read the question, "Do I have to?" Iris placed her hand around her son's shoulder. "Go ahead. Tell us what happened," she urged.

Shane shifted in his chair. He looked at his mom then down at his hands folded in his lap. "He made fun of me," he blurted out.

"Can you tell us exactly what Chuck did to make fun of you?" Mr. Littleton spoke with a calm voice.

"He said I was too short." Shane sat erect in his chair.

"Why would he say that?" Mr. Littleton pressed Shane for more details.

"He wanted to put my books away." Shane answered quickly in little more than a whisper.

Impatient with the progress of the conference, Mr. Stenlund stated, "Speak up, son. Let's get this over with. You were there. Now explain exactly what happened."

Of course, Shane and his parents had discussed in detail the incident the day it happened. Still, the intent of the conference with his parents emphasized the importance of his acknowledging his role in the incident. To fulfill that intent, the principal wished to have Shane explain the situation from his perspective. Shane rested his chin on his chest, then turned to face his dad. He explained the sequence of actions which led to the physical contact. In his explanation, he avoided placing all the blame on Chuck. However, he insisted Chuck started it all by insulting him about his size. Finally he claimed they didn't really fight anyway.

Silence settled over the principal's office. Shane slumped in his chair, his hands gripping the sides of the seat. Briefly, he traveled back in time. For two days he had dreaded the inevitable conference involving his parents. The principal's order that he and Chuck faced a two day suspension shocked him. Never had anything like that happened before. His dad would kill him. To his relief, his mother arrived to take him home from school. His dad worked in the field; nonetheless, he would have to face him later.

Shane remembered vividly the mild alarm shown on his mother's face when she entered the principal's office to pick up her son and to drive him home. Her immediate response was "What on earth happened?"

The twenty minute drive home included a litany of questions eliciting vague, evasive answers from Shane. He insisted on his innocence in the whole incident. What happened was not a fight. He did not like others making fun of him. Though his mom pressed him for details about what he considered making fun entailed, he failed to offer any examples.

That evening the dreaded encounter with his dad occurred. He, too, probed for an explanation of what happened and why it happened. He, too, received little convincing detail. Much to

Shane's surprise, his dad did not threaten to kill him nor did he ignite in anger. Instead, he sat with his son for nearly an hour discussing with him the importance of accepting who we are with all its promise and limitations, and avoiding misinterpreting the response of others to us. Shane said little during this session, one unique in his memory. However, his dad, obviously, understood his son far more than his son realized.

The principal broke the silence. "Thank you for the explanation, Shane. I can appreciate your side of the story." He smiled with eyes fixed on Shane. "I think you may have misunderstood Chuck's intentions to help you. For a variety of reasons at one time or another, we all have been guilty of that." After a short pause, he addressed his comments to all three members of the Stenlund family seated before him. "I want to stress that Shane has caused no trouble in all the years he has attended this school. I think, maybe, most young people could be better students, but according to his records, Shane has performed quite well in his studies. I emphasize he has caused no discipline problems. I don't anticipate he will again." Rising from his chair, Mr. Littleton walked around to stand before the Stenlunds.

"Shane, I'll expect to see you early tomorrow morning to join Miss Elliot's class. Mr. and Mrs. Stenlund, thank you for coming in this morning." He smiled. "I guess you didn't have much choice, but thank you anyway for your gracious attention."

As Shane walked with his parents toward the school parking lot, his broad smile gave evidence of a much brighter day.

Chapter 4

"You damned old bitch!" Shane jerked his hand from under an irascible hen that resented intrusion into her nest. Collecting eggs each morning fell to Shane, in his opinion, only one of his many jobs around the farm. He slipped his hand under the old hen, determined to secure any eggs concealed by her feathery body. She greeted him with another harsh peck of her weapon like beak.

"Damn you!" Shane exclaimed, grabbing the offending chicken around the neck and hurling her out of the nest.

"What the hell you doing, son?" Shane's dad filled the door way in the ancient chicken coop still standing after fifty years of housing mostly chickens.

Alarmed by the sound of his dad's voice, Shane turned to face him. "Every time I try to pick eggs from this old crab, she pecks me." He shook his right hand. "It hurts."

Mr. Stenlund moved closer, reaching out to inspect his son's hand. A small red blotch marked the spot of the latest peck. A smile lightened his face. "You know, son, if all you ever did was make eggs, you probably wouldn't like someone coming in every day to take them either."

A puzzled look was Shane's only response. His dad padded him on the head, a habit Shane disliked and considered appropriate only for little kids, not big kids like him. Shane turned, picked up the egg basket, and resumed his job of collecting eggs.

"When you're done with the eggs, would you dump a couple more buckets of feed in the pig trough?" Mr. Stenlund turned to leave, then paused. "Do you have any plans for the day?"

Shane again faced his dad, placing the egg basket on the dirt floor of the chicken coop. "Yeah, I do. Why?" His tone of voice reflected irritation with the expectation of more work before his dad left him alone.

"Nothing. Just wondered." Shane's dad stepped out of the chicken coop. Over his shoulder, he asked, "What are your plans?"

"Not much. Maybe a short ride on First Mate."

Late spring concluded the hectic time of final cultivation and seeding of crops. For weeks Shane had spent his time after school and on weekends driving a tractor pulling a cultivator or a drill, the machine used for seeding. Why it acquired the name "drill," he did not know nor did he care. By the end of the school year, in early June, he and his dad with the help of neighbors had completed most of the spring planting. Except for the need to cultivate acres of corn to rid the rows of weeds, summer weeks offered a time for Shane to do something other than chores. On this day, he planned a long ride on First Mate, his long time pony, good friend, and companion.

The Red River Valley stretches for miles, defining the border between Minnesota and the Dakotas. Shane's ride took him west toward the Red River, only miles from his home. First Mate traveled slowly, between a trot and a gentle gallop. Avoiding the recently seeded acres, Shane guided his pony on the edges of the fields, space required for the movement of farm equipment from one field to another.

The rhythm of First Mate's motion relaxed Shane, his eyes following the edges of the fields that blended in with the far off horizon. Shane and his family traveled enough for Shane to know that few places were as flat as the Red River Valley. In the distance only a narrow band of trees bordering the Red River interrupted his view. Otherwise, he thought of something someone said about this land he called home: "On a clear day you could almost see for ever."

Family trips to Duluth, only one hundred miles east of his home, gave Shane the chance to see hills, cliffs, and rocks, something other than flat, boring farm land. The few times he traveled with his family three hundred miles southeast to the Twin

Cities of Minneapolis/St. Paul added to his delight in lakes, hills, trees, and crowds of people as well as expanded for Shane the lure of big cities. A summer trip, two years ago, to the Wisconsin Dells further established Shane's preference to land with character, not flatness.

Approaching the banks of the Red River, First Mate stepped carefully over dried mud and debris left by recent spring flooding, an annual event along the banks of the Red River. A fallen tree invited Shane to stop, to dismount and to rest his sore butt. Even after several years of riding, he couldn't escape the inevitable. He lacked sufficient padding where it counted.

Leaning against the fallen tree, Shane watched First Mate, who grazed on the scant grass that struggled to penetrate the silt deposited by the flooding river. The day afforded a perfect opportunity to relax, to forget about farms, chores, and irascible chickens. A bright sun slowly roamed a brilliant blue sky. Days like this, Shane thought, didn't happen very often in the Red River Valley. More often, brisk winds and clouds precluded relaxing outdoors. His eyes resting on a far away grain elevator, he followed the images in his mind. At one time those images nearly always had something to do with cowboys, horses, and riding the range.

At twelve years old, Shane grinned now as he thought about those juvenile dreams. He had moved beyond them, replaced by visions of living in the city free from pesky farm chores, from cold mornings in the barn and long evenings after school. He envisioned riding his bike, not a pony, around the lakes and parks so plentiful in the Twin Cities. He envisioned all the things to do: the movies, the stores in huge shopping centers, the baseball diamonds and, of course, the Twins.

First Mate took his time munching the fresh grass. Shane's mind drifted to a trip only weeks ago to the Twin Cities. A shopping trip for his sister Danni, for him, it added to the lure of the big city. In addition, the confinement to the back seat of the car on the long ride to the Twin Cities only reinforced the animosity that simmered between him and his eighteen year old sister.

Danni, at five feet eight inches, carried herself with pride. Dark hair like her brother's, helping to define bright blue eyes under well groomed eye brows, a delicate nose above full lips, an attractive figure, and permanently tan skin like the rest of her family, all combined to make her proud and confident. She graduated from Twin Pines High School at the conclusion of the school year in June. With relief Shane anticipated the day she would leave for college. Accepted at St. Thomas University in St. Paul, she would move there some time in August, not soon enough for Shane. Was it personality, temperament, chemistry or genes? Whatever the cause, Shane and his sister simply never could avoid verbal confrontations. Maybe the six years' difference in their ages formed the basis for their conflict. Certainly, Danni reminded Shane often enough that he acted like a baby.

On the day of the shopping trip to shower his sister with more money and more attention, Shane determined he wouldn't join them. As much as the big city intrigued him, he wished to avoid watching his parents pander to his arrogant sister. His suggestion that he stay home, his dad rejected. Reluctantly, he climbed into the back seat of the family car to sit next to his sister for the four hour drive to the Twin Cities.

Chapter 5

On the way, the mere suggestion annoyed him of possibly following them around as Mom and Dad wasted tons of money showering Danni with clothes and whatever else she needed to attend college. Shane's hint at Danni's favored place in the family, at one time, would have ignited a fierce response from her. Maturity softened her reaction to her younger brother. As an attractive, eighteen year old, high school graduate, she resisted his inflammatory comments which not long ago would have dragged them into an argument.

Riding next to her brother, Danni shifted her position to command his attention. "Shane, I don't think it's fair for you to whine about favoritism." She grinned. "You don't look neglected. Just remember. In a few weeks I'm gone. You can then have all the attention you want."

Shane could never think of the right thing to say when he most needed to say it. Looking out his side window, he said nothing. Then he blurted, "You think you're so smart. Every time you ask, Mom and Dad jump."

Danni faced straight ahead, aware that whatever she said would fail to placate her abused, little brother. "Maybe if you weren't such a complainer, life would be better for you."

Shane turned sharply to face his sister. "Maybe if you weren't such a smart ass, I wouldn't complain so much."

"Okay, that's enough back there." Mr. Stenlund advised. "Maybe we should just stop and let you two have it out along the road. We have a whole day together. Let's make it enjoyable for a change."

For a change. The words tumbled over in Shane's mind. The real change he waited for would happen when his sister left for college. He stood up from his place next to the fallen tree, stretched, and ran his hands through his thick hair which he insisted hang over his ears and neck. He walked toward First Mate patiently waiting for his captain to decide to return. It was time. As Shane mounted his pony, his smile hinted at satisfaction with his day.

That evening Shane completed his chores with marked alacrity, motivated by his rich, day dreams of the afternoon and impending departure of his nemesis, Danni. The next morning required him to arise early, first to complete his morning duties and then to drive with his dad into Twin Pines for a baseball tournament.

Since preschool age, Shane enjoyed baseball and played each summer in the Twin Pines Little League and next year Babe Ruth League. Consequently, he decided to go to bed early. Good rest before a day of baseball, his dad recommended, could make a big difference in his performance.

That night Shane had a dream, a vivid dream. He lived in Minneapolis, free from parental restraint and free from an arrogant sister. In his dream, he walked the historic Hennepin Avenue lined with theaters, restaurants, and night clubs. The blaze of lights extended for blocks. People crowded the sidewalks; cars inched along the congested street.

In his dream, Shane waited at a busy intersection, crushed against others standing on the curb anticipating the green light. Suddenly, out of the crowd emerged an older gentleman, white hair hanging to his shoulders, a ragged pack hanging from his back. Oblivious to the traffic, the old man stepped onto the street. A taxi cab speeded closer and closer. Shane watched in consternation as the man either failed to see the taxi or simply didn't care.

When a tragic collision seemed inevitable, Shane, in his dream, burst out of the crowd, reached out to grab the old man's back pack. With all his strength, Shane pulled hard, the man landing on top of him as the taxi rushed by. Shane squeezed out from under the man he just saved from a violent encounter with a taxi cab to sit up to generous applause from those waiting at the intersection.

In the morning only shreds of the dream survived. However, Shane could still hear the applause. With a wide smile, he greeted the morning.

Chapter 6

Shane poked more hay into First Mate's manger. He walked around to step into the stall from the back. First Mate turned his head to greet his friend and captain. At fourteen and growing, Shane rode his pony less frequently than he used to. His duties on the farm, his responsibilities at school, and his commitment to baseball left little time for the long, casual rides he so enjoyed earlier. Perhaps his advancing maturity and size also imposed some restrictions on his riding a Shetland pony.

Shane draped his arms around First Mate's neck. "What do you think, Buddy? Should I go or shouldn't I?"

Three days before, Danni had called to invite her family to spend the weekend in the Twin Cities. A junior at St. Thomas University, she took full advantage of her college education, including the celebration of home coming. In the morning, Saturday, Shane and his mom and dad presumably would drive to the Twin Cities to visit Danni, see the football game, then spend the night in a motel.

Shane struggled with his decision to go, not sure if his parents would permit him to stay home for the weekend, another of those unreasonable restrictions he resented. On the other hand, the big city offered much that farm life did not. Since his first visit to Minneapolis several years ago, he had acquired a fascination for the big city, viewing it as a way of life far superior to that on a farm. Besides the relationship with his sister had mellowed. No longer did they engage in the bitter verbal battles of years past. He wasn't sure why their relationship improved except maybe her absence from home removed the opportunity for confrontation and irritation. Though he likely would not admit his role in the sibling contention, he, too, may have matured a bit. Still, maturation failed to alter his intolerance for life on the farm. At the same time, life in the big city retained its appeal for him for reasons he couldn't always explain.

Next to First Mate, his best friend, Shane stood perplexed as all of these conflicting thoughts swirled through his head. He padded First Mate on the neck and repeated the question. "What do you think, old buddy? Should I or shouldn't I?"

For whatever reason, First Mate nodded his head in what Shane interpreted as a "yes." A smile acknowledged his acceptance of First Mate's response. "Why you old son of gun. You must understand me better than anyone else around here. If you think I should go tomorrow, I guess I should. Thank you." He folded his arms around First Mate's neck and gave him a firm hug. Leaving the stall, he applied a solid pat on his pony's rump.

That evening Shane and his parents chatted about their early morning departure. Shane deliberately ignored his earlier debate with himself over joining them or not. With conviction, he believed they would have refused his request to stay home so why, he thought, even bring it up. Their conversation covered what to take since they would spend Saturday night in a motel. Danni lived in a college dormitory offering no chance of accommodating any guests. They also discussed the need to tend to morning chores. Cows, pigs, chickens, and, of course, First Mate needed food to sustain them for more than twenty-four hours. After all this was a farm, and it demanded a very early morning for Shane and his dad. Attendance at the one o'clock game required them to leave home, at least, by nine which meant up by six.

Besides the usual routine with the few farm animals, mid October found the Stenlunds released from the burden of autumn harvest. Except for several acres of corn waiting for picking, all grain fields stood black with recent fall cultivation. That fact gave endless joy to Shane and maybe even to his father.

Blending in with I-94 traffic just east of Moorhead, the Stenlunds sat in silence as on coming traffic rushed on the other side of the median. A familiar route to the Twin Cities, it required them to pay little attention to its curves, hills and interchanges. Iris would make sure her husband did not exceed the seventy mile per hour speed limit. He would keep his attention attached to the road.

"Anybody want to stop up ahead at the Dairy Queen?" Mr. Stenlund broke the silence.

"I don't think so." Iris responded.

"I guess I don't either." Shane agreed.

"That was easy." Martin chuckled.

Silence returned to the car. Shane moved restlessly in the back seat. "What time does the game start?" He asked.

"One o'clock, I think." His dad affirmed.

Shane reached with his hand on the front seat to pull himself forward. "Do we have tickets?

"Danni said she had them already when I talked to her yesterday." His mom turned slightly to address her response to Shane in the back seat.

Shane slumped back in his seat. He stared out his window at the landscape flashing by, concentrating on nothing in particular. Almost three months passed since he last saw his sister. She carried a full academic load throughout the school year. During the past summer she worked in the chemistry lab at the college, good training, she declared, for her goal of graduating as a research chemist. Why she picked that profession Shane refused to speculate. He never did understand much of what his sister did. Besides it didn't matter. It had little to do with their weekend visit.

He discovered when his sister spent a few days home about mid summer she had changed. In Shane's opinion, college life drained some of her sickening arrogance. Not once during her brief stay did she argue with him about anything. She hinted how much he had grown up. Maybe he had, but from his perspective, she changed more. Staring out the window, he thought about what would happen between them now, months later. Though he definitely refused to admit it, he felt a little excited to see his sister.

Nearly two hours later he saw her standing outside her dorm, waving a sign proclaiming victory for the St. Thomas Tommies. A cell phone contact shortly before entering Twin Cities' traffic announced to Danni her family's arrival in minutes depending on weekend congestion. As the family car neared her dorm, she assumed the role of a one-person welcoming committee.

Hugs all around completed the greeting. Danni, for the first time ever, placed a light kiss on her brother's cheek. He gave her a special squeeze. With little time before the kickoff of the game, Danni suggested they park the car in the dorm parking lot and walk the few blocks to the St. Thomas football stadium. Several others did the same. She assured her dad they could check into the motel following the game.

Football, for Shane, lacked the appeal of baseball. His small five feet seven inches, one hundred twenty pounds may have influenced his interest in a sport dominated by athletes much bigger than he. Nonetheless, he enjoyed watching football, and with his family he walked to the stadium expecting a rousing homecoming game between St. Thomas and rival St. John's.

The game, dominated by St. Thomas, ended in a lop sided victory for the Tommies, 42-16. Since the nature of the game demanded little attention, Shane found remarkable the ease with which he and Danni talked. Devoid of any contention, their conversation reviewed each other's life since she last visited home. Whatever caused it, he liked the change. He found his older sister interesting, humorous, smart, and in the bright afternoon sun suddenly pretty, a conclusion only a few months ago he would never have considered.

With the promise her dad would pick her up for Sunday breakfast, Shane and his parents left Danni at her dorm and drove to the small motel on the fringe of downtown Minneapolis. They checked in, unpacked their slight luggage, turned on the TV, and relaxed in the confines of the small motel room after a long day of driving and combating the crush of a rabid football crowd.

For a light dinner, Shane volunteered to walk two short blocks to a large corner Burger King. With the sun setting behind tall buildings, street lights illuminated the way. Shane walked without hesitation, imagining for the moment a life that enabled him to walk to places like a Burger King. Approaching the fast food restaurant, he observed four boys, maybe about his age, seated at an outside table. Even in mid October weather permitted eating outside. Seeing the four boys served as another reminder for Shane of life in the big city. Free from onerous farm duties, they could sit outside a Burger King to eat a snack and enjoy the evening. Shane did not pass unnoticed by the four boys, a snicker shared among them.

With his order in hand, Shane walked out of the restaurant to return to the motel. Stepping through the door, he confronted the four boys who blocked his advance. One of them, taller than the others stepped out from the group.

"You new around here?" He stood facing Shane, hands on hips, shoulders back.

A shiver trickled down Shane's back. Not inclined to physical interaction, and never having engaged in fighting, except for fun, Shane said, "No, just visiting."

"Who you visiting?" The taller boy asked, dropping his arms to his side.

Shane looked at the four boys, confused as to their intention, curious if they were friends or foes. "My sister," Shane declared. Striving to sound confident, he said, "Why do you ask?"

The taller boy doing all the talking glanced at his friends and smiled. He stepped back to look again at Shane. "No reason. Just thought you might need help with all that food."

Shane tightened his grip on the sack he held in his hand. He wasn't sure what to make of the situation he faced. His only recourse, he determined, was to avoid showing fear even though his knees weakened and perspiration formed at the base of his neck. In a firm voice, he stated, "I'm staying with my parents at that motel down there." He pointed. "This is our dinner. I don't need any help." Shane persisted in his effort to circumvent the small group.

Suddenly, the tall one who did all the talking stepped aside. The others followed his lead. Shane moved quickly around them, heading for the motel. Behind him he heard, "Have a good dinner." He breathed deeply as he quickened his pace back to the motel.

What the hell was that all about? He asked himself. He knew for sure that they wouldn't learn to do that shit on the farm.

Chapter 7

Not since homecoming at St. Thomas had Shane seen his sister. Most often, her frequent phone calls received her mother's attention. Fall abruptly jumped into winter with an early heavy snowfall ushering in freezing temperatures. Regardless of the weather, farm animals needed care, hay in their mangers, clean straw in their stalls, feed and water in troughs for both pigs and chickens. Cows required milking morning and evening. Shane and his dad shared these responsibilities, much to Shane's dismay.

Reluctantly, Shane trudged through his chores, each day more dissatisfied with the drag of life on the farm. Only with First Mate did he vent his discontent. His pony always appeared to listen attentively, never showing any irritation with his captain's complaints.

Whenever Shane voiced his opinions about rural life, his parents reminded him of the comfortable conditions he enjoyed. They pointed out the poverty that prevailed in parts of the country, leaving young people destitute and hopeless. He needed to show more appreciation for what his parents provided for him. During private moments he acknowledged the truth of his parents' claim. However, that did little to allay his restlessness.

At school Shane did enough to get by. He caused no trouble and generally complied with school rules both in and out of the classroom. Hardly ever did he think about his two day suspension several years ago, resulting from his reaction to a mere suggestion about his small size. Though he retained a sensitivity about his size, he refused to let it interfere with his relationships with other students. Besides, in ninth grade, Shane measured up to most of his peers. In the last four months he had grown over two inches. If size were a determining factor in social or academic success, he definitely possessed the qualities to enjoy that success.

By mid December, an air of anticipation filtered through Twin Pines High School. Christmas break, gradually losing out to "winter break" for reasons Shane didn't understand, promised students a temporary rest from the demands of school. By December 1, fall sports concluded and winter sports began, leaving a short lull in the athletic schedule. For Shane, who participated in only baseball, the sports scene counted him a spectator. That role satisfied him since in many cases his farm duties usually conflicted with practice times and scheduled games. Not yet a licensed driver, he would have to depend on his parents for transportation. That narrowed his quest for independence.

Danni's winter break nearly coincided with Shane's. This year Christmas occupied a weekend, translating into a four day celebration, Friday through Monday. Three days before that weekend, Shane's mom and dad drove to Twin Pines to pick up Danni, who traveled home by bus. She did not own a car nor did she wish to at this stage in her college career. A frugal strain derived from her parents as well as from her Norwegian ancestry persuaded her to avoid the added expense of owning and operating a car. Her decision puzzled Shane, who envisioned owning a car as a major step in ascending to the adult world.

With a small brief case in hand, Danni rushed through the door leading to the Stenlund kitchen. Close behind came her mom and dad, who carried her light luggage. Her stay would end in less than a week. Shane rose from his place before the living room TV to greet his sister in the kitchen. Placing her brief case on the kitchen table, Danni opened wide her arms, inviting Shane to share a hug. In response to the invitation, he stepped forward into her arms.

"Good to see you, big brother." She spoke with emphasis into his ear.

Shane eased himself back from her embrace, followed by a self-conscious averting of his eyes. "Good to see you, too, big sister." The 'big" held special meaning for both of them. Shane resented her referring to him as "little brother," which she often did in the past. That Danni remembered his resentment suggested a change in their sibling relationship. Since the October trip to the Twin Cities, Shane felt a melting of the frigid relationship that caused so much animosity in years past. Of course, he had not seen his sister since October. He did speak with her on the phone occasionally. He just felt a changing attitude toward her, a change he couldn't explain. He didn't even try.

Chapter 8

The days since her return home found Shane and his sister spending increasingly more time together. Though rarely did she have time for First Mate, the day after her arrival home, she and Shane sat in the living room bored with trying to find entertainment on the TV. Danni, dressed in a St. Thomas sweatshirt and matching sweatpants, sat on the floor, leaning against the sofa. She turned her head to look up at Shane seated on the sofa. "How's the pony? Do you ride him much any more?"

Shane sat a little straighter intrigued that she should ask. "He's fine." Shane stretched his legs and gripped his hands behind his head. "No, I don't ride him much. He's gotten a little stiff in his old age."

"How long have you had him?" She pursued the topic.

Shane sat back, closing his eyes in thought. "I don't know . . . ah, maybe six, seven years."

"Do you know how old he is?" Danni turned and rested her elbow on the sofa seat cushion.

Shane wrinkled his forehead, reaching into his memory. "I don't know." He leaned forward bracing his elbows on his knees. "Dad probably does. All I know is that I got him when I was eight or nine years old. I never bothered to ask about his age."

Danni gripped the sofa, pulling herself to her feet. "Do you want to go out to visit him?"

Shane smiled, finding difficulty believing her interest in First Mate. "Sure if a big city, college girl like you can stand spending time in a barn."

Danni laughed. "Come on. Get your coat. I want to visit my roots. You know. I grew up here too."

First Mate whinnied softly as Shane and Danni stepped into his stall. He stood tethered to his manger. Still he enjoyed the freedom of turning his head to greet his guests. Both Shane and Danni patted the aging pony on his neck and back. First Mate nodded his head slowly.

Danni leaned back to rest against the side of the pony's stall. She studied First Mate, then turned her head to view the cows lined up in their stalls on the other side of the barn. In a moment of introspection she mused, "Too many kids miss the chance to live in this environment."

Shane leaned over First Mate. He stared at his sister. "Ah . . . What do you mean?"

Danni folded her arms over her chest with a shiver from the damp chill of the barn which accentuated its raw animal smell. "I know your feelings about farm life. You've stated them often enough over the years." She tempered a bit of sarcasm with a smile. "I also know how hard you have worked almost since you were a little kid. Dad appreciates it too."

Shane listened with interest, watching his sister over his pony's back.

"I know all that work wasn't always fun. Still, Shane, remember, it develops responsibility, independence, reliability." Danni paused. "It encourages all kinds of good things."

"Like boredom?" Shane interjected.

Danni smiled and tightened her arms around her chest. "I suppose there's that, too. Don't you think, though, that boredom doesn't last? Those other things do."

A frown clouded Shane's face. His head jerked to the side, eye brows squeezed together in acknowledging but not necessarily accepting her conclusion.

"Shane," she continued. "I see too many guys your age hanging around street corners with nothing to do but smoke and harass unsuspecting pedestrians. Almost every night I see these groups of young boys walking near the campus with apparently little to do. That to me is boredom."

Shane backed away from his pony to lean like his sister on his side of the stall. He thought for a moment about the brief October incident near the Burger King. He had mentioned it to no one, confused about what the guys intended with their behavior. He studied his sister for a moment. "I never told anyone this. But on that homecoming weekend when we stayed at the motel, I walked to a Burger King for a little food for the three of us. When I got close, this group of four guys seated outside stared at me. When I came out with the food, they blocked my way and asked stupid questions like if I was new in town and why I was there. They did nothing, but I didn't feel very secure facing four guys."

Danni let her arms hang down. "You were damned lucky. I don't know about those particular guys. I do know others, maybe like them, who do not have anything good in mind. I doubt if they were interested in why you were in the Twin Cities." She repeated, "You were lucky, I think."

"From what you say, I think so, too." Shane moved out of the stall onto the barn's center walkway. "Do these guys pick fights for no reason?"

Danni followed her brother as they walked toward the exit. "Yes, they do pick fights, and they have a reason. Usually, it's to let you know who's boss. Probably, since you only visited, you presented no threat to their territory." She put her arm around her brother's shoulder. "That's boredom, dear brother."

The day after Christmas weekend, Danni and Shane planned a brief ski trip to Lutsen Ski Resort near Duluth. It enjoyed the reputation as Minnesota's premiere ski resort. Weather cooperated with a light dusting of snow on Christmas Day and moderating temperatures. Neither proclaimed any special talent for skiing. However, living in northern Minnesota almost made skiing compulsory, if not skiing then ice fishing. Ice fishing offered little appeal to either Danni or Shane.

Monday morning, early, they dressed in clothes they considered appropriate for a day at Lutsen, neither in possession of fashionable ski apparel. In addition to what they wore, they tossed their warmest jackets into the car, not sure of what they would need for defense against the cold. Danni drove her dad's car the hundred miles or so to Lutsen, north of Duluth.

When they arrived, they found a parking lot jammed with cars, SUV's, and pickups. They also faced lines of skiers waiting to register, rent skies and grab onto the tow ropes. Lutsen offered excellent skiing conditions and facilities for all levels of skill without the inordinately, steep runs of resorts out west.

Because of their limited experience, Danni and Shane restricted themselves to less challenging runs. For over two hours they made the same run several times, delighting in the rush of air around them and the invigorating thrill of speed, skis cutting through the soft top layer of snow in the race to the bottom of the run. Surprised at the energy skiing demanded, they decided to take a break in the lodge. There they discussed which run to try next. Energy restored from a brief rest and equipped with new confidence, they decided to try a more exciting run.

The run they picked would potentially give them greater thrills as well as a series of moguls to enliven the run. Without incident, sister and brother navigated the more difficult slope, maneuvering through the moguls with surprising ease. On the second attempt Shane somehow lost his balance.

In the grueling weeks of rehabilitation ahead, Shane would try to explain what happened. It all did happen so fast. The exact sequence of events eluded him. Whatever the cause, the tip of his right ski caught in the snow, maybe a firm mogul. His speed jerked him to the left. One ski snapped loose from the bindings. The right ski failed to release, bending Shane's right leg off to one side, tearing muscles and ligaments. Pain surged through his leg, pain so intense he blacked out, leaving his body to roll several more yards down the hill.

Close behind her brother, Danni did not see the cause of the spill. She saw what happened next when he twisted in his skies as his body plowed through the snow. She tried to slow her descent to help Shane, who obviously needed it. Finally stopped a few yards below him, she unclamped her skies and stumbled through the snow back to her brother, who lay unmoving, his right leg twisted at an ugly angle. A passing skier hurried to alert the Lutsen rescue team. The team arrived quickly to move Shane to the lodge where, consumed in pain, he lay in a first aid room. Officials at the lodge examined him to determine he needed the attention available at one of Duluth's major hospitals. An ambulance rushed him to the emergency room of St, Luke's Hospital where emergency room doctors assessed the damage which they concluded required reconstructive surgery to repair critical tears of the anterior cruciate ligaments.

Chapter 9

"Mr. and Mrs. Stenlund, your son sustained a vicious, ugly tear of the ACL." Shane sat alone in the living room, his eyes attracted to a spot on the sofa next to him, his leg elevated, an intricate knee brace lying near by. Those words came from Dr. Nevin Banister, an orthopedic surgeon at St Luke's Hospital in Duluth. With frequency they tumbled through Shane's memory. In addition, those words imposed radical changes in his life.

A month had passed since that fateful day at Lutsen. Doctors at St. Luke's diagnosed Shane's injury as a severe tear of the anterior cruciate ligament in his right knee. He had no previous knowledge of such a ligament, nor did Danni or his parents. However, over the past month he learned more about ACL than he wanted to know.

According to the emergency room doctors at St. Luke's, Shane would definitely need reconstructive surgery on the knee. Before the surgery, they suggested the swelling needed to subside. Consequently, they recommended pain killers, a knee brace, and a few days at home prior to the surgery.

Shane moved cautiously in the sofa chair where he spent a part of each day resting his knee or performing exercises designed to strengthen it. He leaned back in the chair, closed his eyes, recalling the agony of the long ride home, stretched out in the back seat of his dad's car. From the hospital on the day of the accident, Danni contacted their parents who hurried to the hospital to learn of the extent of Shane's injury. Of course, shocked by the accident, they stood ready to do wherever they needed to do to help their son deal with a painful injury. The recommended delay before surgery found the Stenlund's, in two vehicles, heading home with the hope the swelling in Shane's leg and knee subsided quickly.

The reconstruction surgery took only about one and one half hours. Because of the seriousness of the tear, Dr. Banister insisted Shane spend one night in the hospital to ensure no unexpected complications. Only days after the surgery, Shane, now in the comfort of his home, could place light weight on his leg with the help of crutches. Just two days after the surgery Shane visited the Twin Pines Rehab Center under the direction of physical therapist Frances Jewel. Since then he returned to the rehab center three days a week in a critical program to strengthen his reconstructed right knee and to prevent stiffening. Never in his nearly fifteen years did treatments under Miss Jewel's supervision or exercises during his private workouts generate such gripping pain.

Shane flexed his knee. Besides the time spent with Frances at the rehab center, he adhered to a rigid schedule of exercising on his own. Already he noted improvement in the knee, less pain when applying pressure or when doing the exercise routine.

During the many hours of recovery, Shane explored his future. At nearly fifteen years old, long term complications eluded him despite Dr. Banister's comments about possible adverse consequences of juvenile knee reconstruction. Obviously, Shane's prime concern was walking again without crutches and without a knee brace. Baseball came next. He asked the doctor and his physical therapist about baseball. The season began in about two and one half months.

In ninth grade, Shane qualified to try out for the varsity baseball team. Though he would certainly make the junior varsity team, making the varsity stood as his goal. He asked, would his knee allow it? Nobody knew the exact answer. To a large extent his playing baseball depended on his commitment to a rehab schedule and on something called "luck of the draw."

On this late afternoon, Shane assessed his status. Never did he have so much time to consider intangible things. He walked without help, a complicated knee brace protecting his healing knee. He had missed more than a week of school following the surgery.

He caught up quickly. He could identify two significant advantages to his injury and subsequent recovery.

First, his surgery released him from many of his chores around the farm. With only a hint of guilt over his dad's assuming most of his chores, Shane definitely did not miss picking eggs, cleaning roosts, and feeding pigs. One job he did resume relatively quickly was milking two cows each morning. Regarding his farm duties, recently he experienced a possible change in his attitude. Maybe they weren't so bad after all. Maybe they had something to do with what Danni talked about during Christmas break, things like responsibility and reliability. These thoughts puzzled him.

The second benefit from his accident pertained to his relationship with Danni. He reflected on the attention she showered on him the day of the accident. Her quick response on the slopes, her hovering attention in the emergency room, and her taking charge to inform Mom and Dad impressed Shane. Added to that, their friendly conversations during her short stay over Christmas break and extending back to October gave him a different perspective of his sister who maybe wasn't such a snob after all. People can change, particularly other people.

Of course, he couldn't ignore the help of his parents. Without their support and patience, he would never have recovered so quickly. Never before did he pause to think about all his parents did for him and had done for him all his life. Someday, perhaps, he would repay them for all they did for him and his sister. Someday he would figure out just how he would do that.

Suddenly, he shook his head as if emerging from a dream, puzzled over spending time on all this stuff he never really thought about before. For the moment, blaming it on the medicine he took for pain and possible infection, Shane reached down to grasp his knee brace. Attached, it enabled him to walk relatively pain free. He walked into the kitchen to grab a can of soda from the fridge, an indulgence not forbidden by his injury.

Chapter 10

"All right you guys, most of you obviously have spent the winter sitting on your butts." Cal Restin, head coach of the Twin Pines High School baseball team, stood at the end of the high school gymnasium watching his potential varsity team. An extended winter delayed any outdoor baseball practice. A short, compact, thirty-five year old history teacher with a commanding voice and bright red hair, Mr. Restin accepted the head coaching position at the same time he accepted his teaching assignment. Since then, now four years ago, the baseball program flourished. Though his arrival in the classroom had altered history very little, his sense of humor added a little color to a subject not always a student favorite.

Mr. Restin insisted on conditioning before any thing else. Conditioning, he asserted, helped prevent injuries. Watching thirty prospective varsity players running around the gym, his playful comment about spending time on their butts carried serious intent.

A blast of his whistle caught the attention of the group. "Gentlemen," he shouted. "Gather around right here in front of me." As the young athletes made their way to where their coach stood, some hurried; some took their time, catching their breath from their brief run around the gym. Silence fell over the group anticipating the coach's words.

"I don't have to tell you about weather in Twin Pines. We all know we can't depend on it in the spring to give conditions suitable for outdoor practice. I hope that soon we can move outside for that purpose. In the meantime, we'll workout here in the gym. It looks like many of you can use the time to get in shape." Coach Restin walked slowly in front of the assembled athletes. "Eventually, some of you will make the varsity team and some of you will spend time on the junior varsity team. Keep in mind that all nine places on the varsity team are open. Those who want one of those positions the most will make the team." A restless shuffle of feet drifted through the group. The coach paced to one side of the group then returned. He made eye contact with a majority of the young boys standing before him. "You also need to know the importance of the junior varsity team. It's where varsity players polish their skills."

Shane Stenlund stood among the group of assembled athletes. For over three months he worked diligently to restore his knee shattered in his skiing accident. Long hours of rehab had given him time to contemplate his future in baseball. He loved the game. His small, trim stature, his quick speed, and his sure hands combined to make him a very good baseball player. He proved this in Little League and later in Babe Ruth baseball. Now he dreamed of a chance to play on the varsity team. The accident nearly crushed that dream. Still, here he stood with twenty-nine other athletes ready to fulfill his dream.

Frequently, during the many hours spent in rehab he discussed with Frances Jewel, his physical therapist, the chances of playing baseball in the spring. Her encouragement gave him confidence he could do it. Only days ago, with his parents, Shane visited Dr. Banister at St. Luke's Hospital in Duluth. A thorough examination of the knee and consultation with Frances Jewel produced a clearance for him to try out for the baseball team.

The months of February, March and part of April found Shane exercising his knee each day. Six weeks of supervised therapy prepared him to assume workouts on his own while visiting every week with Frances at the rehab center. Standing with the other athletes listening to Coach Restin, Shane felt confident in his return to baseball. With a little less confidence, he viewed his chances of making the varsity team.

In a few days, the temperature in Twin Pines rose to make possible outdoor, baseball practice. Shane awaited that practice with some apprehension. His knee felt good. Running gave support to his confidence. Now he considered how running in the outfield or around the bases would affect that knee. To his delight, a week of outdoor practice did nothing to cause him concern. The end of practice left soreness in the knee, but nothing a session in the whirlpool tub couldn't sooth.

Chasing down fly balls, swinging the bat in the batter's box, or running the bases, he did without significant consequences. Shane expected nothing more. He grew eager to play in an actual game. In two days he would have his chance. Coach Restin announced that following a pre-conference game with a neighboring school, he would determine the roster for the varsity team.

Shane did not start the pre-conference game. After all, at only fifteen, he was one of the youngest athletes trying to make the varsity team. In the fourth inning, Coach Restin called upon Shane to replace the left fielder, a position Shane played regularly in Little League and in Babe Ruth. Shane tensed with excitement, waiting for the third out and his team's assuming the field on defense. Only one ball found its way to left field. He made a spectacular catch, racing in and diving for the fast sinking line drive. He caught it to end the inning.

Shane's turn at bat came with two out. He stood poised in the batter's box, waiting for the pitcher to throw him a ball he could hit. With the count two and two, the pitch he wanted arrived. With a level swing, he drove the ball between the left and center fielders. He exploded out of the batter's box and raced to first. The first base coach waved him on as the fielders pursued the well hit ball. Approaching second base, Shane glanced at the third base coach who also waved him on. Shane gained energy as he headed to second base. His step on the second base bag touched only the edge, his ankle buckling, his right knee twisting with excruciating pain, not unlike what he felt on the ski slope. He heard the snap of something in his knee.

Shane crumpled to the ground, pain surging through his leg. To ease the searing pain, he tried pulling his knee toward his chest. He gave up. Surrounded by his coach, his teammates, and officials, he lost touch with the game and with the fate of his first hit of the season.

Chapter 11

Shane fixed his eyes on the bowl of cereal he now found unappetizing. His shoulders slumped, his hair stuck out in unkept bunches after a very short night's sleep.

Mr. Stenlund leaned against the kitchen counter holding a cup of coffee gone cold. "Where were you last night?" He asked setting the cup on the counter.

Shane mumbled an inaudible response.

"What did you say?" His dad moved a little closer to the table, his voice reflecting his irritation.

"No place important." Shane mumbled a little louder.

"What the hell is that supposed to mean?" With his arms hanging at his sides, Mr. Stenlund flexed his hands into tight fists.

Shane looked up at his dad. "Just what I said. Nothing important."

"Nothing important kept you out until . . . what time?" He took a sip of the cold coffee. "What time did you get home?"

Shane shrugged his shoulders. "I don't know. I never checked the time."

"Well, I did. It was about three this morning, too damn late to be out doing nothing."

Shane, a sneer curling his lips, looked at his dad, now backed up against the counter. "If you knew, why did you ask?"

Mr. Stenlund stepped closer again to the table where Shane sat. His arms folded against his chest. Not a particularly big man, his stance and his anger, nonetheless, made him intimidating. "Stop this bull shit, son. Your mom and I expect a little honesty from you, not smart-ass remarks."

Shane pushed his chair away from the table. "Look, I'm seventeen years old. I'm not a little kid anymore. Do I have to tell you about everything I do?" His cheeks flushed with color.

"As long as you live under this roof, you will abide by simple rules. One of those is being honest with your parents about what you do and where you spend your time. For whatever reason, lately you haven't been." Mr. Stenlund stood firm in front of his son, his breathing heavy.

Shane rose from the chair. With a defiant swagger in his step, he approached his dad. "Maybe I should get the hell out of here if I violate your damn rules."

Struggling to restrain himself from striking his son, his dad shouted, "Shane, stop this nonsense. What's gotten into you? Is living here a problem for you?" He took a deep breathe. "We can't go on like this, son. Both your mother and I understand your disappointment brought on by the knee, but life has to go on." He took a deep breath then calmly stated. "It can't go on like this."

Shane stared at his dad then looked away. He rushed to the outside door, pushed it open, and burst outside, proclaiming, "Nothing's the matter with me." In a softer voice, he uttered, "Maybe you should look at yourself."

The bright spring morning did little to soothe his anger. Nothing, recently, seemed to remove the cloud of unhappiness that enveloped him. From the moment he woke up in the morning, he faced the day discontent, rebellious, and ill tempered. At home contentious moments with his parents only fueled his anger. No one understood him any more except, perhaps, First Mate. He helped to cool Shane's temper. Talking to his pony released some of the hostility.

Distraught and seeking some escape from the weight of his distress, Shane headed to First Mate's stall. His pony welcomed his captain with a shake of his head and a snort. Flecks of gray now were sprinkled around his slender body. His eyes had lost the spirit of former years, his function generally reduced to listening to Shane talk about his troubled life. That trouble started two years ago with the second devastating knee injury. Or, maybe, Shane hastened to remind himself, it started on the ski slopes of Lutsen Resort. Certainly, the second reconstruction of his knee spelled the end of his time on the baseball diamond and so far the end of harmony at home and in school.

Shane stepped into First Mate's stall, reached around his short neck to give him a firm hug. He patted him on his back, then sat down on the edge of the manger. He touched his pony's tender nose and scratched under his chin. Only here could Shane find some contentment. Here he didn't have to listen to all the questions, all the complaints. His eyes closed; his fingers gently scratched his pony's nose.

Vivid images of events so drastically altering his life rushed through Shane's mind. He saw himself hustling into second base, jubilant over his first hit as a varsity player. Equally vivid, he could almost feel the surging pain rushing from his shattered ACL, a part of his body that, over the years, had become very familiar to him. Even now, two years later, thinking about the fateful incident sent twinges through his right leg.

With his hand under First Mate's chin, Shane lifted his pony's head to stare into those languid eyes. "What happened to me, old buddy? Things aren't the same anymore." He looked off into the space above his pony's head. "Why can't I get over this knee thing? I can't change what happened?"

Shane stared into a dark corner of the barn. Almost like rewinding an ancient movie film, he relived those agonizing moments immediately after the fall at second base. Worse, those weeks and months of physical therapy paraded through his memory. To face ACL, reconstructive surgery once pushed tolerance to the limit. Twice, Shane concluded, pushed it beyond. As he had the first time, Dr. Banister of St. Luke's Hospital performed the second surgery. Recovery therapy duplicated what he went through before with one overwhelming difference. This one ended his baseball days and tossed him into a fragmented life he never before imagined.

"Is it all my fault, old buddy?" Shane scratched First Mate's forehead. "I have this awful time getting along with anyone, especially Mom and Dad." Staring into his pony's sleepy eyes, he thought he saw a tear form. Or maybe the tear formed in his own eye. He blinked. The knee problem did deny him one of the enjoyments in his life. That denial crushed him at first. It changed his entire perspective. It also changed those around him. Teachers, parents, and friends treated him differently. Yet, according to his parents, at least he interpreted it that way, his attitude changed as did his relationship with them. He detested always fighting with his parents. However, they spoke too often about belligerence, defiance, and irresponsibility. He would not accept taking the blame alone for changes that had taken place in his life.

A final gentle pat on First Mate's nose ended Shane's conversation with his pony. For a short time, it helped to divert his attention away from his troubled life. However, it did nothing to return him to the baseball diamond.

Chapter 12

In the school parking lot, Shane rested against his dad's car, his preferred means of transportation to school in Twin Pines and one concession from his dad during his senior year in high school. Of course, the school did offer bus transportation. For an eighteen year old senior, riding the school bus constituted the abdication of dignity. Sustaining his car privilege often served as the basis for another vociferous argument with his dad, who insisted on Shane's showing some commitment to his duties both at home and in school in return for the use of the car. Weary of the senseless contention surrounding the issue, Mr. Stenlund relented despite Shane's repeated failure to comply with the agreement.

Standing next to his car, Lindsey Cooper faced Shane, curious about his meeting with Mr. Winthrop, the school counselor. Also a senior, Lindsey, a petite young woman, compensated with effusive friendliness for her average appearance and her position at the fringe of the school's social hierarchy. Dressed in ordinary jeans and a V-neck sweater that gave definition to the contours of her body, she carried her five foot, five inch frame with pride, her short brown hair framing a round face highlighted by penetrating eyes now concentrated on Shane's face. A conscientious student, she enjoyed membership in the National Honor Society and already had received acceptance to the University of Minnesota, Duluth.

Shane and Lindsey met literally by accident, an accident months ago in the school parking lot. Lindsey, in a hurry to leave school, backed into Shane's car. Damage was slight. Shane's response was not consistent with the extent of damage.

He possessed no patience for drivers who failed to watch where they were going. Besides, he feared his father would suspend his driving privileges. An initial harsh exchange of words combined with Lindsey's tears, eventually faded into a mature discussion of insurance and repair. Lindsey's calm, friendly nature was instrumental in quelling more aggressive talk.

From this incident emerged a relationship, first allowing only a brief "hello" to longer greetings, finally to Shane's asking for a date. Neither dated regularly. His courage to ask matched her courage to accept. From that first clash in the parking lot developed a relationship which quieted some of Shane's angry moments. They now faced one of those moments.

"What did he tell you?" Lindsey rested her hands on the hood of Shane's car.

Shane rolled his eyes. "Some shit about missing credits I could make up in summer school."

"What happens if you don't?" Lindsey asked.

"I don't graduate." Shane blurted out.

Her mouth dropped open. For a moment emitting no sound then, "Gosh, that's terrible, not to graduate . . . after all this time." Lindsey moved around to the front of the car.

Shane hung his head, shaking it slowly from side to side. "I don't know what the hell's going on in my life. Nothing goes right. I can't even step in the house without getting my ass chewed about something."

Lindsey sighed. "I'm so sorry." She stepped back from the car and reached to touch Shane on his arm. "I wish there was something I could do to help."

Shane looked into Lindsey's sparkling eyes. "Boy, I do too. I can't go on everyday upset about something." Their relationship had accomplished something for him. She commonly served as a calming influence. This time, though, she likely could do nothing.

The pain Shane obviously felt induced silence between them. His anger, frustration and despair exhausted him, depriving him of further comment. Minutes passed. The two young people groped for words to relieve the tension that silenced them. Shane kicked a stone on the blacktop.

Finally, Lindsey moved closer to Shane. She opened her arms, inviting him to a hug. He accepted. They held each other, Lindsey resting her head on his chest, he turning his cheek in her soft hair.

Lindsey pulled back. "Maybe we'd better get going. My parents will start worrying about their dear daughter." A smile spread across her face. She quickly licked her lips and reached up to kiss Shane on the cheek. "It will get better. Don't give up."

Shane's brow wrinkled. "I sure hope so. I can't go on like this." He paused and glanced down at the blacktop. "Maybe I'll just screw it all and take off someplace."

Lindsey stiffened. "You don't really mean that, Shane."

He shrugged his shoulders in a gesture of surrender. "I don't know. Sometimes, I can't think of any thing else to do. I probably can't graduate. I'm failing in two required classes. My parents will have a fit when they find out."

"What about the summer school thing?" Lindsey refused to end the conversation with Shane so distraught.

Shane stared at the blacktop of the parking lot and shoved his hands into the front pockets of his jeans. "Yeah, maybe I could go through the graduation ceremony if I promised to sign up for summer school." The strain in his voice revealed what he thought about that option.

"Shane, I'm sorry, but I do have to get home." She squeezed his hand. "Please think about that summer school plan before you make any decisions." She turned to walk toward her car parked a few yards away.

Shane did not move. He watched her walk to her car, reminding himself at least one thing went right in his life, Lindsey Cooper. That night he called to ask her to attend the senior prom as his date. She quickly agreed. Shane closed his cell phone, breathed deeply, ending the day with a smile.

Chapter 13

Danni Stenlund stooped to pick up the morning paper she earlier ignored in her rush to arrive at work on time. She unlocked the door to her one bedroom condo fifteen floors above Minneapolis' Nicollet Mall. Inside, she paused to admire the colorful entry tile and straight ahead the large picture window giving a spectacular view of downtown Minneapolis and the Nicollet Mall below.

Along with her large purse, which doubled as a brief case, she dropped the paper on a small bench by the entrance. Her condo gave her great satisfaction. The few months she lived there had added to her pride in ownership and delight in its design and decor. It afforded her all the comforts and conveniences she needed in a home. A compact kitchen with a center island blended with the living room furnished with, of course, contemporary Scandinavian designed furniture, acquired with the help of her parents. At twenty-four years old, she valued, more than ever, her Scandinavian heritage. Off to one side of the living room, a hallway led to the powder room, a small den or office, and ended with the bedroom and master bath suite.

On this late afternoon, Danni stood in the entry way admiring the condo she had worked diligently to buy. Running her hands over the delicate wall paper decorating the hallway, she couldn't refrain from savoring the success she enjoyed in her life. Four productive years at St. Thomas University, a vigorous search for a job as a research chemist which ended with her joining a private research company in suburban Minneapolis, and the owning of this beautiful, high rise condo combined to make hers a life of gratitude and contentment.

Danni opened the fridge to reach for a Sprite, a major violation, she admitted, of her concern for healthful living. She promised herself numerous times she would give up soda. So far, her promise stood unfulfilled. Still, not much in Danni's life escaped her control, except that nasty addiction to Sprite. Her commitment to a healthy life style helped her sustain her trim, attractive figure. At five feet, eight inches, one hundred twenty pounds, she had changed little since high school. If at all, she had changed for the better, maturity adding to her friendliness and poise.

Like her father's, her dark complexion betrayed her Norwegian heritage. Her dark complexion provided a perfect setting for bright blue eyes and a gracious smile that created charming dimples. Adding to her appeal, wavy dark hair framed her slender face.

While in high school, Danni dated often, as often as she wished. However, she avoided any serious attachments to any one boy. Modest and without presumption about her appearance, she still attracted the attention of boys her age, even some older. An outstanding student, she applied her intelligence not only in the classroom but also in her social life.

Since graduating from college, she established a serious relationship with Grayson Quinn, a former college classmate and current computer software salesman. Despite her relationship with Grayson, Danni valued her independence and resisted any talk about living together.

Returning to the front entrance bench to retrieve her purse and briefcase, she glanced at the morning newspaper left there. A headline on the front page immediately caught her attention: "Homeless Teen Found Dead." She dropped her purse on the floor, grasped the paper with both hands then sat down on the bench. She scanned the article which contained details about the young man's life and tragic death. From a middle class family, the young man apparently couldn't deal with his father's sudden death months ago. Leaving a St. Paul home he found incapable of satisfying his emotional needs, he wandered around with other homeless, Twin

City teens before meeting his death, an apparent suicide, under the Hennepin Ave. bridge.

Danni looked up from the paper. Her eyes absently focused on a small tear in the wallpaper covering the opposite wall. In her mind she saw her brother helplessly plowing through the snow on a Lutsen slope. His agony was deeply imprinted in her mind. She recalled the conversations with Shane about life in the big city compared with the boredom of the farm. The article awakened for Danni the numerous times she witnessed young people hanging around without discernible purpose. She worried about her brother.

Not often enough did she visit home. Her job, Grayson, and the condo left little time for her to drive north to Twin Pines and the farm where she grew up. However, she did know about Shane's bitterness and depression. She worried about his inability to deal with the crushing disappointment of the second knee surgery which ended a much too short baseball career.

Danni folded the paper and placed it on the bench. She got up and walked to the kitchen where on the counter sat her soda. Deep in thought about her brother, she took a generous swallow, dismissing the chance Shane would take the route of the young, homeless teen in the article. Nonetheless, she was aware of the fragile grasp young people sometimes had on reality. They did strange things for strange reasons. She remembered private moments when she questioned her confidence to move from high school onto college or even earlier, from middle school to high school. With apprehension, she confronted these moments even though, unlike her brother, a devastating injury did not dramatically alter her life.

She kept in touch with her mother about Shane's knee and its critical effect on his life. She knew nothing about his academic problems which endangered his graduation. She spoke with her parents, mainly her mom, at least two or three times a week, seeking information about Shane but rarely talking to him on the phone. Her mom didn't expand on her son's emotional turmoil, likely facing it each day proved enough. Words really weren't needed for Danni to sense the struggle her parents faced dealing with Shane's inability to accept the consequences of his injured knee.

Danni anticipated with interest her brother's impending graduation, hoping that achievement would allay some of his bitterness. What he planned to do after graduation she did not know. She did know unless his attitude and outlook improved, not much would change for him.

Placing the soda can back on the counter, she stepped in front of the picture window, giving her a wonderful view of the world outside. How grateful she felt about her own world. She hoped someday her brother could feel the same about his.

Chapter 14

"Martin, please stop your pacing and sit down." Iris refilled her coffee cup, turned, and sat down at the kitchen table. The Stenlunds took great pride in their country home. Its first floor living room, dining room, den, and kitchen made available room for most family needs. Invariably, in times of serious discussion, the family gravitated to the kitchen where they always seemed to find easier the resolution of problems. Right now Martin and Iris wrestled with a problem, a letter from officials at the high school.

When agitated, Martin found sitting down virtually impossible. He moved from one side of the kitchen to another, at times stepping into the adjacent dining room. Iris positioned herself at the large, rectangular family table where over the years they gathered for their meals. With coffee cup before her, she studied the pattern on the table cloth. She repeated, "Martin, please come and sit down. You're making me nervous."

Martin paused by the coffee maker on the counter, refilled his cup, and turned to face his wife. "What the hell happened to him?" He shook his head slowly, his eyes fixed on his wife.

"I don't know," Iris sighed. "His knee injuries surely had a lot to do with it." She sipped her coffee. Silence enveloped the kitchen.

Martin moved a few steps toward the table. "Yes," he nodded his head, "that seems like the beginning. What I don't understand is why he can't accept what he can't change and move on."

Iris studied her cup as she moved it in a small circle. With sad eyes she looked up at her husband. "I've asked that question a hundred times over the past few months. We've heard all about the tough times some teens have adjusting to changes in their lives. Shane surely is one of them. Knowing that doesn't make any easier watching him become so angry and bitter."

Martin decided to pull a chair away from the kitchen table and sit down. He placed his coffee cup off to the side and folded his hands on the table. "Where's the letter from the school?"

Iris pointed to the basket in one corner of the kitchen counter. "Right over there." Rising, she said, "I'll get it for you."

Returning to her place by the table, she handed the letter to her husband. Earlier in the day, the letter arrived informing the Stenlunds their son would not graduate due to his failing record in two classes required for graduation. The Stenlunds greeted the information with shock and dismay. Definitely, they knew of Shane's neglect of his studies and his slipping grades. However, they had no idea that neglect threatened and, worse, could possibly preclude his graduation and, in their opinion, adversely influence his future.

With hands gripping the one page letter, Martin studied it again, this time with a little more composure. His initial reading, upon his return from work in the field, overwhelmed him. As his eyes followed the sentences explaining the situation, he noticed suggested options for Shane, options Martin, in his outrage, overlooked before. Summer school caught his attention. He read the detail more carefully. A commitment to summer school would permit Shane, at least, to participate in the graduation ceremony.

"Honey, did you read the information about summer school?"

Iris looked up at her husband seated across the table. "Yes, I scanned that part. I guess my mind was a little preoccupied at the time with the thought he wouldn't graduate."

"Well, it gives Shane a chance to graduate with his class if he successfully completes summer school." Martin explained.

Iris' face lightened, eyes wide. "That's not such a bad deal. I don't know why Shane wouldn't go along with it."

"I don't either, but Shane lately hasn't shown much sound thinking or cooperation."

From outside they heard the sound of a car in the driveway, likely Shane's return from school. They both tensed, anticipating another noisy confrontation with their son. They remained seated, a position they considered the least intimidating. They waited. Each sipped coffee. A car door slammed. They both turned to face the outside door off one end of the kitchen. Suddenly, that door burst open, and Shane stepped in. Seeing his parents seated at the kitchen table stopped him just inside the door.

"Welcome home, son." His mom spoke first. "How was your day?" Even to her, those comments were so artificial.

Shane stood speechless, a look of surprise frozen on his face. Rarely did his parents waste time at the kitchen table in the middle of the afternoon.

Martin pushed back his chair and rose to greet his son. "Good afternoon," was all he could manage to say.

Shane looked at his mom then at his dad. "What's going on?"

Realizing the urgency of the situation and the artificiality of the moment, Martin cleared his throat, "Shane, please sit down here at the table. Your mom and I have something to discuss with you."

Shane rolled his eyes and stretched his arms to the side, palms up. "What did I do now?" He blurted.

"Sit down, son." His mom directed.

He complied with her request, dragging a chair out from the table and plopping down on it.

Iris sat rigid in her chair as Martin, leaning against the kitchen counter, responded, "It's not what you've done. It's what you haven't done."

Shane let out an audible breath. "What is that supposed to mean?"

Martin took two steps toward the table. "Shane, today your mother and I received a letter from the school informing us you cannot graduate. Your are short two required credits."

Shane gritted his teeth; a hint of red spread over his face. He gripped the edges of his chair. He mumbled, "What God damn difference does it make?"

Martin stepped closer to the table. "We're not going to listen to language like that," he reprimanded, his eyes wide, a quaver in his voice. "We think it does matter, and we would like to discuss it as adults."

Shane averted his eyes and hung his head. He looked up, first at his mom and then at his dad. "What do you want me to say? I screwed up."

"Yes, you did," his dad affirmed. "Right now we don't have to get into why. We need to get into what to do about it."

Tension diminished in the Stenland kitchen. Shane slumped in his chair. His mom moved her coffee cup in a small circle. His dad moved back to the counter.

With a calmer voice, Martin spoke, "Son, not graduating is such a waste of time and energy. To go through eleven years of school only to screw up in year twelve makes absolutely no sense." He took a deep breath. He ran his hand through his hair and set his eyes on his son. "Not graduating can also make a big difference in your future."

Shane studied his dad then turned away to stare at his hands resting in his lap.

"Son, how long have you known about this problem?" His father ended the silence.

"A while." Shane spoke softly.

"Have you talked to anyone at school about it?" His mom joined the conversation.

Shane closed his eyes, head down. He exhaled. "Yeah. I talked to Mr. Winthrop a while ago."

"What did he say?" Iris persisted.

"That I wouldn't graduate because of not enough credits."

"Did he say anything about summer school?" Martin asked.

Shane didn't respond. He looked around him as if searching for some escape.

"Well," his dad urged. "Did he?"

Shane nodded his head.

"Did he also say you could possibly go through the graduation ceremony if you committed to summer school and passed?"

Shane pounded his fists on the table, slammed the chair back against the wall, stood up shouting, "Fuck this shit! I'm not going to any damned summer school. That's for retards!"

His parents stared astonished at their son's violence and vulgarity. Shane rushed toward the door he entered only minutes before.

Martin's voice vibrated through the kitchen. "Shane, you will not talk to your parents that way!" He moved toward the door to prevent Shane from leaving.

Iris jumped up from her chair. "No, Martin. Let him go. Nothing we say will do any good right now."

With a bang the outside door shut, leaving Shane's parents alone in their kitchen, disconcerted and distraught.

Chapter 15

Martin and Iris Stenlund arrived at the Twin Pines High School minutes before the end of the school day. They parked in the visitor parking lot, avoiding the imminent rush of students streaming for their cars in a packed, student parking lot. Stepping out of his car, Martin scratched his head in amazement at the student parking lot filled with expensive cars. He grinned when he reminded himself that their own son drove a car to school.

How kids could afford the cars they drove to school was not the issue which brought the Stenlunds to the high school. Instead, they arrived to meet with school officials about their son's academic deficiency. Walking to the front entrance of the high school, Martin would welcome the car issue over one related to graduation.

The scheduled meeting coincided with the end of the school day so that Shane could join his parents after his last class. Martin followed his wife into the school's main office where the staff greeted them and directed them to a small waiting room outside the principal's office. Equipped with four lounge chairs, a small table containing literature about the school, and a large map on one wall depicting the Twin Pines School District, the room gave Martin a feeling of confinement. If this room served as the cooling center for aberrant, misguided students, it definitely served its purpose well.

The Stenlunds waited only minutes before the office staff ushered in their son. Unresponsive, he stuffed his hands in his front pockets, ignoring his parents' greeting, and slumped into one of the chairs.

"How was your day?" His mom asked.

Shane shrugged his shoulders without a verbal comment, the gesture a sufficient reply.

Martin looked at his son and slowly shook his head, regretting the degree to which the relationship with Shane had deteriorated. Nearly everyday brought another heated argument about everything from using the car to cultivating a field to his failure in school. Only days before, Martin and Shane verbally collided in the barn over the meeting for which they now waited.

As he sat in the small, crowded waiting room, the scene emerged vividly in Martin's memory. They were performing a job they both disliked, cleaning the stalls occupied by the cattle and Shane's pony. The combination of wet, straw bedding and manure produced a pungent odor strong enough to make their eyes water.

"God, I hate this job." Shane uttered, throwing another fork full of manure out on the center isle of the barn.

Martin, working in another stall, emptied his fork then leaned on it. "I'll second that, son," delighting in something they could agree to. "It's not something I like either." He moved into the stall to dig his fork into the soggy bedding.

The two worked in silence. Soon they worked next to each other as they advanced from one stall to another. With the recent hostile confrontations with Shane about his failure to graduate, neither of Shane's parents had broached the subject of graduation or of summer school. However, the letter they received included an invitation to meet with school officials to discuss alternatives. The Stenlunds would not sacrifice the opportunity for that discussion.

Martin set his fork into the bedding and again used the fork to lean on. "Shane, stop for a minute. Step over here."

Without comment he did what his dad asked.

Martin fixed his eyes on his son. "Now, I don't want to start another battle, but we need to consider what to do about your graduation. School ends in only a few weeks."

Shane stood, offering no response. He kicked at a clump of manure.

Martin shifted from one foot to the other. "That letter we got from the school included an invitation to meet with school officials to discuss options for you."

Shane's head popped up from his gaze at the dirty barn floor. "I know the option. I don't want to go to summer school. I said that before," he adamantly announced.

"Okay, okay," Martin extended his arms, hands up in a gesture of surrender. "Son, do you realize the importance of a high school diploma?"

Shane shrugged his shoulders dismissively.

His dad stepped back, running his shoe over the top of the fork to remove an accumulation of manure. He stood straight, eyes studying his son. He spoke. "A few minutes ago you said you hated this job we're doing. For years you have expressed your dissatisfaction with life on the farm. You have grumbled over the many chores we expect you to do. Do you think you can go beyond these petty farm chores without a high school diploma?"

Shane looked away from his dad. He closed his eyes as in thought. Shaking his head, he answered, "I don't know, Dad. I don't know what I think." Another pause. "I'm not going to sit with a bunch of duds in summer school."

"Even if it means you graduate?" Martin pleaded with his son.

Shane turned to walk away from his dad.

"Wait. Don't go. Would you, at least, agree to meet with the people at school?"

Shane stopped, faced his father. "All this is bull shit. What are they going to say that they haven't already said? If that diploma is so damned important, maybe you can buy one for me." Shane tossed his fork and stomped out of the barn.

"Good afternoon, Mr. and Mrs. Stenlund, Shane." The greeting of the high school principal, Mr. Baxter, jerked Martin back to reality. Following the futile discussion between father and son, a calmer discussion with his mother had persuaded Shane to join his parents at the meeting.

"Sorry to keep you waiting," Mr. Baxter apologized. "Please come on in and have a seat." He gestured to chairs positioned in front of his desk. The principal's office, modest but accommodating, contained the usual office furniture, a desk, accompanying chairs, file cabinets and book cases lining two sides of the room.

"Thank you for coming." Mr. Baxter sat forward in his chair, his attention directed to the Stenlunds seated in front of him. "Graduating from high school represents a giant step in each person's future. I certainly understand your concern for the threat Shane faces in his future without a high school diploma."

He opened a file placed on his desk. "Mr. Winthrop, the school counselor, has given me Shane's academic record." Shane moved restlessly in his chair, eyes focused on the floor. "For whatever reason, Shane is failing an English and a government class, both required for graduation. With less than a month left of the school year, he doesn't have time to achieve passing grades in those two courses."

Martin placed his hand over his wife's. She glanced at her son seated on her right.

Mr. Baxter turned a page in the folder. "I believe Mr. Winthrop has discussed with Shane the possibility of graduating following a successful, summer school session. Beyond that, about the only other option is returning this fall to complete, successfully, those two courses during the fall semester."

Mr. Stenlund shifted in his chair. Mom and Dad noted their son's reaction. Martin folded his arms across his chest. "What about the ceremony itself? Could Shane participate?"

Mr. Baxter sat back in his chair. "Yes, I believe that option was explained to Shane by Mr. Winthrop. If Shane agreed to summer school, yes, he could participate." The principal looked at each of the Stenlunds. He faced silence.

Finally, Iris turned to Shane. "Well, what do you say?"

For a moment he said nothing. He moved his head from side to side as if looking for something under his chair. He pushed back his chair, jumped up and blurted, "I'm not going to summer school." He turned toward the office door. With his hand on the door knob, he looked back at his parents and the principal. "If you think I'm going to come back in the fall, you're nuts!" He opened the door, stepped out, and slammed it behind him.

The Stenlunds sat mildly shocked by their son's behavior. Previous episodes over the same issue had failed to prepare them for the response they just witnessed.

"I'm sorry he feels the way he does." Mr. Baxter sympathized with the Stenlunds.

Martin again gripped his wife's hand. "We are sorry too. We apologize for our son's behavior." He paused. With a shrug of his shoulders, he continued. "I'm not sure what will happen. We have not given up hope that he will come around to reason."

The Stenlunds rose together. "Thank you, Mr. Baxter. We appreciate your time," Iris commented quietly then reached into her purse for a tissue which she used to dab her eyes.

Chapter 16

Shane sat on the plush tractor seat. Sitting down made easier turning the Green Monster for the second half of the round. A huge John Deere tractor with four jumbo tires, a spacious cab, a dash panel of gauges and lights, and the power to pull a sixteen foot field cultivator, Shane had dubbed the Green Monster. A mere thirteen years old when he first took the controls of the monster, the intervening years found him spending hours each spring and fall turning the black, rich Red River Valley soil.

On a warm, partly cloudy Saturday, Shane's job for the day entailed making one last pass with the field cultivator before seeding. The turmoil of the early spring with news of his not graduating and the emotional confrontations with parents and school officials made welcome the solitary day driving a tractor all alone in an isolated field. In truth, the tractor required very little skilled driving. Simply sit back in the captain's chair and steer in a straight line.

Like so many other farm duties, this one demanded very little thinking. *Maybe*, Shane thought, *over the years performing duties requiring very little thinking influenced his work as a student.* He was too accustomed to working without thinking. He smiled as that thought floated through his mind. Recently, little in his life gave him reason to smile. In private moments like those he now experienced, he regretted the disruption in his life and in the lives of his parents created by the graduation issue.

Placing blame for the drastic changes in his life was elusive. However, he could never dismiss that fateful day skiing with his sister on one of Lutsen's hills. Long ago, the number of times he relived that day reached countless. Occasional twinges in his damaged knee over the years only added to the number.

With one hand on the thick padded steering wheel of the Green Monster, Shane leaned against the side of the cab that enclosed the driver. Despite his effort to resist any thoughts of graduation, he couldn't suppress them. Crowding his mind were thoughts about the importance of a high school diploma and the relationship between a college education and success or failure in life. After all, his dad didn't have a college education. Shane considered his father successful even if that success was on a farm.

Shane sat back in the tractor's seat again to maneuver the Green Monster and its enormous cultivator to complete the round. *What would he do with his life*? He doubted attending summer school would give him greater opportunity in the future. Maybe he could find a life in the big city. Danni did. That she brought with her to the big city a thirst for learning and the pursuit of a goal, at the moment, Shane ignored.

He quickly corrected the tractor's path which for a few yards left a strip of soil untouched. Considering the size of the field, no one would notice the gap in his cultivation. His eyes surveyed the vastness of the fields around him, ending only when they met the horizon. He had to admit a definite, primitive beauty to the flat, black ground that stretched for miles around him. For just an instant he wondered if those big city guys, who a few years ago approached him outside a Minneapolis Burger King, found any beauty in their surroundings?

Shane shifted his weight, moving to the other side of the cab, the huge tractor powering straight ahead. Looking back at the cultivator, he detected a faint trail of dust at the far end of the field. Obviously, some vehicle headed his way. Quickly, he could make out a light colored car, one he didn't recognize, certainly not his dad's. With curiosity, he watched the car approach the end of the field where he would make another turn around.

As the tractor and the car converged on the same spot at the end of the field, the driver of the car waved. The car, a late model

Mazda, he thought, stopped, leaving more than enough room for Shane to turn to start a new round. He slowed the Green Monster. Out of the car stepped his sister dressed in shorts and a brightly colored top. She waved with both arms. Shane swung his right arm back and forth in recognition of her wave. Only feet before making the turn around, he stopped the tractor, shut off the powerful engine, and hopped down to greet his sister.

They met with open arms, a firm hug confirming an affection rarely displayed, at least, by Shane.

"Are you lost?" he grinned.

"No, remember, I lived here once myself." Danni poked at her brother's chest.

More serious in tone, Shane asked, "Is something wrong?"

Danni backed up to her car. "No, not really. I just brought you some lunch."

Shane smiled. "That's great. I need something to wake me up." He stretched his arms and straightened his back. "You know, it doesn't take a genius to do what I'm doing."

Danni reached into her car to bring out a small basket along with a picnic blanket.

Shane's mouth dropped open. "What is this, a picnic?"

"Why not. It's a beautiful day so why not spend it in a different way?" Danni chuckled at her unintentional rhyme.

Settled down in the shade of the Green Monster, Danni reached into the basket for sandwiches, a small container of salad and a portion of potato chips for each of them. In silence they organized their lunch on the blanket.

Shane looked up at his sister. "Thank you for coming." He ran his hands through his thick hair. "But why are you here?"

"Oh, just an escape from the big city." Danni stretched out her legs.

Shane turned to look at the car. "Is the car yours?"

Danni smiled with pride. "Yes, I bought it about a month ago."

"I like it." Shane said between bites of his sandwich.

Silence filled the quiet of the cool spring air. Danni took a swallow of her favorite soda. Carefully setting the soda bottle down on the blanket, she folded her arms around her legs, resting her chin on her knees. "Shane, Mom told me you wouldn't graduate this spring."

He looked at his sister, then with his hand pushed a clump of dirt off the blanket. "I wondered how long before she told you." He closed his eyes then nodded. "Yes, it's true."

Danni shook her head. "I'm so sorry to hear that. What happened?"

Shane drew a deep breath. "A long story. A short version is I lack two required credits."

"What happened with them?"

Shane extended his legs in search of a little more comfort on the blanket. "I don't know. I didn't get the work done, I guess." He paused, his eyes connecting with hers. "I got behind and finally just gave up."

"Can't you make up the work missed?" Danni asked even though she knew the answer. Their mother had explained the entire situation to her.

"Yeah, in summer school or in the fall semester." Shane grumbled then took a deep breath. "Danni, I really don't want to talk about this damned graduation thing. For weeks Mom and Dad have been on my ass about it. I'm sorry, but summer school is bull shit. If I have to do that, screw the diploma."

Danni rescued a napkin threatening to blow away. She brushed crumbs off her lap. Again, she drew her knees up and surrounded them with her arms. "I think I understand your attitude about summer school." She stopped, wishing to avoid any sibling hostility. "I don't understand about the diploma. It does make a difference."

Shane stood up to lean against one of the Green Monster's jumbo tires. "Danni, I've heard that argument all spring. Nobody has convinced me that life will end without a high school diploma." He stared down at the black soil at his feet. "I'm not sure if high school has prepared me for anything."

Danni flattened her legs on the blanket. "That's a harsh indictment of the twelve years you spent in school."

Shane turned to push his arms against the jumbo tire. Shaking his head, he said, "I don't know what the hell to think. I don't know what the hell I want to do. I just know I want off this God damn farm." He looked off into the distance.

Danni got up and moved closer to her brother. With her hand she gently rubbed his back. "I don't think you're the first teen to have those doubts. Facing the world after high school can be daunting for most of us."

"It wasn't for you." Shane replied.

"Oh, you don't know that. Yes, it all looked good on the outside. On the inside, all kinds of questions tumbled in my mind."

Shane turned to face his sister. "What did you do about the questions?"

"I took my time to think about them. I discovered I didn't have to rush into decisions. I don't think you do either."

Shane stepped back from his sister. With arms open, palms face up in a pleading gesture, he asked, "What the hell should I do?"

She smiled. "Mom tells me you have a date to the prom."

Shane nodded.

"Who's the lucky girl? Do I know her?"

Shane relaxed his shoulders. "I don't think so. Her name is Lindsey Cooper. She's a senior and lives in Twin Pines."

"That's great." Danni gripped Shane's hand. "Why don't you plan to have a fun time at the prom? Forget about the graduation thing for now. When school's out let's talk some more.

Shane opened his arms to his sister. She stepped forward to accept the invitation for another hug. He held her firmly, whispering in her ear, "Thank you, Thank you."

Chapter 17

Excitement drifted through the halls of Twin Pines High School. At least it did in those halls where juniors and seniors gathered. In but two days the junior-senior prom would find most of the members of upper classes assembled in the high school gym, site of this year's prom. In three weeks all students and likely most teachers as well would celebrate the conclusion to another school year. More important, seniors would walk across the stage to receive a diploma signifying the conclusion of twelve years of education.

Shane faced his locker, searching for the government text book he had ignored too long. Though the government class was one of the credits preventing his graduation, it still didn't excuse him from attending the class. How many other students knew about his missing graduation he had no idea. A topic he didn't willingly discussed with his peers, it also represented one reason he didn't share the excitement and anticipation of the culmination of twelve years of education. However, he did feel some of the excitement for Saturday's prom.

Until he met Lindsey Cooper months ago, Shane rarely dated. Baseball and farm responsibilities commanded his priorities. Consequently, Saturday marked his first prom. With Lindsey he discussed his academic problems. A conscientious student, much like his sister, she applied herself assiduously, capitalizing on the talent she possessed. They discussed their future, hers starting with enrollment at the University of Minnesota Duluth. They touched on Shane's future, but when they did, they bumped into the summer school issue which he vehemently refused to discuss. To avoid animosity, they agreed to ignore discussions of his future.

That may have been the agreement between Lindsey and him. However, questions about his future lay at the very edge of his conscious awareness. Few idle moments failed to include thoughts of his future. Danni's advice to take it easy, to avoid rushing to hasty decisions, eased some of his concern. In three weeks graduation would send one hundred fifty-six young people out into the real world, as Shane often heard it described. The only real world he knew was the world of farming, and he hated it as he hated all the attention to a stupid, high school diploma. Shane rested his hands against the edges of his locker, his eyes staring into its blank, back wall.

"Did you lose something?" Lindsey stopped behind Shane on her way to her next class.

Her soft voice gently pulled Shane back to reality. He turned and smiled. "Hi. Just looking for my government text book."

Not a popular topic between them, Lindsey frowned. "Do you need it today?"

Shane shrugged his shoulders. "I don't know. Sometimes we do; sometimes we don't. I don't need any more hassle in that class." Shane slammed shut the locker door.

Lindsey's English class was on the way to his government class. They walked together.

"You all set for Saturday night?" Lindsey reached for Shane's hand.

He glanced over at his prom date. "I guess so. Mom pressed my one suit; I polished my shoes. What else is there?" He laughed as he pushed against her hand.

"For you probably not much. You boys are lucky. You don't have to worry about hair and . . . ah, well, you know all that girl stuff."

"I know. I have a sister." He looked up at Room 203, her English classroom. "By the way, I did make reservations for dinner at the Country Side Country Club," Shane announced with pride in his diligence.

"That's great. What time?"

Shane stopped. They stood before Lindsey's English classroom. "About seven o'clock. Is that okay?" He asked.

"Sounds good to me. Things won't get started here until after nine anyway." Lindsey stepped to the door of her classroom and dropped Shane's hand. "Talk to you later." She waved as she disappeared into her English classroom.

Shane ambled toward his government class questioning why he even bothered. Maybe some minor miracle would rescue him from the ranks of the failed. However, he never believed in miracles.

Chapter 18

Saturday morning Shane awoke early to start on several routine tasks he needed to complete before about four o'clock when he expected to get ready for the big night. He promised to pick up Lindsey by six thirty for their seven o'clock dinner reservation. He assumed he needed no more than an hour to get ready. Uncharacteristically, he had laid out his clothes that morning. Still, he didn't want to rush. Definitely, he wished to arrive on time to Lindsey's home.

While he performed mindless tasks like feeding the chickens, picking the eggs, and lugging pails of a mixture of grain and water for the pigs, he thought about prom night, a new experience for him. Lindsey and he dated frequently during the last few months. He considered her a compatible friend and partner, attractive, smart, with a good sense of humor. Only recently did thoughts occur to him of going beyond simply making out. Recently, Lindsey responded tenderly to his limited advances, even including his ventures under her top. He smiled remembering the supple softness of her breast but hesitant to contemplate engaging in serious sex.

At times when boys gathered in the school bathroom or the lunch room, he heard talk of "scoring" on prom night. Of course, he knew what scoring meant. However, he respected Lindsey. He didn't wish to do anything that would offend her. Also overheard from those boy conversations were rumors about couples who would rent motel rooms on prom night. Shane found hard to believe parents permitting that. He knew his wouldn't. Despite all the talk and rumors, he couldn't dismiss a little romantic opportunity prom night might have for him.

"My, you look so handsome." Shane's mom reached to adjust his tie. Not very often did he wear one.

"Thanks, Mom." He stood stiff and uncomfortable in his crisply pressed suit and starched shirt.

"You have a good time. Keep in mind your dad and I don't want you coming home when the sun rises."

Shane closed his eyes and shook his head. "Oh, Mom, I'm not gonna do that. Lindsey's parents expect her home at a reasonable time, too."

Shane's dad came in from a day in the field. He voiced compliments about his son's gallant appearance, forgotten for the present the hours of bitter dispute that disrupted their home over Shane's missed graduation.

Shane looked at his watch. "I've gotta go. I don't wanna be late."

Mom gave him a brief hug, again suggesting he have a good time. Dad reached out to pat his son's back, adding his wish for a good time. Vivid in his mind were thoughts of the anguish suffered by his son in recent weeks. Dad also added a caution to drive carefully.

His parents then followed him out to the car insisting on taking pictures before he drove away. As he backed the car around to head out to the main road to Twin Pines, he honked the horn to start his evening of entertainment and potential discovery.

Lindsey lived with her parents and two younger brothers in an impressive, colonial style home at the edge of Twin Pines. A successful automobile dealer in town, Mr. Cooper provided very well for his family. Certainly he spared no expense for the formal his daughter wore. Lindsey welcomed Shane at the front door.

She smiled, "You're right on time."

For an instant Shane could find no words to express his reaction to appearance of his date. To him Lindsey looked gorgeous in her nearly floor length formal with a thin shawl covering bare shoulders, her hair tiered elegantly on top her head, her face aglow with anticipation. "I guess I am, thank you." Shane stared at Lindsey. "You look great." He shuffled his weight from one leg to the other. In one hand he held a corsage designed to fit on her wrist. He stepped closer, striving to conceal his nervousness. "I got this for you."

Lindsey reached to accept the corsage. "Thank you. It's beautiful." She slipped the corsage over her wrist. "Look, it matches by dress perfectly. Thank you." Her sparkling smile reinforced her gratitude. She extended her hand.

His hand met hers, "You're welcome."

Her parents also insisted on taking pictures. Like Shane's mom and dad, they wished them a good time, advised them to be home at a reasonable time, and cautioned them to drive carefully.

Walking to the car, Shane smiled, thinking parents must all share the same script.

Chapter 19

Dinner at the Country Side Country Club enabled Shane and Lindsey to relax, following for both but particularly for her a day of anticipation and preparation. Over dinner they refrained from talk about subjects related to school and graduation. Instead, they talked about the new model cars her dad saw on his recent trip to Detroit and about the whole business of cultivating and seeding which Shane knew intimately.

With dinner concluded, they drove to the high school, this year's site for the prom. The last two years the country club where they just ate dinner also served as the prom site. The lack of careful supervision allowed four couples to spend more time drinking in the parking lot than dancing in the main hall of the club. Consequently, school officials determined this year the high school gym would serve as the prom site. Initially, some students and parents grumbled about the change. The opposition faded in a few days since most students and parents considered the event more important than where it took place.

Shane and Lindsey arrived in time for the grand march, a tradition featuring the prom couples parading around the gym one time for the benefit of proud parents who wished to take pictures. Neither Shane's nor Lindsey's parents believed that necessary since they already took the pictures they wanted.

The pageantry of the event, the glamor and sophistication of fellow students he saw nearly every school day impressed Shane.

Soon the couples found tables where they could relax, talk to friends, and observe the couples who excelled on the dance floor or thought they did. Shane and Lindsey sat with two of her friends and their dates. They danced several sets before taking a break for a glass of punch and a taste of delicate pastry.

The night raced by, much faster than Shane expected. He and Lindsey had made no particular plans for after the prom. Word of a party at the home of the senior class president spread around the gym. Attending a party didn't interest either of them. When the band leader called the last dance, most couples responded. A slow dance, it enabled Shane to feel Lindsey's body against his. A sensation trickled in his groin and up into his stomach.

She pulled him close as his arm tightened around her back. She looked up, a radiant smile brightening her face. The music stopped. They stopped, prolonging the firm embrace. Lindsey kissed his cheek and whispered, "Time to go."

Chapter 20

With no plan, they drove aimlessly around the main streets of Twin Pines, striving to extend the night and meeting several other classmates doing the same. Finally, Lindsey suggested they drive out beyond her home where a rest stop would give them a chance to enjoy the beautiful spring night. In addition, it would give them a chance to sit and reflect upon their night at the prom. The rest stop, a simple turn off from the main highway, sat nestled at the edge of a grove of pine and oak trees, giving it a hint of romantic privacy.

Shane drove into the rest area, parked and shut off the car. They stepped out to walk a short distance to a bench in the shelter of a spreading oak tree. Before reaching the bench, they turned to face each other. Emotion, under control throughout the evening, now surged as they virtually leaped into each other's arms. They kissed long and hard. She offered no resistance. More kisses generated more emotion.

Suddenly, Lindsey stiffened. Breathless, she whispered, "Maybe we shouldn't." She tried to turn away. He refused to allow her to do so.

She pleaded, "Don't! Please, don't!"

"Damn you!" Shane yelled. "What the hell's the matter?"

"Please let me go. Take me home!" She begged. "I can't do this." She burst into tears.

Chapter 21

Shane found an inconspicuous corner of the twenty-four hour restaurant that served as the Twin Pines bus terminal. On this Monday morning students at the high school would now be moving to their second hour classes. When he would attend another class, he had no idea.

A bulging backpack filled with extra clothes and a few personal items clinging to his back, Shane waited for the eight thirty bus to the Twin Cities. Concerned he would see someone he recognized or who would recognized him, he stood in a remote corner of the waiting area, restless but resolved. He was getting out of Twin Pines. The thought of leaving the only place he'd known as home came with moments of intimidation which he successfully suppressed.

In recent months he suffered enough turmoil, disappointment, anxiety, and finally shame. He had to separate himself from the accumulation of problems that made his life intolerable. He shifted his weight from one foot to the other, a slight twinge trickled from his right knee to this thigh. Maybe other causes lay at the foundation of the difficulties he faced, but that drastic moment at Lutsen, in Shane's mind, was certainly one of them. He shifted the backpack to reach into his pocket to feel the money he withdrew from the ATM, depleting his meager account.

At eight fifteen the Greyhound bus pulled into the circular driveway at the front of the restaurant. An announcement greeted the bus's arrival. Shane moved to the restaurant exit. Three other travelers, none familiar, joined him in line at the bus. The driver stood off to the side welcoming his passengers. Shane declined the driver's request to store his backpack under the bus. Easing himself up the three, narrow steps, he gazed over a nearly empty bus. He found a seat about halfway back, wiggled free from his backpack, and stuffed it in the overhead bin. His seat next to the window gave him a fleeting view of the restaurant as the bus pulled onto the highway that would take it to the Twin Cities.

Shane leaned back in his seat and closed his eyes in a futile attempt to relax. Never in his life had he suffered such a disastrous weekend, one that had started out with such promise but ended in such pain. He glanced around the near empty bus. Never in his life had he ridden in a regular bus. Of course, years ago he rode in school busses, much different from the one in which he now sat.

He stretched out his legs under the seat in front of him, his average size conducive to comfort in the relatively confined seats of the bus. Out his window he watched as the bus passed buildings and businesses he had driven by countless times. Leaving the city, he observed country so incredibly familiar to him. Yet he was leaving it. He was leaving the only place he ever called home. The thought produced a lingering sensation in his stomach.

With his seat tipped back, he stared into the small reading light embedded in the bin above his seat. He concluded that prom night was the worst night he could remember, even worse than Lutsen. He could hear Lindsey begging him to stop. A wave of emotion traveled from his stomach to his throat. For an instant he felt nauseated, struggling with what the hell had possessed him to push himself on Lindsey, the only girl he considered not only a date but also a companion. He screwed up that relationship too like he had screwed up everything else in his life.

Big boys don't cry. In Shane's opinion, at eighteen years old he was considered a big boy. Still, Shane fought the tears which gathered in his eyes. His first prom ended in utter humiliation for him and especially for Lindsey. He rubbed his eyes experiencing anew the crushing desperation of his endless drive home after watching Lindsey dash out of his car as soon as he stopped in her driveway. He regretted having no chance even to say he was sorry.

Now, looking out the window at the country side rushing by, he wondered if anything he said would have made any difference.

Shane turned in his seat, striving to cancel the images clouding his mind. It didn't help. Those images only grew more vivid. The hours he spent late Saturday night turning in his bed, grasping for sleep, helped him impose resolve on his shattered life. All day Sunday he prepared himself mentally for the escape that now found him on the bus.

He had spoken little to his parents who insisted on talking about his night at the prom. He resisted their attempts to hear details of the evening. Just thinking about the devastating ending to that evening renewed the lingering agony he felt at the remote rest stop. With some success, he avoided his parents. However, he needed to talk to his sister. In his determination to leave the farm and his home, she offered some rescue.

In his room, he quietly assembled a few clothes he would take with him. He called the Twin Pines bus terminal to check on service to the Twin Cities. His call confirmed an eight thirty departure on Monday morning. Shane reserved a one way ticket, charged on an ATM card he rarely used. He also decided to drive the car to school as usual, leave it in the school parking lot, and ask his sister to let his parents know about the car. Explaining to them why he decided to leave home would require much more careful consideration than he cared to think about. With most preparation completed, Shane called Danni on his cell phone. As his bus headed southeast away from Twin Pines, he could almost hear, word for word, that conversation.

"Shane, to what do I owe the pleasure of your call?" Danni answered with a hint of humor and sarcasm. So rarely did he call her or even talk to her when she called home, his call served as a distinct surprise.

With his phone pressed to his ear, Shane sat on his bed speechless, struggling for words to explain the reason for his call.

"Are you there?" Danni urged.

He cleared his throat. "I need your help." Concerned his parents might overhear his call, he spoke softly.

Alarmed, Danni asked, "What's wrong? Are you okay?"

"Yeah, I'm okay, I guess. I just need your help." His voice barely above a whisper.

"Yes, you said that. What's wrong?" Her voice reflected the concern she felt.

"I want to come stay with you." He blurted out.

The comment caught Danni without a response.

"I need to get away from this God damn farm, school, the whole fucking thing!" Shane spoke in a firm voice with conviction and resolve.

"Wow. Wait a minute. What brought this on?" Shane's problems at school she knew about. Did those problems justify leaving home?

"Look," Shane's frustrations imposed an urgency in his voice. He breathed in then exhaled. "It's a long story. I can't talk about it now. I'm sorry, but I . . . ah, I need someplace to stay for a while until I can get some corner on this life of mine."

"Have you talked to Mom and Dad about this?" Danni asked.

"No."

"Don't you think you should?" Danni persisted

"They're, like . . . part of the problem, I think." Silence again. "Look, can I stay with you or can't I?"

Danni realized she would not receive the details of his troubles over the phone. "Sure, you can stay here. When are you coming?"

"Tomorrow," Shane announced.

Danni caught her breath in surprise, halting the conversation. At last, she replied, "We obviously need to discuss this but not now. What time are you coming? How are you getting here?"

"I leave on the bus at eight thirty in the morning. Should be there by about noon."

"Okay. Call me when you arrive."

With little else to say for either of them, the conversation ended.

The announcement by the driver of a brief stop in the next town for additional passengers, brought Shane back to the reality of this remarkable day which not long ago he would never have dreamed of.

At twelve fifteen the bus entered the Twin City freeway system. During the nearly four hour ride, Shane captured a few moments of sleep. The driver's announcement of their impending arrival interrupted one of those moments. Shane stretched as much as the confinement of his seat would allow. He rubbed his eyes, searched out his window for anything he remembered about Minneapolis from previous trips to visit his sister. A melancholy smile worked its way across his lips as he remembered previous visits to see her, occasions representing a much happier time indeed.

Shane reached into his shirt pocket for his cell phone to inform Danni of his arrival. She could use her lunch hour to pick him up and drop him off at her condo. She was waiting for Shane when he stepped off the bus with all he owned in the world right now stuffed in his backpack. She greeted him with a brief hug. They moved quickly to the parking lot and Danni's car for the short ride to her condo.

Chapter 22

Shane stood next to his sister before the large window overlooking the Nicollet Mall. All afternoon he did very little except watch some TV and wait for his sister's return from work. She brought with her a couple orders of hamburgers and fries to serve as their dinner until she could determine exactly what arrangements would suit her brother.

"Great place." Shane commented.

"Yeah, I like it. It's perfect for my needs."

"By the way," Shane turned to his sister, "would you call Dad for me. As I told you, I left the car in the school parking lot. He needs to pick it up. I'd rather not talk to him right now."

Danni nodded her head. "Sure."

Avoiding a discussion she knew inevitable, a discussion of Shane's future, Danni moved to the kitchen to unpack the hamburgers and fries she brought home for their dinner. With two plates prepared, she turned to ask her brother, "Where would you like to sit down?"

"Wherever you want." Shane shrugged his shoulders.

"Why don't you take the sofa? I'll join you there." Danni handed him a plate.

Shane stepped across the living room to sit on a large, leather sofa. Danni followed. For a few moments they concentrated on their hamburgers and fries, halting only for a sallow of Danni's forbidden soda.

With their plates nearly empty, Danni asked, "Do you need anything else to eat? We can get more food if you want."

"No, I'm fine." Shane leaned back on the sofa, savoring, more than his meager dinner, a relaxation he hadn't felt in days.

Danni got up to collect his plate and with hers returned them to the kitchen sink. She returned to regain her place at the end of the sofa where she rested against the end cushion

Shane crossed his legs and shifted his position. With hands clasped gently around his right knee, he fixed his eyes on the blank TV.

"Do you want to watch TV?" She asked.

"Fine," Shane answered. He stood up and stepped to the TV, eyes searching. "Where's the remote?"

"Right next to the TV, on the right."

Shane reached for the remote, turned and handed it to his sister. "Here, you do it."

Danni leaned forward. She turned on the TV, clicking through the channels. "Not much on. How about the news?"

"Okay." Shane shrugged his shoulders.

They sat in silence watching the news. Danni straightened up at her end of the sofa. Her eyes rested on her brother. Taking a deep breath, she asked, "Okay, what happened at home to make you want to leave?"

Shane stared at the TV, oblivious to what he saw there. Momentarily distracted, what he did see was a large, flat screen TV, the kind he urged his dad to buy. Beneath the TV he noted a DVD player and an AM FM receiver. He closed his eyes. He shook his head. "I don't know what happened. Nothing went right."

"Did you talk to Mom and Dad?" a question she previously asked but one of importance.

"No, not really," Shane mumbled.

"What do you mean?"

Shane shifted his position, stretching his right leg. "Ah . . . I don't know. All our talk ended in arguing about graduation."

"Did you think any more about graduation after our conversation a while ago?"

"No. What's to think about?" He asked in a bitter tone.

Danni sat back on the sofa. Sensitive to her brother's fragile mood, she refrained from pursuing the subject of graduation. She rose from the sofa to walk to the kitchen. From the fridge she grabbed a can of soda. "Would you like another Sprite?"

"Sure," came the terse response from the living room.

Returning to the living room, Danni handed Shane the soda then positioned herself in front of the picture window. For a few moments she observed the activity on the Nicollet Mall below, always a source of interest. She brought the soda to her lips to take a swallow. She turned to face Shane, still seated on the sofa, paying casual attention to the TV.

"Shane, you are certainly welcome to stay here. The den doesn't make the best bedroom, but it will work if you're not too particular." A smile crossed Danni's lips.

Shane looked up at his sister. "Thank you."

Danni took a deep breath and slowly exhaled. "What you're going to do all day long is another issue. Have you thought about that?"

Shane averted his eyes. He studied the floor beneath him. Shaking his head, he said, "No," to the floor.

"Remember, a long time ago we talked about life on the farm in contrast to life in the city? You mentioned the boredom of life on the farm. Without something to do, without some plan, what you will find here is only more boredom."

Shane got up from the sofa to stand next to his sister by the large window. He trained is eyes on all the people moving about on the mall. "I guess I'll have to look for a job or something." He reached into his pocket. "I have some money, not a lot but all I had in my savings."

"It isn't just about money. It's about having some purpose each day." Danni tipped up her can of Sprite, took another swallow, then turned to set the can on an end table. She faced Shane. "In that conversation we had in your pony's stall, we also talked about idleness. Remember, I told then about the number of young people I saw hanging around in idleness doing nothing. Eventually, some of them likely found something to do which ended in clashes with the police."

Shane's gaze never left the window. "I know," he uttered. "I know all about work. I don't remember any idleness on the farm." He turned toward his sister. "Don't you think I could find a job here?"

Danni nodded her head. "Of course, I'm sure you could at least until you decide what you want to do with your life." She picked up her Sprite, took a last swallow, and walked the few steps to the kitchen where she dropped the can in the recycling bin. Over her shoulder she advised. "Look, why don't we get you set up in the den?" Leading Shane the short distance to the den, She advised, "We can talk more tomorrow. By the way, I'm sorry you have to sleep on the floor. We'll have to invest in a small cot or something."

"Don't worry about that." Shane answered. "I really appreciate your letting me stay here."

Laughing, Danni replied, "It's what sisters are for." She directed Shane into the den. "While you're getting acquainted with your room for now, I'll call Dad about the car."

"Thank you," Shane acknowledged in a voice barely above a whisper.

Chapter 23

Dressed in a tan pant suit over a brown blouse she had worn to work, Danni sat down on the bed, holding her cell phone. Though she hesitated out of concern for especially their dad's response, Shane's request that she contact their parents about his leaving home and the location of the car demanded she make the call. In the phone's directory she located one of the most frequently called numbers. She pressed the phone to her ear. Her dad answered on the third ring.

"Hello, Danni. How are you?" A hint of worry in his voice.

"I'm fine." She spoke in a soft but tense voice. Since Shane asked her earlier to call home, she thought about how she would approach the subject with her dad. Direct, without preface, was her decision. "I'm calling about Shane."

"Well, I wonder where the hell he is." Her dad grumbled. "He should have been home from school a long time ago. I assume something delayed him for some reason. He left earlier this morning."

Danni gripped the cell phone tight against her ear. "I'm afraid he isn't in school, Dad. He's here."

Her dad caught his breath then barked into the phone. "What? You've got to be kidding. What the hell is he doing there?"

Danni waited before responding, searching for the right words to explain the situation. "Dad, listen to me just for a moment. I don't know what's happened there at home with Shane. Sunday he called to ask about staying here for a while. He didn't give a very specific reason why."

"What the hell . . ." her dad interrupted.

"Dad, please, just listen for a bit." Danni took a breath then swallowed. "Today, he arrived by bus about noon. He will stay here as long as he wishes until he can get his life straightened out. Right now I don't think he wants to discuss it with you. Please give him time."

Silence filled the line. Then her dad cleared his throat. "Things have not gone well for him this spring in school, but did he give you any reason for his strange behavior?"

"Well, as I said before, he didn't say anything specific. He did mention the graduation thing, but nothing beyond that except to declare how he had screwed up everything."

"What does he plan on doing?" Her dad asked.

"Right now I'm not sure. We'll have to deal with this one day at a time. He needs time to think about what's next for him. I don't think we should pressure him about why he did what he did." She paused, her initial anxiety fading. "By the way, he wanted me to tell you the car is parked in the school parking lot."

She heard a brief sigh then, "Thank you. A bit of a shock, but your mother and I appreciate your call and your willingness to step in for your brother. I don't understand what's going on, but we know he's safe there with you."

"Of course he is, Dad. I think we need to give him time to deal with the problems he has."

More silence. "I suppose. He's obviously made a decision we all have to live with."

"Yes, I agree." Danni reached across the bed, grasping a tissue from the night stand. She dabbed her forehead. "Look, Dad, try not to worry about Shane. He's not the first eighteen year old to bump up against a personal crisis."

Her dad exhaled audibly. "I can't promise we won't worry, but thank you for letting us know. Please keep in touch and remind Shane that he's welcome back home any time."

"Yes, I will. Bye now."

Danni closed her eyes for an instant, relieved with the conclusion to a conversation she regretted but felt compelled to make. She definitely did not place the blame on her parents for the problems which forced her brother to leave home. Still, she understood the demands her dad imposed on him over the years. Even those carefree years of baseball included pressure to do well.

With the thought of baseball came the thought of the knee surgeries which marked a crucial time in her brother's life. In recent months, hearing about Shane's academic deficiencies, made her think about what would have happened without the knee surgeries? She frowned, quickly got up off the bed, stuffed her phone in her purse, and hurried out to the kitchen, passing the den where Shane was getting acquainted with his bedroom.

While Danni rinsed dishes in preparation for placement in the dish washer, Shane left the den and stood behind her. "Need any help, sis?"

In surprise, Danni turned around to face her brother, who stood with hands in his pockets. "No, I have only a few things to put away in the dish washer. What do you think of your room?"

Shane smiled. "Great."

Danni laughed. "Not sure it's great. Sorry about the hard floor."

"It won't be so bad. Besides I can't be choosy." He moved over to lean on the counter. "Did you call?"

"Yes," Danni nodded her head.

Shane straightened up pushing away from the counter. "What did he say?"

"Not much, obviously a bit shocked but kind of understanding your need to get away." She placed a plate in the dish washer then looked up at her brother. "He wished you well and said anytime you were welcome to come home."

Shane smiled a melancholy smile, a gentle shaking of his head accepting his sister's brief explanation.

Danni rinsed out her coffee cup, two more plates, and a glass, placing them in the dish washer. Closing the dish washer, she looked up at her brother. "Why don't we go back in the living room? Just a couple things about life in the big city." She smiled while guiding her brother back to the sofa.

Seated she turned to face Shane. "Obviously, I need to get off to work tomorrow. In the morning I'll leave an extra key on the bench by the door. Make sure, if you go out, you lock up. I should be home about five o'clock depending on traffic. I don't know your plans, but you'll have to decide what to do. There should be food in the fridge for lunch. We'll do something else for dinner after I get home." Danni paused. "Any questions?"

Shane shook his head. "Sounds good. Don't worry about me. I will take care of myself."

The evening passed quietly as sister and brother watched two TV sitcoms before Danni confessed to working a long day. She rose from her place on the sofa. "I think I need to get to bed. Stay up if you wish. Not much on TV but it's something to do." She laughed.

Shane also stood up. "No, it's been a long day for me too."

They stood in the middle of the living room. Danni moved closer to her brother, opened her arms and gave him a firm hug. "Good night, brother," she whispered.

"Good night. See you tomorrow." Shane answered.

They both headed in the same direction, Shane to the den, Danni to the master bedroom.

In the den, Shane lay on the floor sandwiched between two light blankets. He stared into the darkness of the den, reliving in his mind the emotional turmoil of the last forty-eight hours. At the core of the turmoil was his decision to leave home and the chances that decision would help him begin a new life or sentence him to the old, bitter one. Lindsey's pleas echoed in his mind as he waited for an elusive sleep.

Chapter 24

Shane returned to the den where he folded the blankets serving as his bed. He stepped into the master bath which he would have to share with his sister. The other bath, the powder room he heard it described, contained no shower. Danni had provided towels for him the night before. He showered and brushed his teeth. He stood looking at himself in the mirror. He studied his reflection, a sadness shown in his eyes; the edges of his mouth turned down slightly. He slowly moved his head back and forth, reflecting on how the hell he got to this point in his life. He threw the towel on the floor, started to walk out of the bathroom then stopped, reached for the towel and hung it up. In the den he dressed in jeans and a T shirt, the only kind of clothes that fit in his backpack.

In the kitchen, Shane ate a piece of toast and drank a glass of apple juice for breakfast. At nine o'clock in the morning, with absolutely nothing to do, he stood in front of that window to the Nicollet Mall world below. What a contrast to his life on the farm when each morning before school he performed his chores. At school right now he would sit in his second hour class. An instant of nostalgia intruded on his view of the Mall. School, chores, farm, none of that mattered any more. He gazed down at the Nicollet Mall, fifteen floors below, crowded with people doing whatever people did on a Tuesday morning on Nicollet Avenue.

He grabbed the TV remote. Rarely did he watch TV at nine o'clock in the morning on any day. Surfing through the channels, he found nothing of interest except a reference on the morning news to a serious problem with homeless teens. The news item captured his attention since he realized without his sister he could be one of them. The news reporter claimed that each night over twenty-five hundred young people ages sixteen to twenty-one wandered the streets of the Twin Cities, homeless. The statistic shocked him. He sat down on the sofa to listen to the rest of the report. He learned that very few facilities existed for the homeless young people, mostly teens.

Shane leaned back on the sofa, his hand gripping the remote control. He attempted to grasp the reality of what he just heard, perplexed by where these young people came from or what had forced them out of their homes and onto the street. Like him they weren't in school. Like him they had screwed up. *Did he risk ending up on the street*? He stared at the TV and saw only a commercial. He shut it off. He would not spend the day watching TV. Nonetheless, the news item about the homeless young people captured his attention much more than it would have a few days ago.

He got up from the sofa, replaced the TV remote, and stood again in front of the large window. The crowd on the mall had thinned. Still, people walked in and out of the stores, he knew nothing about, that lined the Nicollet Mall. He had a day to kill, probably lot of days to kill. He would not spend this day standing in front of the window watching the action on the Nicollet Mall. Instead, he would join the people on the Nicollet Mall.

Slipping his hand into his front pocket, Shane checked to ensure he had the key to the condo. In the hallway, he turned to make sure he locked the door. With a sense of anticipation, almost adventure, he took the elevator down to street level. He stepped out onto the Nicollet Avenue, intrigued by all the people, the buildings and the shadows almost printed across the wide sidewalk. He looked both ways.

Danni's condo building apparently was near one end of the mall. On his left he glimpsed a park. He elected to head for the tall office buildings on his right. He had no idea what went on in these buildings and really didn't care on this Tuesday morning, the first since he left home. He simply wanted to walk, to forget about the farm and Twin Pines, and to explore.

His walk took him toward Macy's a few blocks away. Not far to his left he saw a Target store. That the mall restricted traffic to only buses and taxis Shane found interesting. In his limited travel, he had not seen streets that prohibited regular car traffic. He passed several small boutiques and specialty shops as well as restaurants. At near noon, people lined up for lunch at some of these restaurants featuring outside eating. He hadn't witnessed that before either. A grin stretched his lips as he realized how little he knew about the world off the farm.

Reluctant to stray too far from the condo, Shane halted his walk to determine how far he had gone. The condo was still visible a few blocks back. He relaxed and turned to explore more of this urban world. Soon he approached a towering building, taller than any around it, bordering the Mall. The ground level of the building, readily accessible, included an area almost like a park in the middle of down town Minneapolis. Shane stood impressed and intrigued with this indoor park, decorated with a fountain, tables under umbrellas, benches, real trees and a stage for, he supposed, entertainment of some kind. People gathered in small groups around the tables and benches, some ate lunch from bags, some sat simply enjoying an early summer day.

Shane questioned where all these people came from. A group of people about his age assembled near the fountain. He thought about the news item he saw earlier on TV. *Were these some of the homeless people mentioned in that report*? He saw a young couple in an embrace. His mind quickly pictured Lindsey and him on the dance floor, only days ago. A pang of sadness and regret trickled through his body. Since the dreadful mess he made of his first prom, he thought often of Lindsey, wondering if she ever thought about him? He sat down on one of the benches perplexed by a world he knew so little about.

For a while, he lost track of time, he sat on the bench content to feel the sun's warmth through the wide entrance and to observe the flow of people coming and going in the apparently very popular place. He considered what his days in the big city would include. He couldn't spend his time walking around the Nicollet Mall even though right now it offered a welcomed diversion. He thought about his sister who definitely had adapted well to life off the farm. He rose from the bench, stretched, and started back to the condo, thinking, maybe, he, too, could adapt.

Chapter 25

"How was your day?" Danni entered the condo lugging a grocery bag and her purse.

Shane sprawled on the sofa. "Oh, great." His comment dripping with sarcasm.

Danni unloaded her burden on the kitchen counter. "I brought some pizza from Papa Murphy's. All we have to do is bake it for a few minutes."

"I'm not stupid. I've heard of Papa Murphy's," Shane mumbled.

Danni walked toward her bedroom. She paused in front of her brother. "What did you do today?"

He pulled his feet up to the sofa, averting his eyes from his sister. "What do you think? Not much I can do."

She rolled her eyes at the comment then continued on into her bedroom where she changed into shorts and a comfortable, cotton top. Hanging up her clothes she wore to work, she couldn't help but reflect upon her brother's attitude. It simply was not good. In truth, it had worsened in the three weeks since his arrival. His hanging around the condo, doing nothing and seeking to do nothing gave her additional reason to worry. But he was eighteen years old, an age which carried with it, presumably, increased independence and self reliance. Still, Shane evinced neither. Instead, he floundered in a world of idleness.

When she returned to the living room, Shane pointed the remote at the TV, searching for anything of interest beside the evening news. Danni sat down on the end of the sofa and watched his skipping from one channel to another finally giving up to the

NBC evening news on Channel 11. He sat back, looking with vacant eyes at the TV.

"Would you like some pizza?" She asked.

"Yeah, why not?" He tossed the TV remote onto the nearby sofa table.

Danni carried in a plate of pizza, set it on the coffee table, and eased herself onto the sofa. She reached for a piece of pizza. "By the way, I talked with Mom this afternoon."

Shane took a bite of his pizza, chewed slowly, then asked. "So, what did she have to say?"

"Well, she asked about you. She wonders when you're coming home or when you'll call."

He would not make eye contact with his sister; instead, he stared at the TV. "I suppose they miss someone to boss around."

"Shane, stop this nonsense!" Danni stood up; her face turned red; her hands gripped her hips. "Mom and Dad love you and miss you. How can you talk like that?" She hurried into the kitchen, refusing to wait for another belligerent response.

Shane sat up, placing his elbows on his knees. A sudden twinge reminded him of maybe why he was here and not at home. A knee shattered, not once but twice, can make a hell of a difference. He shook his head. Everything he tried he fucked up. He fixed his eyes on the TV, the smell of pizza lingering from the kitchen.

Danni returned to the sofa, carrying a small plate with more pizza. She dabbed her lips with a napkin, balancing the plate on her lap. She turned to face Shane seated at the other end of the sofa. "Can we talk like adults for a minute?"

Shane looked over at his sister. "Sure, what's there to talk about?"

"One thing is your attitude."

"What's the matter with it?" He asked with a sneer curling his lips.

"You see nothing the matter with the way you react even to a reasonable question?"

"Don't start on me. I had enough of that shit at home." He took another bite of his pizza, chewed then asked, "What do you expect from a loser?"

"Shane, listen to me." She set her plate on the sofa arm and leaned forward with elbows resting on her knees. "You're not a loser. You need to stop that kind of talk. Some things have not gone your way. That doesn't make you a loser."

"What does it make me? You have all the answers." Shane spit out his response.

"No, I don't. It's obvious, though, that something has to change or things won't get better." Danni stood up to carry her plate to the kitchen. She reached out her hand in an invitation for Shane to give her the plate before him on the coffee table. She placed the plates on the kitchen counter. Bracing her hands on the edge of the counter, she inhaled. Releasing her breath, she stepped back into the living room.

Standing in the middle of the floor, she calmly stated, "Look, Shane, you've been here for three weeks. You can stay here as long as you wish, and I mean that." She paused, placing her hands on her hips. You do need to find something to do. You can't spend all your time sitting here or wandering around the Mall."

"What would you suggest I do?" A sarcastic edge cut through his response.

"Have you considered looking for a job?" Danni echoed his sarcasm.

"Sure, I have. What kind of job should I look for? Not much demand for a farm boy who couldn't even graduate from high school."

Danni recognized the fundamental truth to his answer. They talked previously about the importance of a high school diploma. However, she rejected addressing that subject now. "Why not check with one of the restaurants on the mall or how about Target right around the corner?"

"What good are any jobs there? Earn ten bucks an hour for a dead end job sweeping floors or cleaning up other people's shit."

"It's not a career. It's only until you decide what you want to do." Danni sensed the futility of the discussion. Nonetheless, she believed until her brother found something productive to occupy his time, he would become increasingly vulnerable to a long list of temptations swirling around the streets of downtown Minneapolis.

In the kitchen she cleaned up the pizza dishes. Passing through the living room on her way to the powder room, Danni mentioned to Shane that she and Grayson, whom Shane had met only briefly, planned to spend part of the evening walking through Loring Park, a short distance from the condo. "Why don't you join us?"

"No thanks." Shane mumbled, still sitting on the sofa.

"What are your plans for the evening?" She worried about his strolling aimlessly around the mall and nearby Hennepin Avenue at night. He earlier made a comment which embodied a truth whose full impact, she believed, he failed to grasp. That he was, indeed, a farm boy who hadn't even graduated from high school did add to his vulnerability.

"I don't know. Maybe just sit here for a while." For a while he did sit there. However, after Danni left with her boy friend, he decided to find relief on the mall from the boredom and angst that each day closed in tighter around him.

Chapter 26

Shane picked through the few clothes he brought with him, laying a clean pair of shorts and Twins T shirt on the futon which replaced for a bed the blankets on the floor. At least he could venture out on the Mall in different clothes. What he had worn for more than two days gave him a feeling of vagrancy. Stepping into the shorts, a frown creased his brow. *Maybe he was just a vagrant.* He shook his head, reminding himself to forget that shit.

In the corridor outside the condo, Shane secured the door and tucked the key in his shorts. He took the familiar steps to the elevator and the familiar ride to the street below. In his short stay with Danni, he discovered that no matter the day of the week or the time of the day or night people crowded the Nicollet Mall. In three weeks he had spent much of each day there himself.

On this Thursday evening he walked toward what he learned was named the Crystal Court, the area he found interesting on his first introduction to the mall. With no particular purpose he moved with the crowd paying little attention to those around him.

The discussion or more accurately the verbal interchange with Danni replayed in his mind. This talk about him and his future was getting tedious. The bitterness and anger that plagued him for months hung over him like a cloud. Since he left home, he hadn't talked to his parents. That he really didn't care bothered him but not enough to call home. In one week his classmates would graduate. In recent days, during private moments around the condo, he found considerable time to think about the life he left behind. Not graduating, more than he would admit, captured a significant share of that life.

Up ahead he could see the IDS Tower's Crystal Court with lights now spilling over the small groups and individuals milling around the fountain, the tables or sitting on the benches. People also casually strolled through the court on their way to a restaurant or a boutique. Shane spotted a bench off to one side of the court, about the only available seat. He sat down, shoulders slouched, hands resting on the edge of the bench. His eyes traveled around the court. Near the fountain several, apparent, senior citizens traded taking pictures. The tables accommodated some who snacked and some who just sat. Standing off to Shane's left, a young couple faced each other, engaged in an animated conversation punctuated with bold gestures, either a happy conversation or an angry one.

As he watched the couple, he thought of Lindsey Cooper. He heard again her pleas for him to stop. He winced, rolling his eyes, wishing he could think of all the good times they shared rather than that horrible prom night. However, even thoughts of Lindsey and prom night occurred less and less, replaced by a daily struggle with a life without meaning. Shane leaned forward, resting his head in his hands, fighting against the threat of tears.

"Hey, guy, you okay?"

The question jerked Shane away from his musing. He looked up to see before him a short, stocky guy about his own age wearing black pants and a golf shirt with Eighth Street Grill printed across the front. "Yeah, I'm fine." Shane cleared his throat.

"Mind if I sit down?" The young man asked.

"Sure. Be my guest." Shane moved closer to the end of the bench.

They sat in silence, one at each end of the bench. The young man stretched out his legs in front of him, then leaned back on arms resting on the edge of the bench. "Do you live around here? I think I've seen you before."

"Yeah, down there a few blocks, in a condo." Shane pointed.

The young man reached out his hand. "Hi. I'm Max Hawkins. I work at the place printed here on my shirt. It's close. Just taking a break."

Shane reached over to shake hands with Max. "I'm Shane Stenlund, unemployed.

Chapter 27

"Shane, dammit, would you stop pacing and sit down." Mr. Stenlund moved off the sofa into one of the two chairs stationed near each end of the sofa. "We can't talk with you marching around."

Shane stopped long enough to address his dad. "What's there to talk about that we haven't talked about before?" His voice retained the caustic tone it acquired in recent months.

"Just do as your dad asks." Danni intervened, accustomed to the bitterness and belligerence of her brother. During the five weeks she shared her condo with Shane, she had dissuaded their parents from visiting. She insisted they wait until he gained more control over his life. He had changed little with the passage of five weeks. Their parents grew more eager to visit, to try to talk sensibly with their son. Repeated requests to visit forced Danni to relent.

Martin and Iris drove to the Twin Cities early Saturday, arriving at the condo about mid morning. Despite his threats to leave before they arrived, Danni persuaded Shane to stay to meet with his parents in some attempt at conciliation. In her mind, the conflict separating them had gone on far too long. Adults should attempt to resolve their differences.

Reluctantly, Shane plopped himself onto the sofa shared by Danni and his mother. He looked over at his mom, her face pale and drawn, her eyes tinged with redness, then at his dad in expectation of some comment. His demeanor shouted, "You wanted to talk so let's talk."

Danni sensed the almost palpable tension hovering over the living room. "Dad, how are things on the farm?"

Martin folded his arms across his chest. He took a deep breath. The strain of the conflict with his son shown clearly on his face too, his hair noticeably sprinkled with more gray. "Okay. Seeding almost done. A few acres left."

Silence descended again over the living room.

"How's your job?" Iris shifted nervously in her place next to Shane.

"Busy. More requests all the time for testing." Danni replied.

"What are you testing?" Her mom asked.

"Oh, all kinds of things, mostly food related." Danni explained.

Martin dropped his arms to his sides in obvious impatience. "I'm sorry, but we drove down here this morning to talk to our son who we haven't seen or talked to in weeks. We are worried. We want to know what's going on."

The comment aroused Shane from his lethargy. "What's going on is not a damned thing. I've learned a lot about the Nicollet Mall if that means anything." He looked around at his family. "Other than that not much has changed."

"Danni told us some time ago that you intended to look for a job." His dad asked tentatively, aware of his son's volatility.

"Did she tell you about my great qualifications for a job?" Shane spit out with contempt.

Danni jumped up. She moved to the large picture window where she sat on the narrow ledge. "Mom and Dad, we have discussed the job thing several times. Shane can't see himself working what he calls a dead-end job. I've tried to reason with him about starting somewhere." With a tip of her head, she shrugged her shoulders. "He hasn't listened very well."

Shane spread his arms in supplication. "As far as you people are concerned, I can't do a damned thing very well."

"That's not true, and you know it." His dad barked. "For you, that has become an excuse to sit on your butt and do nothing."

Tension mounted in the room. Eyes darted from one family member to another. Shane studied the floor.

Mr. Stenlund swallowed and continued. "We don't need excuses anymore. We need action. At almost nineteen years old, Shane, you need to start looking realistically at your future. Mistakes you have made are in the past. Forget about them, and as we do every spring on the farm, start over."

Shane glared at his dad. "Yeah, that's easy for you to say. You don't have people constantly telling you what to do. I . . . I think I can figure a few things out for myself. It doesn't take a genius to see I'm qualified to do very little in the world."

"Yes, you have imposed some handicaps on yourself. That doesn't have to mean you give up." Iris spoke softly, careful not to inflame the discussion.

To reduce the tension hanging over them, Danni got up from the window ledge. "Does anyone want a cup of coffee or a soda?" With her mother's help, Danni served coffee to her parents and a soda for herself. Shane wanted nothing. A restless quiet settled over the Stenlund family.

"You'll stay for the night, won't you?" Danni asked her parents.

"No, we have rented a motel room in a Super Eight not far from here." Her dad announced.

"You don't have to do that." Danni replied.

"I know, but we don't want to intrude here." Martin confessed.

"Okay, Dad, but parents are not intruders." Danni smiled.

"That's my role." Shane blurted out. His comment engendered no response. He got up from his place on the sofa. He hadn't moved since his dad asked him to stop pacing the floor. "Say, Mom and Dad, did you attend the graduation thing, let's see . . . last weekend, I think?"

Both shook their heads.

In feigned surprise, Shane said, "Why not? You kept telling me how damn important that graduation was." A malicious grin distorted his face.

"Shane, stop it. Maybe when you recognize how right Mom and Dad were, you will start seeing some meaning to your life." Danni stared at her ungrateful brother, unable to contain her anger.

Shane's eyes opened wide; his breathing came in bursts. "I don't have to put up with this shit. You people have no idea what I recognize and what I don't." He turned to look first at his dad then his mom. "Mom and Dad, you came here to talk. Okay you talked. You said the same God damn things you said before." He moved toward the condo exit. "I don't know what's gonna happen. I do know I'm not gonna listen to your bullshit anymore." He turned abruptly, stormed out the door, slamming it behind him.

Danni and her parents sat in stunned silence, each considering how this all happened.

"I'm sorry," Danni pleaded. "He doesn't mean what he says. He can't let go of his anger."

"Don't blame yourself," her dad consoled. "It's not your fault." He stepped toward his daughter, reaching out to grasp her hand. "I'm not sure it's anyone's fault. We all need to move beyond assessing blame before something even more serious happens."

Without saying it, they all suspected that placing blame need go no further than the slopes at Lutsen Ski Resort.

Chapter 28

For twenty-four hours Shane walked the streets around his sister's condo. His aimless wandering after he stormed out of the family clash took him to very familiar places, ones where he spent most of his time for the past several weeks. Of course, he walked the Nicollet Mall. He ventured by the sprawling convention center and for a short time from a pedestrian bridge stared absently at the traffic under him on the freeway below, his only thought, *did people never stay home*? Most of the night he spent in Loring Park, sprawled out on a hard, wooden park bench partially hidden from view by a bush and a sign advising users to keep the park clean. On the many walks Shane took during his time living with Danni, none of them occurred late at night. What restrictions applied to sleeping on park benches he had no idea. Vagrancy was a word rare in his vocabulary.

Intentionally, he ended the long night with a walk to the Crystal Court where he always seemed to find some peace and contentment. At six o'clock in the morning he observed very little activity in the court. He selected a favorite place, one giving him a full view of the fountain and the Mall beyond visible through the wall of windows separating it from the IDS Center.

Tired, troubled, and confused, he sat down heavily on the bench. He ran his hands through his hair, snarled and sticky from neglect. Never had he envisioned a time when he would spend the night walking big city streets. Weeks had passed and still little had changed to make his life more tolerable. He repeatedly asked himself about the direction of his life. One thing for sure, he needed to look for some kind of job. Floating around aimlessly had to stop. With his sister, he now agreed; boredom wasn't confined to life on the farm. He faced enough of it here in the big city.

He felt no regret leaving in haste his family feud the day before. His parents refused to release their oppressive hold over him. They simply failed to understand his need for freedom to make his own decisions. With disappointment he witnessed, yesterday, his sister joining his parents in dictating his life.

Shane stood up, stretched, and rubbed his eyes. The night in the park didn't offer much sleeping comfort. That he spent the night virtually on the street amazed him. The thought produced a tiny smile. The smile quickly faded when he considered facing Danni, whose calls on his cell phone he ignored. Soon he would have to confront her but not until evening. After she left for work, he would return to the condo and its quiet emptiness.

He sat down again and glanced at his watch, only eight o'clock. Danni would soon leave for work. She made no attempt to call him in the last couple hours. Preoccupied with Danni's reaction to his staying out all night, he paid little attention to the person sitting down at the other end of the bench. It was Max.

"You're up early." Max's comment startled Shane.

"Hi, ah . . . Max isn't it?"

"Yeah, we talked not too long ago. You're unemployed, right?" Max grinned, alluding to their previous conversation.

Shane lowered his head. "Yeah, that's me. What're you doing here so early?" Shane looked over at his first acquaintance since leaving the farm.

"On my way to work, just down the street, the Eighth Street Grill, remember? By the way have you found a job yet?"

Shane shook his head. "No."

"Have you looked?" Max pursued the topic.

"No," was Shane's terse response. Getting a job ranked very low on his list of favorite topics. He heard enough about jobs from his parents as well as from his sister.

Sensing Shane's reluctance to talk about a job, Max asked, "You live down the Mall a ways, don't you?"

"Yeah, with my sister."

"How long have you lived there?" Max reached into his jacket pocket for a lighter to light his cigarette. He inhaled deeply then released a stream of smoke through his nose.

Shane grasped his knees and straightened his arms forcing him to sit up. "Four or five weeks, I guess."

"What did you do before that?" Max flicked ashes from his cigarette.

Shane grinned. "Picked eggs and cleaned chicken shit off roosts in the chicken coop."

Puzzled, Max looked over at Shane. "What the hell is that?"

Shane laughed. "I lived on a farm. Chickens were my responsibility."

"How did you get here?" The more they talked the more their conversation fueled Max's curiosity.

Shane stood up from his place on the bench. He shoved his hands into the pockets of his shorts. He looked down at Max sitting at the other end of the bench, his cigarette squeezed between his thumb and forefinger. "It's a long story, as the saying goes. I don't want to bore you with the details. In short, I . . . I guess I got tired of life on the farm."

Max got up and stuffed out his cigarette in a large concrete waste container with an ash tray at the top. "I need to get to work over at the grill a couple blocks away. I mentioned it to you before." He moved away from the bench. "Maybe we can talk again. I've seen you here many times. You can tell me some of your long story."

"Yeah, maybe we can to that." Shane watched Max walk away, thinking he might have found a friend.

Chapter 29

"So, Mr. Shane, Max tells me you are a farm boy." Jacques Millet, head waiter at the Eighth Street Grill, leaned with both hands on the back of the chair.

Shane interrupted his wiping off the table and gently shook out the towel. "Yeah, I was a farm boy for eighteen years." He grinned, shuffling the towel from one hand to the other.

"Why did you leave the farm? In Minnesota isn't that the best place to be?" Jacques laughed, while he pushed chairs closer to the table.

Shane joined in the laughter but offered no explanation.

Jacques patted him on the back. "Farm boy or not, it's good to have you here. We can always use help who knows what hard work is." He moved on adjusting chairs around other tables.

For six days about eight hours a day Shane had worked at the Eighth Street Grill which occupied a former warehouse only a few blocks from Danni's condo. His hours varied depending upon the day and upon the schedule of other general help or bus boys.

During a quiet moment near the conclusion of the lunch rush, Shane stepped off to one corner of the dining room. He stared out over the large dining room distinguished by large windows making up one whole wall and decorated by heavy curtains pulled back and tied at the edges of the windows. Shane quickly counted fourteen tables of various sizes, each surrounded by padded chairs. Customers were now seated at only about half of them. He visually marked off the tables that were his responsibility. From his position in the corner designated for the bus boys and servers, he savored the smell of the famous grill upon which popular lunches were prepared.

With no tables, at the moment, needing clearing, he stood erect with his towel draped over his arm. He looked out over the dining room, seeing no one in particular. His thoughts drifted to another quiet Sunday evening only days before.

On that other quiet Sunday evening he sat watching the people strolling through the Crystal Court.

"Hey, guy, how you doin?" Max Hawkins appeared out of nowhere and plunked himself at the end of Shane's bench.

"Not working tonight?" Shane asked, used to meeting Max in the court.

Max reached for a cigarette and lighted it. "No, just a slow Sunday evening at the grill. Gives me a little longer break."

At first just coincidence but recently more intentional, Max and Shane met in the court. Several of these meetings generated a mutual interest in backgrounds and futures.

Max stretched out his legs and took a drag on his cigarette. "Have a big day?" he asked stealing a side glance at Shane.

"Oh, yeah, Sundays are always big days, like all my days." Shane stared down at his feet.

The two sat in silence before Max turned to look at Shane. "Say, last time we met you mentioned you coming to the big city was a long story. You said someday you'd tell me. How about it? Why are you here floating around the Nicollet Mall doing nothing?"

Shane blushed realizing the truth of Max's reference to doing nothing. He placed his hands on the front edge of the bench and straightened his arms. Looking at the fountain highlighting the Crystal Court, he smiled and asked, "Are you sure you want to hear my stupid story?"

Max tipped his head and shrugged his shoulders. "Why not? I haven't heard a good tale for a long time." He reached over and gave Shane a gentle poke on the arm.

"Well, okay. It's no big deal." Shane's brow narrowed. He took a breath and started to explain. He talked of the agonizing moment on the ski slope and again on the baseball diamond. Refusing to place all the blame on the ski accident, Shane traced the changes that occurred in his life after the knee surgeries. The failure to qualify for graduation and the animosity that created at home concluded his long story. He did not mention Lindsey Cooper, the memory of prom night still painfully fresh.

As Shane slowly and quickly shared his story, Max listened without comment. An occasional smile or nod of the head expressed his response to the details of Shane's path from the innocence of the farm to aimlessness of the city.

Shane got up from the bench and looked down at Max. "Don't you have to get back to work?"

"Pretty soon. Awfully slow tonight. My boss told me to take my time. So I will."

Shane grasped his hands behind his back. "You know . . . I, ah, I'm curious how you got here. I've seen you here often. Do you live around here? I know where you work." Shane stepped closer to Max. "Maybe it's your turn to tell the long story."

Max laughed. "It's not nearly as dramatic as yours." He shrugged his shoulders. "I have a few more minutes to kill so why not." He rested his elbows on his knees, clasped his hands, and took his turn explaining how he came to working at the Eighth Street Grill.

Like Shane, he was almost nineteen years old. He did not have to explain what was obvious about him from the first time they met. He was short, stocky with biceps bulging from the short sleeves of his shirt with Eighth Street Grill printed on the front. He had obviously spent time working out. Hair cut short accentuated his round face, dominated by a frequent and generous smile that produced a distinct cleft in his chin.

He explained that like Shane sports played an important part of his earlier life. Wrestling his favorite sport, he participated on the White Bear Lake High School team until he fell victim, like Shane, to conflicts with parents and with school officials. With falling grades, he discussed with his parents his dropping out of school to do something he didn't hate. Except for wrestling, school gave him little to enjoy.

Max reached for another cigarette and his lighter. He paused long enough to light the cigarette and take a long drag. He glanced at his watch then up at Shane. He resumed. His parents had announced he either stay in school or leave. Their home provided no haven for a high school drop out. Incensed, he left.

His departure, over a year ago, left him alone, on his own and living in a 2001 Honda Civic. Jobs at a car wash and a Burger King preceded his current job as bus boy and general helper at the Eighth Street Grill, for the time being adequate for his basic needs. Despite his meager circumstances, he remained confident in his decision to leave home. The future, he claimed, would prove the wisdom of that decision.

While Max talked, Shane returned to his place at the end of the bench, captivated by Max's story. Hearing about Max's path to independence, Shane recognized the commonalities of their young lives. Learning that he lived in his car shocked Shane, who never imaged anyone living that way. Each time he talked with Max confirmed the degree to which life on the farm had shielded him from the realities of life in the big city.

Max stopped talking and looked over at Shane. "There you have it, the thrilling story of a bus boy."

Shane grinned. "Interesting." He folded his arms across his chest. "You ever get bored?" Shane alluded to the wretched boredom of the farm, the stifling repetition of day to day chores.

Max laughed at the subject of boredom. "Sit in your car for hours with nothing to do for a while, and you'll learn about boredom."

Shane got up off the bench and moved a few steps back. He stretched his arms overhead. "What did you do about the boredom?"

"I got a job." Max replied. "I think you need one."

Shane turned his back to Max, hands on hips. "Yeah, I got to do something damn soon, or I'll go nuts."

"Why don't you talk to the people at the grill? Not a bad place to work." Max suggested.

Instantly, Shane reflected on his earlier thoughts condemning dead-end jobs. "I have not had much interest in dead-end jobs."

Max stood up and faced Shane. "What do you expect for those of us who dropped out of school, some kind of executive position?" The comment brought silence.

Shane started walking away. "Wait, don't go. I realize working as a bus boy is not much of a future. But, hey, it's something to do."

The next day Shane took Max's advice and applied for a job at the Eighth Street Grill. In one more day he would receive his first check for one week's work.

Several tables emptied at one time. Both Max and Shane responded to the need to clear and clean the tables. Completed, they retreated to the kitchen for a temporary break. They took advantage of the short break to sit down at a small employee table in an inconspicuous corner of the kitchen. Just a few feet away the head chef and a fry cook stood over the hot grilled where sizzled the Grill's famous hamburgers under preparation for the few remaining lunch customers.

"Got any plans after work?" Max asked.

Shane looked across the table at Max and shrugged his shoulders. "Maybe walk back to the condo."

Max leaned over the table. "We have a little get-together after work. Ah . . . with a couple other guys who kind of float around town."

Shane had missed companionship during his stay with his sister. Never a social leader, he still always shared friendship with his peers. In recent months with all the personal turmoil he faced, socializing failed to interest him.

"What did you have in mind?" Shane asked.

Max settled back in his chair and clasped his hands behind his head. "Some buddies and I plan to have a little conference." Max grinned. "A little conference overlooking the Mississippi at a quiet little place, perfect for discussing the future of the world."

Not knowing just how to interpret Max's conference, Shane looked puzzled. "I don't think I can add much to a discussion of the future of the world." His brow wrinkled.

Max laughed. "Look, we're going to drink a few beers and relax for a little while. No harm done. You can meet a couple of my friends. You'll like em."

Shane pushed his chair back and got up. "I guess that sounds okay." He agreed.

That night was the second night Shane spent on the streets of the big city.

Chapter 30

"Welcome to my home." From behind the wheel of his Honda, Max turned, sweeping his arm over the back seat. Converted into a bed, the back seat of the Honda gave him a thin mattress, a pillow and a blanket.

Shane's eyes opened wide as he surveyed where Max spent most of his nights. "Do ya sleep here every night?"

"Almost." Max gripped the back of his seat, staring at his bed. "Sometimes in the winter I try to use one of the few shelters around here for people like us."

Shane looked over at his friend. "If there aren't many shelters around, where do people like us go?"

Max turned back to grip the steering wheel. "Good question. Some of them find some park or some place out of the wind. Never very warm."

Shane studied the near empty parking lot in front of them. Basic necessities like a place to sleep had not occurred to him. He could always find a place with his sister. He turned to face Max. "I heard one day on the news that hundreds of young people spend the night on the streets in the Twin Cities."

Max nodded his head then rubbed his eyes. "I don't know how many. I just know there's a lot of them."

Shane reflected on the reality of hundreds of young people without a home. Why? Did all of them, like him, have conflicts with parents? Why were there so many problems between kids and parents? What would he do without his sister?

"Hey, buddy, we aren't gonna solve any problems tonight. Let's party." Max started his Honda and backed out of his parking space next to the Eighth Street Grill.

"Where we going?" Shane asked, buckling his seat belt.

Max cautiously entered the I-94 freeway a short distance south of the restaurant. "To the river, my friend." A mischievous grin spread his lips and deepened the cleft in his chin. "Really, above the river on the St. Paul side near the Lake Street Bridge."

Not very familiar with the Twin City area, Shane asked, "What's there?"

"Well," Max glanced over at Shane, "a bunch trees, rocks, and a fantastic view of Minneapolis across the river."

"Is it some kind of park?" Shane's curiosity increased.

"Ah, it . . . ah it isn't a park exactly, just a good place to hang out."

They drove in silence, only sparse traffic on the freeway and the exit that took them to Cretin Avenue and access to the special river bluffs. In minutes after leaving Cretin Avenue, Max turned onto Lake Street and then onto Mississippi River Road. He slowed and turned onto a quiet road hidden in thick foliage on both sides. He pulled off onto a slight clearing and stopped behind another car.

"This is it." Max released his seat belt and opened his door.

Shane did the same and stood next to the car looking into the dark, thick foliage. Max moved around the front of the car to stand next to Shane.

"A little reminder," he cautioned. "There's a path through these trees and bushes, but it's very steep and rocky. Be careful not to fall. It's a long way down to the river." He poked Shane on the shoulder. "Okay, follow me."

Shane stepped behind Max. Before they disappeared into the dark, dense woods, Shane saw the sign, "Danger. Keep Out." He tensed, a nervous twinge in his stomach. What was he getting into?

Max turned to notice Shane pausing near the sign. "Don't worry about that. Just be careful. You'll be fine."

Carefully, stepping over twigs, rocks and through low hanging limbs, Shane obediently followed Max. They eased their way down until they arrived at a plateau or ledge of solid rock protruding from the steep cliff. On the flat surface three guys sat, each holding a can of beer.

"What took ya so long?" One of them asked.

"Some of us have to work on Sunday nights." Max offered a sharp retort.

"Well, good for you," came another playful response.

Max stepped to the middle of the group. "Hey guys, this is Shane. He's this farm boy I told you about, lately my partner at the grill." He looked over at Shane standing off to the side. "Forgive them if they don't get up. They're a bit crude when it comes to manners. Besides, they might tumble down the cliff."

Max gingerly reached for Shane. "Shane, meet Ricky Brooks, Ramon Cardena, and last, the stud, Derek Hayes."

Shane greeted them with a quiet, "Hi, good to meet you." In the darkness and cover of the surrounding trees, he could scarcely see the three people he met. Still, the one named Derek seemed the biggest of the three. He sat on his knees while the other two sat with knees pulled up in front of them. Shane could see his head of dark curly hair and even in the darkness his white teeth.

"Come on in and sit down." The white teeth glistened through the big smile. "Have a beer to celebrate Sunday night." Laughter trickled around the group.

Shane sat down on the hard ground. Derek handed him a can of beer. He accepted. All through high school including his tumultuous, shortened senior year, he rarely attended beer parties. Not that he opposed drinking beer. He simply didn't like it. His parents didn't either. At least he never found beer in the house. Most of the guys he associated with shared his distaste for beer. He did like an occasional rum and coke. Tonight the drink menu did not include rum and coke.

Settled into as much comfort as possible on the rock ledge, the five young men talked haltingly at first, sensitive to a stranger among them. The beer, however, soon loosened tongues. The conversation ranged widely from what they did to how they got to where they were in life. Shane listened carefully to the explanations, intrigued by how and where these guys lived and worked. In time he learned about each one.

Ricky Brooks, sitting in the shadows of the thick foliage, appeared short and slim with blonde hair cut short. He had graduated from a Minneapolis high school three years ago. Now at twenty-one he worked as a mechanic, living at home most of the time with his mom and alcoholic Dad.

In the shadows of the ledge Ramon Cardena sat with his hands draped over his knees, gripping a beer can. His brown skin accentuated sparkling dark eyes. At eighteen, he had dropped out of a St. Paul high school at the end of his junior year. No regular job, he lived in a subsidized apartment with his mother, a maid at a Minneapolis hotel. When Ramon was ten, his father left, never to return.

Finally, Derek Hayes came from a middle class, suburban home. Even on the dark and shadowy ledge Shane could see Derek's long legs stretched out in front of him as he relaxed on the hard ground. He could also see his broad shoulders on which rested thick, dark hair. Not surprising, a basketball player in high school, he graduated to move on to complete one semester at a local community college. Restrictions imposed at home forced him to leave for more than a year to spend his time on the Twin City streets. Now at twenty years old, he worked on an assembly line operating a computerized machine creating packaging for a variety of products. He lived at home most of the time.

The details of each guy's story distracted Shane, who didn't realize the ease with which the beer went down. Already three empty cans lay before him. He, too, related what led to his departure from the farm, only touching on the details about his knee. Talking about it served no purpose anymore. It was the past. There it should stay.

Conversation slowed as Max and Derek each reached for another beer. Suddenly, blue and red lights skipped over the tree tops high above them. They all craned their necks, looking up through the foliage.

"The cops," Max announced.

Frantically, Ricky and Derek tossed beer cans into the brush and over the edge of the ledge. In minutes two spots of light bounced toward them through the trees.

Ricky and Ramon scattered deeper into the dense foliage. Max and Derek had cars to worry about. Shane stood in near panic, lost on the ledge of solid rock. He caught a glimpse of Ricky and Ramon disappearing into the darkness of the trees. He tried to follow them, but they vanished, swallowed by the darkness. Grabbing onto a tree, he tried to figure out the area around him. Behind him a sheer cliff dropped to the Mississippi below. Above he caught a glimpse of flickering red and blue strobe lights. To each side heavy foliage blocked his way. He clung to the tree, breathing heavily, the harsh voices of the police magnified by surrounding rock.

Confident the trees and the darkness concealed him from view, Shane squatted, still clinging to the tree. He waited. Below he could hear the splash of water against the rocks. He shivered in the early morning chill. He questioned what the hell he was doing clinging to a tree on a steep cliff over looking the Mississippi. He needed to use his head about Max and his Sunday night get togethers.

Shane lost touch with time. How long he squatted next to the tree he didn't know. He searched the trees above for evidence of the police car lights. He saw nothing. Briefly he considered what had happened to Max and Derek and their cars. However, concern for his own predicament claimed top priority.

Cautiously, Shane stood up to move back to the ledge where the group had gathered, only a few beer cans the last remnants of the celebration of Sunday evening. Resolved to get off the cliff and unaware of what happened to Ricky and Ramon, he started back up the cluttered path he and Max descended hours ago.

Finally at the top, Shane looked in all directions for police cars or for Max and Derek, nothing in sight except a well lighted street a short distance away. He tried to remember the route they took to the river from the Mall area. He walked to the street lined with lights. His watch showed four A.M. The well lighted street he discovered was Lake Street. Standing on the sidewalk, he viewed the Lake Street Bridge and the Minneapolis skyline in the distance. With hands in his pockets he started his walk west in a direction he hoped would bring him eventually to the Nicollet Mall.

Chapter 31

Shane pushed the elevator button. He rested his arm against the wall, waiting for the door to open. Confronting Danni at six in the morning bothered him. Maybe she wasn't up yet. Nonetheless, his work schedule dictated he clean up and report to work by ten.

The elevator door parted; Shane stepped in pressing the button for the fifteenth floor. He found brief comfort in leaning against the round bar fastened to three sides of the elevator. The image of the Minneapolis skyline passed before his eyes. *How did he ever find his way back?* A smile confirmed his satisfaction in doing just that. Loring Park offered a few minutes of rest before his work schedule forced him back to Danni's condo.

Shane fitted the key into the lock of the entrance door. Careful to avoid disturbing his sister, he closed the door with a gentle push. He moved to the kitchen and around to the hall and his room, the converted den. Sliding a discarded pair of shorts and a shirt to the end of the futon which served as his sofa and his bed, he sat down heavily. Little time remained before he walked to work. He leaned back and closed his eyes.

"Good morning, Shane." Danni stood framed in the doorway to the den. "Where have you been all night?" she asked in a nonthreatening voice. During the weeks since Shane's arrival to share her condo, his erratic schedule, though still a concern, no longer shocked her. She had grown accustomed to his late night and sometimes all night absences.

"No place in particular," Shane mumbled.

"It must have been some place to keep you out all night." Danni commented.

Shane stretched out his legs in front of him. "Max asked me to join him and his friends after work for a little celebration of Sunday evening." Shane spoke with a caustic grin.

"Celebration of what?" Danni's eyes opened wide and wrinkles grooved her brow.

"Nothing. It was just a chance for a couple beers, okay?" His voice acquired a sharp edge.

Danni's shoulders drooped. "I'm sorry I asked." She turned and walked to the kitchen.

Shane shook his head, rolling his eyes with irritation over why she always had to know what he did. He left that shit on the farm. Recent days brought other minor confrontations with his sister provoked by her insistence on asking more questions about how he spent his time. Earlier she urged him to get a job. So he got a job. Now she had to know what he did and where he went. At almost nineteen he didn't need another Mother monitoring his life.

Danni returned to the den, holding a cup of coffee. "Can I get you a cup?" she asked in a conciliatory tone.

"No," Shane snapped back.

Still standing in the doorway to the den, Danni said, "By the way, Dad called last night."

The statement attracted Shane's attention. "What did he want?" He kicked off his shoes.

Danni sipped her coffee. "You know, Mom and Dad worry about you. Dad asked about you and your new job."

Shane reached down to pull off his socks. "Did you tell him I make a whopping twelve fifty an hour?"

Danni frowned and exhaled. "No, I didn't. I did tell him you were doing well. At least you hadn't complained."

"Thank you for small favors." Shane stood up to pull his shirt over his head.

"You don't have to be so sarcastic." Danni stepped back from the entrance to the den. She took another sip of coffee, hesitating to deliver the sad news about Shane's pony First Mate. "Dad told me to tell you the vet had to put down First Mate."

Shane stopped, his shirt half way over his head. He yanked it down, his eyes staring hard at his sister. "What happened?" His voice lost much of its earlier edge.

Danni rested the coffee cup in both hands near her stomach. "I guess mostly old age. He wasn't eating well and could hardly walk. The vet determined it best to put him out of his misery."

Shane dropped his head onto his chest, closed his eyes and for a fleeting moment relived the thrill of the companionship and the many rides on First Mate.

"Why the hell couldn't they tell me? Call me or something?"

A benign smile spread Danni's lips. "It's not as if you want to talk to them or are even around if you did."

Shane threw his shirt on the floor. "Screw it. It's always me, isn't it. Always my fault. Nothing ever changes."

"Shane, that's not true." Danni took one step into the den. "You really haven't made any effort to talk to Mom and Dad. When you do, it's in anger."

"Fuck it. Now I have absolutely nothing to return to the farm for." He turned his back on his sister. "I've got to get ready for work," he growled.

Danni's mouth dropped open. She stared appalled at her brother's harsh, insensitive response. She returned to the kitchen and rinsed out her coffee cup. She, too, needed to prepare for work. She definitely did not need to contend with her brother's belligerence and indignation.

Shane did not notice when his sister left for work nor did he care. Hearing about his beloved pony caused a return of the distress that for months had hovered over his life. In his mind he faulted himself for ignoring his childhood companion. With all the frustration, with all the despair of the past few months, he simply neglected his pony. He privately confessed to a selfishness he previously never acknowledged. Standing in the shower, washing away the residue, both physical and emotional, of the last twelve hours, he vowed never to forget his First Mate.

As Shane reached for the door to the corridor, his cell phone vibrated and sounded in his pocket. He let the door close and reached for his phone. It was Max.

"Hello," Shane answered.

"How you doin? Did you find your way home last night?" Max asked.

"Yeah, I'm home now. What happened to you guys?" Shane sat down on the bench in the condo entry way.

"Not much," Max explained. "The cops got Derek and me for trespassing. Two hundred bucks each."

"God, that's a kick in the head," Shane sympathized with his friend.

"What happened to you?" Max inquired.

Shane described his adventure finding his way off the cliff then the long journey back to the condo.

"Good you made it back. Sorry about the problem. That's never happened before."

"You don't have to feel sorry. You didn't force me to go with you for the celebration of Sunday evening." Shane chuckled, thinking about the interesting evening before the arrival of the law.

In a serious tone of voice, Max asked, "Did you see what happened to Ricky and Ramon?"

Shane paused before answering. "No, I didn't. I kind of panicked. I tried to hide and then find my way off that steep cliff."

"I tried to call them this morning," Max explained, "but I haven't got an answer from either one. I thought maybe you saw them."

"I'm sorry. I really didn't except to see them disappear into the trees. Do you think there's a problem?" Shane stood up from the bench.

"No, I don't think so. It's just funny they don't answer their phones."

"Maybe they're sleeping," Shane suggested.

'Maybe," Max concurred.

After a brief silence, Shane announced, "I'm off to work. What time do you show up?"

"Not till three."

"Keep me posted if you hear anything." Shane closed his phone and stepped out into the corridor.

The lunch crowd gave Shane plenty to do clearing, cleaning and resetting tables. He worked alone until three o'clock when Max showed up. At two thirty, during a quiet time at the grill, Shane's cell phone vibrated in his pocket. Again it was Max.

Shane snapped open his phone. "Hey, aren't you coming to work in a few minutes?"

With an audible strain in his voice, Max uttered, "No, I'm taking the day off."

"You sick or something?" Shane asked playfully.

"No, I'm fine. I did get ahold of Ramon. He said he and Ricky got separated last night. He didn't know what happened to him. He's tried to call but no answer. I'm going back to the bluff just to look around."

"God, that's kind of scary, isn't it?" Shane gripped his cell phone.

"I don't know if it is or not. He's been there several times before, not like you."

"Look," Shane said. "I have to get back to work. Please keep me informed if you find out anything."

"Will do. Talk to ya later." Silence filled the line.

Shane completed his work shift, preoccupied with the mystery surrounding Ricky's whereabouts and the sad news about First Mate. At seven o'clock he removed his apron and headed back to the condo, no social commitments on a Monday night. On the walk back to the condo, his mind played with the thoughts of First Mate and now with Ricky. Reluctant to face his sister and another bitter verbal exchange, he nonetheless, could not consider another night on the streets or in Loring Park.

In the condo Shane avoided any quarrel with his sister. They watched the TV, lost in their own private worlds, Danni concentrating more on paper work from her office than on the TV.

At ten thirty Max called again to explain in a tense, rapid voice he still had not contacted Ricky, no word about him at all. Max had called Ricky's mother who could add nothing to her son's disappearance. He had not contacted her. Together, Max and Ricky's mother decided to contact the police to explain what happened the previous night. The officials agreed to begin, in the morning, a search of the bluff as well as the river.

That search ended when the St Paul City Rescue Squad dragging the river found Ricky's body a half mile from the bluff.

Chapter 32

In his nineteen years Shane had never experienced the death of a friend. Rarely did he experience the death of anything, except, perhaps, a chicken or pig. Learning of the death of a recent acquaintance shocked him. He hardly knew Ricky Brooks, having spent only a harrowing night with him clinging to a steep cliff. Nonetheless, Ricky was a real person, not just a name in the paper.

Added to the somber event was the passing of First Mate, Shane's childhood pony and companion. For so many years he took his pony for granted. First Mate would be there when Shane needed him. Shane remembered the discussion he shared with Danni that fateful Christmas break when Danni and he drove to Lutsen Ski Resort. They stood in First Mate's stall in an atmosphere of mutual respect to discuss Shane's impatience with life on the farm. Not for months had he thought about those memorable moments. Now, images crowded his mind of the countless times he clung to his pony's back as they raced across a field or walked carefully on the edge of a road.

In the days since Ricky's funeral, Shane devoted more of his private hours in a philosophical mood. For the first time he contemplated the fragility of life. What happened to Ricky could easily have happened to him. *Why was it Ricky*? He asked himself. *Was there some force out there to decide when your time was up*? Growing up he attended church regularly. After confirmation he drifted away from church attendance. Thoughts like these bothered him.

Never very literary, Shane read only what he had to read. He couldn't remember sitting down reading a book simply for pleasure. However, during those introspective moments he recalled reading for an English class a book entitled *Death Be Not Proud*. The author's name vanished from his memory a long time ago. The title and the subject, the author's son battling a lethal brain tumor, stayed locked in a remote corner of his memory.

The title now awakened in his mind the strength and courage of the young boy in his futile fight against a vicious tumor. Death indeed had nothing to be proud of. To Shane, pride came from saving a life, not taking the life of a young man no older than himself?

This period of reflection brought a calm to Shane's life. He followed a strict, daily routine, deliberately refraining from any clashes with his sister. Each day they went to work. Each day they attended to their own personal needs without infringing on each other's privacy. He abandoned thoughts of spending nights on the street because of petty differences with his sister. One morning before leaving for work he spoke with his mother for the first time since the verbal tangle a few weeks ago in the condo, ending with an angry Shane rushing out the door. A short conversation on the phone, it dealt with Shane's job, his relationship with his sister, his pony, his attitude toward his life, and ended with expressions of a Mother's love.

At work he and Max carried out their responsibilities without complaint. The management of the grill did not fail to recognize the commitment displayed by the two young men. After two months of work, Shane's twelve fifty an hour increased to thirteen fifty. In this slight raise he took great pride.

The near absence of enmity in the condo delighted Danni. Her position as lead chemist on an important project involving a law suit against a soft drink company consumed her days as well as her evenings at home.

On an evening free of work she watched TV alone while Shane worked a shift ending at nine o'clock, the conclusion of the dinner rush. At nine thirty he entered the condo. Not since Ricky's death had he ventured out at the end of a work shift.

"How was work?" Danni asked when he passed through the living room on the way to the den.

"Okay," he answered without stopping, his first priority to deposit the evening's tips in his special, personal bank under the futon. Sitting on the futon, he kicked off his shoes, pulled off his work shirt, and stepped out of his trousers.

Dressed more casually in a Twins T-shirt and a pair of shorts, he returned to the living room to slump down in one of the stuffed chairs next to the sofa. Danni spread out on one end of the sofa with her feet resting on the cushions. When Shane reappeared, she swung her legs off the sofa. "Here, have a seat," she offered.

"No, that's okay. This if fine." Shane stretched out, bracing his body against the back of the chair.

The late TV news attracted the attention of both. They listened in silence to a report of another shooting in downtown Minneapolis. Apparently, an argument ended in the use of guns.

"Did you hear any thing about this at work?" Danni twisted her body, placing her feet on the floor.

"No, nothing." Shane replied.

Again silence prevailed between them as they listened to more of the evening news.

"Have you heard anything else about Ricky's parents?" Immediately following the tragic accident, Danni joined Shane in talking about mortality, a topic neither previously considered.

Shane rested his hands on top his head. "No, I haven't heard a thing. Max did mention a few days ago that Ricky's mother called to thank him for all he did."

A sport report on the Twins' season captured Shane's attention. Through all the turmoil of the last two to three years, he retained an interest in baseball, even harboring, maybe, a chance to play again. His knee rarely bothered him, but at times he did feel twinges of sensation if he moved the wrong way on his leg.

With the conclusion of the sports, Shane moved forward on the chair. "How is that project of yours going?" He asked Danni.

She looked over at her brother and smiled. His showing an interest in her work was surely a good sign. "It's going but, oh, so slow. Dealing with state and federal laws really complicates things."

A puzzled look took over Shane's face. "What's it all about?"

Danni frowned, the space between her eye brows narrowing. Though she explained it before, she tried again to describe the project and her part in it as simply as she could, avoiding the professional and legal jargon. She talked about the law suit and her company's role in determining the potential harm of a popular health drink, a product of the corporate defendant.

"Sounds complicated," Shane acknowledged.

Danni laughed, "That's an understatement." She eased herself up from the sofa. "Talking about that law suit reminds me it's time to get to bed. Maybe I'll see you in the morning. What time do you work?"

"Not till noon." Shane confirmed.

Danni hesitated before moving on to her bedroom. "Maybe I won't see you in the morning." She laughed.

Lying on his futon, Shane reflected on his brief evening with his sister. Not for a long time did they converse in harmony without contention and bitterness. He turned onto his side, relaxed, ready for sleep to transport him through another night and into the routine of another day.

Chapter 33

Nick Karpin sat alone quietly eating a lunch of soup and club sandwich. For months he ate his lunch at the Eighth Street Grill just off the Nicollet Mall. Recently, he noticed one of the bus boys who, in Nick's opinion, did his menial job conscientiously. This young man responded quickly to a vacated table, efficiently clearing and resetting it for the next customer. Nick admired efficiency. He could use more efficient help.

A second generation Russian, at four years old Nick immigrated with his parents to the United States in search of less oppression. Nick's father, a pharmacist, struggled under the burden of rigid government control. Finally his parents made the decision to flee the country and take their chances in America where they heard the opportunity for success awaited them. With some disappointment they discovered the limits of that expectation.

With little success in finding work in New York, Nick's father packed up his family and floated around the Midwest searching for the elusive opportunity in the pharmaceutical industry. Finally, after several failures Nick's father found a home and a business in St. Paul, Minnesota. He started with a part time job at a national pharmaceutical chain. Soon, the company hired him full time. Three years of working for someone else convinced him he could do better on his own. He opened a neighborhood pharmacy thirty years ago. Though his father had retired, he retained ownership of the store. It still served customers from a large section of residential St. Paul.

Nick attended several schools while his father searched for a place to settle down. Only an average student, he excelled at making friends and persuading them to do what he wanted. In a St. Paul high school from which he eventually graduated, he organized a minor rebellion when the school administration threatened to prohibit students from leaving the school grounds during lunch time. A fast food restaurant a mere block away, in Nick's opinion, offered a far better lunch menu than did the school. He won.

At forty-five years old Nick had capitalized on his organizational and persuasive talents. Gregarious and voluble, he carried his slight six foot frame confidently. His thick black hair clung to his head in tight curls. A prominent nose accentuated penetrating eyes, a significant part of his persuasive arsenal.

Since graduating from high school, he had attended for two years a Twin Cities community college. After that he toyed in the business world employed by, at various times, a car wash, a carpet cleaning business, and a lawn service. His plunge into the business world precluded any serious attention to women or interest in marriage. He enjoyed the life of a bachelor. With the passing of his parents, he sold the pharmacy which had provided so well for the Karpin family. He used that money to invest in apartments. Currently, he owned two apartment buildings located in south Minneapolis near Lake Street.

Nick Karpin's role as a landlord involved more than simply collecting rent from the apartments. The business served as a shield for a vibrant trade in illegal drugs. Most of his life found him associated with the drug world, the legal drug world. Nonetheless, Nick recognized the potential of the drug world only marginally different from that of his father's.

In time his frequent visits for lunch at the grill gave Nick the chance to introduce himself to the bus boy whose name he learned was Shane Stenlund. Most often Shane worked when Nick lunched at the grill. Each time Nick would snatch a bit of Shane's time to learn about his background growing up on the farm and his move to the city. Finally, Nick asked if Shane would have a few minutes to talk longer. They agreed to meet the next day at the conclusion of Shane's shift. They met in the Grill's parking lot where they sat in Nick's black BMW.

"How long have you worked here?" Nick asked after they settled into the plush leather, front seat.

Shane closed his eyes in thought. "Oh . . . ah about four months. I started this past summer."

"Do you like what you do?" Nick twisted in his seat to face Shane.

Shane smiled. "It's . . . okay. Something to do."

Nick hesitated. "Ah . . . ah, I don't mean to pry into your private life, but would you mind telling me how much you make working here?" His business experience gave Nick a very good idea of the wages for bus boys. He simply wished to assess Shane's level of confidence in sharing the information.

"Thirteen fifty an hour," Shane answered.

"Can you live on that?"

Shane rubbed his hand over the delicate leather on the dash board in front of him. "Barely," he replied.

Nick straightened up, placing his hands on the padded steering wheel. "You know, I could use someone like you, someone responsible, efficient, and reliable. It wouldn't take much of your time. You could still work here and at the same time make a little extra money."

Shane's face revealed his interest in what he heard. "What would I do?"

Nick took his time explaining his apartment business, careful to avoid any mention of what that business concealed. Maybe twice a week Shane would deposit, what Nick termed, rent money into one of two different bank accounts, one in the suburbs, one in down town Minneapolis not far from the Grill. For his service Shane would earn, in the beginning, fifty dollars each deposit. Nick stressed the need for discretion for reasons Shane failed to understand, and Nick dismissed with the excuse he didn't always have the time to interrupt his busy day with trips to the bank.

Furthermore, he wished to have a less frequent presence at the banks.

The proposal puzzled Shane though he chose not to question Nick about why he needed someone to deposit rent money. The chance to make another possible one hundred dollars a week impressed him. Of course, he had no idea it wasn't rent money. Shane folded his hands in his lap and stared out the front window.

Nick interpreted the absence of any more questions from Shane as likely acceptance. He ended the conversation saying, "Look, think about it. I'll talk to you tomorrow at lunch. You do work tomorrow, right?"

Shane reached for the door handle, opened the door and stepped out. "Yeah, I do. I'll see you tomorrow." He shut the door, moved back away from the car, watching it leave the parking lot. Deciding didn't require much thought. The next day Shane agreed to make Nick's deposits.

Nick sipped his ice tea and reached for another French fry. He caught Shane's attention and nodded his head. In the past month Shane had made two deposits each week bringing home an extra four hundred dollars for the month, an almost unbelievable sum he added to his personal savings bank under his futon. Soon he would have to open a real savings account, perhaps, at one of the banks he visited weekly.

The discussion with Nick that late afternoon in the parking lot had tumbled through Shane's mind on his walk back to the condo. He couldn't understand the need for what Nick asked him to do. For fifty dollars a shot, he really didn't care. The next morning he mentioned the proposal to Danni, who reacted with suspicion. However, she refused to interfere with Shane's chance to earn more money.

Two weeks later his first delivery took him to a prominent bank on Hennepin Avenue. Entering the bank, Shane had walked confidently to the window behind which stood a male teller. He handed the teller a small pouch which contained the money. Shane did not know how much money it contained or how the teller would know into which account it belonged. A little nervous about the whole transaction, Shane relaxed when the teller accepted the pouch without question, emptied it on the shelf below him, and with a smile handed back the pouch. He said, "Thank you and have a good day." Shane left the bank satisfied he wouldn't mind this job.

Chapter 34

"What's with that guy?" Max jerked his head in the direction of Nick Karpin's table.

Shane and Max stood off to the side of the Eighth Street Grill dining room attending to the lunch crowd. A steady hum of numerous conversations permeated the dining room as did the clinking of forks and knives on plates and saucers.

Shane shuffled his feet. "A friend."

"What does he do? He's here damn near every day."

Shane never forgot one of the major conditions of his working for Nick, secrecy. He leaned against the wall. "I don't know, but I think he's some big landlord who likes the food here."

"You certainly made an impression on him. He talks to you whenever he's here." Max gave Shane a friendly bump on the shoulder.

Three tables emptied at once putting into action both Max and Shane. With the tables cleared and reset, they moved back to their inconspicuous place in one corner of the dining room. They kept a close watch on the other tables.

Max clasped his hands behind his back in an alert position. "How you handling the cold?" He asked Shane.

Shane cringed, folding his arms around his chest. "It's a bitch."

"I know," Max concurred.

On several nights Shane had shared Max's car. On others he had sought escape from the cold at a Lutheran Social Services shelter. He will never forget those nights huddled in a sleeping bag beneath a bench in Loring Park.

"Have you talked with you sister lately?" Max dropped his arms to his sides.

Shane shook his head. "No."

For more than three weeks Shane had avoided seeing or talking to his sister, even on his cell phone. For a time around Christmas a fragile calm had settled over the condo Shane shared with Danni. He took great pride in the extra money he earned nearly every week making, what he still considered, mysterious deposits in two banks. His small savings account tucked under his futon grew. His supervisor at the Grill complimented him on his performance. Despite Shane's considering it a dead-end job, he, nonetheless, strived to do the job well. Except for Danni's occasional inquiries about his strange delivery job, harmony prevailed in the condo.

The approaching winter had introduced minor complications for Shane making the deposits. As he watched his assigned tables, in his mind he relived recent moments waiting for the bus to take him to, now, a familiar bank in Wayzata, a wealthy suburban community clinging to the eastern shore of Lake Minnetonka. The cold wind blowing down Hennepin Avenue that day reminded him of those winter mornings on the farm, getting up to complete his chores. Another sweater had helped to reduce the chill of the bus stop. Paying more attention to the bus schedule had helped even more.

After attending to three of his assigned tables, collecting soiled dishes and partially eaten lunches, Shane returned to his station where he would await the next table to clear, clean and reset. Instantly his reverie dragged him back not to the recent, cold trip to Wayzata but to that first one weeks ago which served as a welcome diversion from his usual territory in downtown Minneapolis.

The experience unfolded so vividly in his mind. As the bus headed west on I-394, he had noted the huge General Mills office complex and farther down the road the Ridgedale Shopping Center. Vague memories had reminded him of traveling this route when he came with his parents to visit Danni. Beyond Ridgedale the road changed in number only to Highway 12 and brought him to the Highway 101 exit and finally to a bus transit station and parking lot high above Wayzata's main street. A short walk back to the bank and the almost wordless transaction had left Shane on his own, fifty dollars richer.

In sharp contrast to his recent, wintery visit to Wayzata when all he wanted to do was to step on a warm bus back to Minneapolis, Shane retained his attention to that first visit under much warmer conditions. Then he had ventured to the main street which bordered the eastern shore of the sprawling Lake Minnetonka. Shane remembered standing for the first time on the shore looking out across Lake Minnetonka at an explosion of autumn's vivid reds, yellows, and oranges. It had awakened memories of fall in Twin Pines, the hometown he hadn't visited or even thought much about since the dreadful prom weekend months before. Rarely had he thought about his previous life; dealing with his present life demanded all his attention. The quiet, near rural atmosphere of this small community impressed Shane and engendered a moment of nostalgia for what used to be.

That time before Christmas saw Shane and Danni busy with their own lives with little time to discuss his future or his often late nights. During this period Shane spoke with his parents once or twice, reassuring them that life in the big city treated him okay.

Shane jumped to attention as more tables emptied. The lunch crowd thinned. His friend and part time boss, Nick Karpin, walking out of the dinning room, slipped him a twenty dollar tip. With all tables reset, Shane took his turn at the employee table in the kitchen. Much to his delight his job as bus boy entitled him to free meals. Today he nursed a large bowl of French onion soup and munched an egg salad sandwich. He thought about those days of near tranquility with his sister only weeks ago. His spoon half way to his mouth, he stopped. In his mind he recaptured that moment that began the unraveling of the tranquility.

On a winter Saturday afternoon, clearing tables side by side, Max mentioned to Shane. "How about another celebration of Sunday?"

Shane's eyes opened wide, trained on Max. "You serious?" He never forgot the tragic night on the sheer river cliff. He had pushed it into a remote corner of his mind. Max's alluding to it quickly unlocked the memory. That Max would make facetious reference to the tragedy surprised him.

"Yeah." Max wiped clean the table top. "Derek, you remember Derek. Well, he plans to have a gathering at his parents' house in the suburbs. He does spend some of his time there."

Shane paused before replying. "Maybe."

"Do you work tomorrow?" Max asked.

"Yeah, eleven to seven," Shane answered.

"Think about it. You need to get out and unwind a little." Max grinned. "Don't worry. There's no dangerous cliffs around Derek's place."

Shane pushed his soup bowl back and took another bite of his sandwich. He had attended that party, the first in a series of incidents which ended in another significant change in his life.

Shane's mind drifted back to that party. It had lasted most of the night, delaying his return to the condo until seven in the morning. Danni expressed a mild disappointment for her brother's careless behavior, the first time in weeks any contention existed between them. Their relationship deteriorated from there.

Annoyed by the return of his sister's attempts to control his life, Shane spent more time with Max and his friends, eager to find some diversion in his daily routine, eager to avoid the boredom which too often hung heavily over his life. The frequency of all night absence from the condo increased. Danni spoke to him repeatedly about what he did during these all night affairs. Her probing only irritated the scars from clashes with his parents over the restrictions they imposed on him. The more frequent the arguments the more intense the disagreements. Danni persisted in questioning his job as courier for an apartment landlord.

The culmination of their renewed conflict occurred following a long cold night sitting around a pit fire roasting wieners and drinking beer with Max, Ramon Cardena, who joined them above the river the night Ricky drowned, and Hector Garcia, Ramon's friend. To Shane a winter wiener roast carried little appeal. Returning to the escalating unrest in the condo carried less. He accepted the wiener roast invitation.

Max had dropped Shane off at the condo in the cold early morning darkness. Quietly pushing open the door, Shane could think of nothing else but curling up on his futon to sleep before his one o'clock shift at the grill. He slipped through the living room toward the den. At the entrance to the den, he reached for the door, closed it, leaving enough space for his hand to reach in to switch on the light. He didn't want to disturb his sister. He didn't need any more reprimands from her about his late nights.

He switched on the light and slipped into the den. In his futon lay another person, a man. Momentarily startled, he moved closer to the futon to discover Grayson, Danni's long time boy friend, stretched out on his bed. Grayson moved but didn't wake up.

"God dammit," Shane mumbled to himself. "What the hell?" He quickly shut off the light to return to the living room to spend what remained of the night on the sofa. In the morning Shane awoke to his sister and Grayson sitting by the kitchen table drinking coffee.

Shane moved his plate away from the edge of the table and pushed back his chair. The encounter with Danni and Grayson was imprinted vividly in his mind. His questioning Grayson's shacking up with his sister besides presumptuously using his futon had ignited a prolonged, vociferous argument. All the old issues emerged, the disappointment, the belligerence, the irresponsibility, and the animosity. The intrusion of Grayson, rarely a topic Danni and Shane addressed, only added to the intensity of the argument. After the shouting, Shane rushed to the den, threw all his meager belongings, included his savings stuffed under the futon, into his back pack, and slammed the door on the comfort of a warm condo.

Chapter 35

Partially concealed by the ATM machine, he rested against a broom. For days he watched as a young man regularly came to the bank, made a quick transaction, apparently a deposit, then left. He speculated about his behavior, maybe an employee of a fast food joint depositing the day's cash or bringing in his tip money. Whatever his purpose, the young man aroused his suspicion.

Ambrose Blakeship's eyes followed Shane all the way to the bank's exit. Long straight hair parted over those eyes and rested on his shoulders. A tattered jacket covered his frail, upper frame often denied proper nourishment. Years of confrontations with the law, of time in prison, and of time on probation had inscribed on his face a perpetual frown which reflected a belligerence not consistent with his size. Still his life of hardship and deprivation had produced a dominant bitterness.

With a shrug of his shoulders, Ambrose resumed his job of keeping the bank's lobby clean, a job he despised. He hated watching bank customers come and go, depositing and withdrawing money, money he wished he had. He could use an easy hit. He would have to pay closer attention to this young guy.

Born in Chicago forty years ago, Ambrose grew up near the famous Chicago Stock Yards where his parents worked most of their lives. He vowed he would never follow in his parents' footsteps. Seeing his parents come home each day smelling of manure and wearing clothes stained with animal hair and blood convinced him his future lay some other place. After graduation from high school, he joined the Army. Two years later, the theft of five hundred dollars from the officers' club earned him a dishonorable discharge and five years probation.

He returned to Chicago to a life of petty crime rather than one of productive employment. Violations of his probation, three arrests, two for breaking and entering and one for assault, landed him in prison for two years.

Out of prison he stumbled around Chicago working at whatever menial jobs he could find. His aging parents tolerated his living at home but refused to support him beyond that. In 2005, weary of the pointless struggle of his life, he sought refuge in the Twin Cities where he heard of more fruitful opportunities to make a living without exhaustive effort.

With little more success in his job search than in Chicago, Ambrose reverted to his former specialty, stealing from others. Arrested again for breaking and entering, he spent additional time in the Hennepin County Workhouse. Released, he was assigned a parole officer who helped him secure a job, ironically on the maintenance staff of a bank on Marquette Avenue in down town Minneapolis. Coincidentally, his job brought him to the same bank Shane visited once or twice a week. As Ambrose moved his broom around the customer high tables in the center of the lobby, he concluded he would pay more attention to this young man, maybe even where he went after leaving the bank.

Shane did his job for Nick without asking questions and without, he thought, attracting attention. He received brief but specific instructions. He sought the assistance of the same teller with each deposit. Furthermore, his instructions included a prohibition on opening the pouches. He had no idea how much money he deposited each visit to the bank. In addition, he had absolutely no idea anyone paid him special attention.

Since storming out of his sister's condo nearly a month ago, he had fought the cold winter weather day and night. Seeking a place to sleep each night exposed him to an entirely new life. During the summer he had spent a few nights on the street. Doing so in the winter presented an entirely different problem. Yet he refused to give in to the temptation to return to his sister's condo.

He desperately clung to his freedom, vehemently rejecting those who attempted to rule his life. At nineteen years old, coming up on twenty, he could take care of himself. However, on nights when luck found him outside in below freezing temperatures, he questioned his judgement about lodging.

Leaving the downtown bank, Shane zipped up his jacket and tightened the scarf around his neck. In an hour he needed to check in for work, only a ten minute walk from the bank. With nowhere else to seek shelter from the cold north wind whipping around the towering office buildings, he headed for the Eighth Street Grill.

The next two weeks gave Ambrose the chance to observe more carefully Shane's mysterious banking activity. On his day off, Ambrose risked wasting it by hanging around the area outside the bank with the possibility of seeing where the young man went after making the presumed deposit. Besides, he had nothing better to do on his day off except sit around his cramped, chilly apartment.

As Shane left the bank, Ambrose followed him at a safe distance but close enough to avoid losing him in the crowded sidewalk. He trailed Shane to a bus stop on Hennepin Avenue two blocks from the bank. There Shane boarded a bus that headed for the western suburbs.

Shane's schedule of deposits varied from week to week but not by much. A man of meticulous detail, Nick made sure he or someone he appointed delivered the money pouches to Shane at times that didn't interfere with his hours at the Grill. Since Nick ate his lunch there so often, he learned of Shane's work schedule each week. Typically Shane received one pouch at a time either for delivery to the downtown bank or to the one in Wayzata. Occasionally, he received two pouches requiring delivery on the same day.

Shane sat in the Crystal Court sipping a cup of hot coffee. A break in his work schedule freed him to accept another deposit assignment. He waited impatiently for the arrival of either Nick or Paul, the only other person besides Nick, with whom Shane had contact.

Paul showed up carrying the familiar shoulder bag. He approached Shane with a smile and a brief greeting, the purpose of their meeting not conducive to lengthy conversation. He subtly reached into the shoulder bag and withdrew his hand holding not one pouch but two. Though it would earn Shane one hundred dollars, the assignment to both banks did not please him on this cold brisk day. Nonetheless, a job was a job for which he received a more than fair wage. Paul gave Shane an encouraging pat on the back, turned and hurried away from the court.

With the two pouches safely concealed inside his heavy winter coat, Shane made his way quickly to the Marquette Avenue bank, only a short walk from the Court. As he did so many times in the previous weeks, he entered the bank, stepped up to the same teller who each time completed the transaction, saying no more than a soft hello. Shane stepped back from the teller window and left the bank to walk to the bus stop on Hennepin Avenue. He never noticed a man, dressed in a ragged coat and a brimmed cap with ear flaps, watching his every move.

Convinced by means of his own crude logic that this young man had access to a lot of money, Ambrose envisioned getting his hands on some of it. For months he tediously swept the bank lobby, each day experiencing more discontent with his meager salary and the weekly requirement to check in with his parole officer. A little extra money would remove some of the tedium.

Ambrose, earlier, had followed the young man to the bus stop but no farther. He was eager to determine where he went on the bus. Misgivings about plunging into the unknown deterred him. Nonetheless, inspired by his careful observation and patience, Ambrose, over the last several days paid close attention to the young man and his regular visits to the bank that Ambrose helped to keep clean.

On this cold, late afternoon Ambrose caught sight of the young man hurrying into his bank. About ready to get off work, Ambrose hung around outside the bank, intent on confirming his suspicions about the guy. Dismissing his former misgivings, he would, today, join the young man on a bus ride to an unknown destination.

Shane clutched the two pouches inside his jacket. Time compelled him to hurry making the first transaction. The pale winter sun had already set and darkness began to settle over the Twin Cities. The Wayzata bank closed at six o'clock. Shane went through the deposit routine at the down town bank and rushed to the bus stop for the ride to Wayzata. Ambrose watched him push open the bank exit and head for the Hennepin Avenue bus stop. He followed.

On the bus Ambrose paused to note that Shane sat by himself about half way back in the bus, intent on looking out the window. Ambrose selected a seat which would enable him to keep his eye on his prey.

At the Wayzata transfer station, Shane quickly jumped down off the bus and hurried on the familiar route to the bank. Ambrose followed. Shane reached the bank's parking lot where lights cast shadows around and under several pine trees and parked cars. Ambrose followed, forced now to make a quick decision. Either act in the darkness of the parking lot or lose the chance to make extra money for the day.

Shane moved under the shadow of one pine tree. Ambrose breathed deeply. Despite the cold, perspiration formed around his neck. He wiped his gloved hand over his brow. With only a few feet separating him from Shane, he charged, hitting the unsuspecting Shane in the middle of the back, sending him to his knees.

Shane emitted a groan as his right knee slammed into the blacktop. His heavy winter coat gave him some protection from the attack. However, the pain from his knee and the surprise of the assault rendered Shane momentarily helpless. He tried to regain his feet, confused by what was happening, pain surging through his body.

The initial collision with Shane had ignited in Ambrose an almost feral hostility. He reached back and struck a solid blow to the back of Shane's head. Shane slumped onto the cold blacktop. Ambrose stood above him, his breathing heavy and in gasps. He delivered a vicious kick to Shane's ribs.

Pain exploded in Shane's chest. Desperate and in agony, he rolled onto his stomach. Ambrose moved closer to kick him in the kidneys. Shane doubled up in agonizing pain. Still he tried to rise up on his good knee. Ambrose kicked him again in the rib cage. Shane dropped to the blacktop and went limp.

Regaining more control, Ambrose reached down to turn Shane over on his back. He reached into his winter coat to find the pouch attached to Shane's belt. He pulled the pouch lose and ripped it open to find a roll of bills tightly wrapped. Greedy hands yanked them from the pouch. Shane groaned in pain. Ambrose stood up to apply, with greater deliberation, one more solid kick to the side of Shane's head. Shane lay silent, unmoving. Ambrose reached inside Shane's jacket, seeking his wallet. It might contain more valuables.

Ambrose moved away from the motionless body. He glanced at the roll of one hundred dollar bills. He grinned, made one last inspection of his victim, and ran toward the bus stop several hundred dollars richer. He left Shane sprawled on the blacktop, unconscious, blood trickling from one ear.

Chapter 36

Hot water cascaded through her thick, black hair and down over her trim, supple body. Alisha Sanders rubbed vigorously, soap suds swirling around the shower drain. For how many years she tried to scrub away the shame and guilt she lost count. She remembered exactly when the shame began. Only twelve years old, she stood at the threshold of adolescence with accompanying physical and emotional changes. Physically, she had developed early. She had taken pride in the gradual transformation of her body.

Standing in the shower allowing the water to wash over her, Alisha acknowledged that night would never lose its power to influence her life. In her mind she repeatedly returned to that evening. Her mother attended a concert with friends, leaving Alisha at home with her dad. An only child, she had enjoyed a special status with both her parents, especially her dad who recently had looked at her with a mysterious smile. As she undressed for bed, her father knocked at her bedroom door.

Not waiting for a response, he slowly pushed the door open and entered. Alisha looked at her dad with eyes wide. She tensed, frozen in place. Never before had anything like this happened. She stood nearly paralyzed trying to determine what to do. She reached for a sweatshirt tossed on the bed. At the same time her father moved closer.

"You know, Alisha, you are a beautiful girl."

With the sweatshirt she attempted to cover herself as best she could. This was her father. Why should she feel frightened? Confusion tangled her mind.

Alisha covered her eyes in a futile attempt to erase the dreadful image of her father's salacious grin. She stepped out of the shower, grabbed a towel and dried herself. She wiped the steam off the mirror over the sink in the cramped motel bathroom. Her hands paused over her breasts. She shook her head. Despite what happened so many years ago, she took pride in her five feet, five inch figure, the firmness and size of her breasts, the flatness of her stomach and the gentle contours of her hips and thighs.

Alisha completed her post engagement routine. For longer than she wished to admit prostitution served as her main source of income. The fateful moment with her dad marked only the beginning of repeated crushing episodes with him who employed fear to discourage his daughter from talking about them with anyone. Her transition into adolescence made her body more appealing and her dad's violation of her young body more frequent.

When a junior at Wayzata Senior High School, where she enjoyed membership in the National Honor Society, she dated a popular boy, a classmate and sports hero. After the homecoming football game when he scored two touchdowns in a Wayzata win, he escorted Alisha to the homecoming dance. After the dance they drove to a secluded spot north of Wayzata where he raped her in the back seat of his car. The devastating experience plunged Alisha into depression. Still she refused to report the incident, believing she and her beautiful body were at fault. Before the end of her junior year, she could tolerate no longer living at home under the lecherous eyes of her father or what she interpreted as the accusing eyes of her classmates.

The woman who now looked back at her in the mirror retained the physical appeal of that junior in high school. Months on the street in the cold and sun had deepened nascent creases around her eyes and when she smiled, around her lips. Nonetheless, her months on the street had left unaltered her hypnotic, dark eyes, her thick, black hair which encircled a delicate face, or the lure of her smile which revealed gleaming white teeth despite the lack of regular care.

Each night with another client awakened for Alisha the guilt and the shame. Each night also served, ironically, as a form of revenge against men who had so profoundly scarred her life. The power she believed she exercised over her clients as they grunted and panted on top of her offered a small sense of control. They, not she, were the victims this time.

After she left her home in Wayzata, her parents pleaded with her to return. Especially her mother, choked with emotion, over the phone had begged her to come home, completely oblivious to her husband's sexual abuse of their daughter. Alisha refused all entreaties. Eventually she ended any contact with her parents. Finding a place to sleep created a serious problem, one common to young people living on the street. Contact with other street teens helped her find some place to sleep most nights including couch hopping at the homes of friends and mere acquaintances. More than once that place to sleep was a heavy card board box.

As days and weeks dragged on, Alisha worked typical menial jobs at fast food establishments and even for a short time at Target, stocking shelves in the middle of the night. Ultimately she relented to the reality of her most important asset, her body. Since that realization, she had developed a list of eager and often wealthy clients most of whom she met in motels for which they paid. She did her job well for which her clients also paid well.

Standing in the middle of the latest motel room, she turned to check if she had left anything on the bed or dresser. She pulled on her coat, stuffed the money into her purse and walked out of the motel into the evening darkness and cold.

Rarely had she agreed to meet a client in her home town. The impressive fee changed her mind for this client, an executive from a local insurance company whom Alisha met online. Consequently the engagement required her to ride the bus to Wayzata and from the bus transit station walk several blocks to the motel. The walk took her by the bank regularly visited by Shane Stenlund.

On this dark, cold evening Alisha cut through the bank parking lot on her way to the transit station located blocks literally above Wayzata's main street. Since the bank very likely was closed, she looked at all the cars parked in the lot with some curiosity. Stepping around cars parked in the middle of the lot, she saw, partially concealed by shadows cast by a large pine tree, what looked like a bundle of clothes. No light to illuminate that particular area, she stepped closer to look more carefully. She immediately recognized the bundle was more than simply clothing. It was a person sprawled on the blacktop. Cautiously, she moved closer. Maybe just a drunk sleeping it off, she thought. In the past few months she had seen plenty of that under bridges and in building door ways.

Ready to ignore the person and head for the transit station, she gasped at the sight of blood puddled around the person's head. Shivers trickled down her back. She couldn't leave the person lying on the cold black top. Maybe someone from the bank could find him. She wouldn't have to get involved. The person moved, moaned, and lay still. Alisha remembered when she needed help desperately. No one was there to help her. This person needed help. With sudden resolve, she reached for her cell phone and dialed 911. She shivered from the cold, stomach muscles quivering. Kneeling down, she took a deep breath ready to await the arrival of emergency personnel.

Chapter 37

From the cell phone the melodic tones of *Rhapsody in Blue* dragged Danni from a deep sleep. With blurry eyes she glanced at the clock which recorded a time of 1:17 A.M. She reached for her cell phone normally on the night stand next to her bed. Her fingers touched only the surface of the stand. The music tone filled the bedroom. Danni sat up on the edge of the bed to spy the phone on the dresser across the room.

She hurried to grab the phone, her hand tense, nerves tightening the muscles in her stomach.

"Hello," she answered with a thin voice.

"Hello. I'm sorry to disturb you at this hour. My name is Heather. I'm a nurse at the Methodist Hospital Emergency Center."

Danni's hand gripped the phone tighter. She reached to turn on the light.

Heather continued. "A short time ago a young man entered the Emergency Center with no identification. He has . . . has sustained some serious injuries. We found his cell phone. The directory listed a sister at this number."

Danni gasped. Catching her breath, she explained. "I do have a brother . . . ah, about nineteen years old. I don't think anyone else would have my phone number." She paused, then as if in a hurry, blurted out, "What happened?"

"I can't tell you much without the patient's consent, but he was discovered unconscious in a parking lot near a Wayzata bank."

Danni inhaled sharply remembering Shane's mysterious deposit job. "Is he conscious now?" She asked.

"Right now he's under sedation. I'm sorry, but privacy laws prohibit my giving you much detail about his condition. Perhaps you could come to the Emergency Center to help to establish the young man's identity." Heather spoke in a professional tone.

Frustration combined with fear swept over Danni. "Yes, I will be there as quickly as I can. You said Methodist Hospital, right?"

"Yes, that's right." Heather confirmed.

"I'll be there shortly. I live only a few minutes away." Danni snapped shut her cell phone.

She jumped into a pair of jeans and a sweat shirt. Riding down the elevator she buttoned up her jacket. In her car she faced little traffic on her way to Lake Street and then west to St. Louis Park and Methodist Hospital. With both hands squeezed around the steering wheel, she gazed at the nearly empty road ahead.

A blur of questions tumbled through her mind. *Could the young man really be Shane? Should she have done more to provide for her younger brother? Did she and their parents impose too many restrictions on his quest for independence*? She thought, too, about Shane living on the streets or wherever he found a place to sleep. She shook her head, fearful of what she might discover at the Emergency Center.

Danni stepped back from the bed in a crowded room encircled with drapes attached to a track in the ceiling. She nodded her head, tears gathering in her eyes.

"Yes, he's my brother, Shane Stenlund." She confirmed.

Heather, the nurse who had made the early morning call, placed a hand gently on Danni's arm, profoundly sensitive to moments like these. "Thank you for getting here so fast. We've sedated him while we determine the extent of his injuries. Ah . . . ah some of them are obvious. We need to learn what internal injuries he suffers."

Danni moved closer to the bed. She breathed deeply struggling with her emotions. Her shoulders slumped. Tubes and wires attached to monitoring devices ended in or around Shane's arm. She faced the nurse. "Do you know what happened?"

"Not in any detail except it was likely a vicious assault and robbery. His wallet was missing. Thankfully the assailant missed the cell phone."

Danni turned away from her brother. She found difficult looking at him, his face swollen and discolored. "How did he get here?"

Heather hesitated on her way to check the monitors. "Well, the ambulance brought him here. Somebody discovered him on the blacktop parking lot and apparently called 911. At this time we don't know any more than that." She reached to adjust the intravenous tube.

An orderly appeared in the opening of the curtain. He pushed in a different table, explaining the Emergency Room doctor had ordered further testing to determine Shane's injuries.

Distraught over her brother's condition, Danni heeded the advice of nurse Heather and settled in the waiting room where a late night talk show offered some diversion to three or four people, presumably, awaiting news about a loved one. Danni restlessly moved in her seat, feelings of fear and guilt blocking out the activity in the waiting room.

An hour later Heather approached Danni slumped in a plastic covered arm chair. "Excuse me." Heather spoke quietly. "Your brother has been moved to a room in the Intensive Care Unit. If you could come with me, I will take you there. The doctor will meet with you to explain your brother's condition."

Danni jumped up from her place. "Thank you."

They entered the room on the third floor, a private room. Danni followed Heather as she eased the door open and entered. An eerie quiet filled the room. A typical hospital room, it contained, beside the bed, a closet, a bathroom, two chairs, a TV mounted to the wall, and most important a bank of monitors with blinking lights illuminating digital devices.

Heather moved closer to the bed. She studied the monitors. She then turned and walked to the door. "The doctor will be here shortly."

Danni stared at her brother, forgiving him any transgressions he may have committed. He lay motionless in the bed, his breathing obstructed. A bandage encircled his head. His left eye disappeared in the bulge of swelling. Two cotton splints surrounded his nose, his lips twice their normal size. Danni hung her head in despair. *Who in the hell did this? How could people be so brutal?*

"Excuse me. You must be Danni Stenlund?" A young doctor, tall, thin with hair combed straight back and clutching a clip board, reached out his hand. "I'm Dr. Carson."

Danni grasped the doctor's hand.

Dr. Carson motioned to the chairs in the corner of the room. "Please sit down. I'll explain what we have found out about your brother's condition."

Danni eased herself onto the chair.

The doctor sat beside her. He glanced at the clip board resting in his lap. Turning to Danni, he emphasized that Shane's injuries were not life threatening, but he had sustained serious injury to his head, likely kicked several times or hit with a blunt object.

Danni cringed but said nothing.

The doctor flipped up the page attached to his clip board. He cleared his throat. "Our examination confirmed a concussion but no fracture of the skull." He looked at Shane in the bed. "You obviously have noticed the injury to his face and mouth. He has a broken jaw, two missing teeth, and damage to the left eye which could adversely affect his vision. Time will determine that." He stopped and laid aside his clip board. "For a while he'll be very sore, but with time he will heal. He will have to take it easy until that happens." The doctor's eyes met Danni's. "Any questions?"

Danni sighed deeply. She closed her eyes in thought then opened them under a furrowed brow. "Besides his eye, will he have any other serious repercussions?"

The doctor sat back in his chair. "Of course, we can't always determine that with complete accuracy. Everyone heals differently." His eyes connected again with Danni's. "But I don't think so."

"How long will he have to stay in the hospital?" Danni shifted in her chair.

"Here in the ICU only another twelve hours or so. We will then transfer him to a regular room. How long he stays there will depend on how he responds to treatment and how fast he heals. He appears strong and in good health. That will make a difference in the healing time."

The doctor rose from his chair and grabbed his clip board. "Your brother will be all right. It just takes time and patience, yours and his." He smiled and stepped to the door. "The nursing staff will pay close attention to his progress." He paused. "I hesitate to mention this at this time, but reality is reality. One of the staff will arrive shortly to complete admission requirements. I'm sorry." The doctor glanced down at his clip board. With his hand on the door, he stopped to make eye contact with Danni. "Could I help you with anything else?"

Danni got up from her chair. "No, thank you very much for the information. I will contact our parents later this morning. I will return this afternoon to check on Shane."

As he walked out of the room, the doctor said over his shoulder, "Believe me. He's in good hands here."

Danni smiled, inched closer to Shane's bed. Placing her hand on his free arm, she whispered, "You need a lot of good hands."

Chapter 38

The call came as Martin and Iris Stenlund shared breakfast in the kitchen of their farm home. With a quiet but firm voice Danni announced to her parents the hospitalization of her brother following a severe beating. She gave few details other than describing his injuries and affirming, though serious, they were not life threatening.

For months following Shane's abrupt departure from home, his parents searched for an explanation. What had happened to their son who as a young boy had made them so proud of his willingness to assume his share of responsibilities around the farm? During the many hours Martin spent working the fields or doing the chores around the barn, he found abundant opportunity to think of his son who for so many years shared the farm work.

The quiet evenings that prevailed in the Stenlund home in the absence of both Danni and Shane gave Martin and Iris time to discuss what they could have done differently to weaken their son's expanding discontent with life on the farm. They often questioned if something else provoked the restlessness that marked his teen years. *Did he suffer from some emotional disorder that they should have recognized? Should they have consulted a psychologist? Were they simply too naive in failing to respond intelligently to their son's growing bitterness?*

They talked about signs of his gradually changing nature. They agreed that Shane's rebellion received a significant boost on the slops of Lutzen Ski Resort where he tore ligaments in his knee. The reality of life without his favorite sport dragged heavily on Shane's attitude toward school, home, and his relationships with his peers. He simply behaved differently after that accident and subsequent complications.

They wondered, too, about his sudden departure following the prom. His date with Lindsay Cooper seemed to brighten his mood. Excited about the prom date, he entered into its preparation with delight, seeking advice from his mother about details, such as flowers and whether to have dinner before the dance and if so where? Yet all of that excitement ended in his decision to leave home, hinting that something did happen during his night at the prom?

The Stenlunds couldn't remember how many times they relived the ugly scene in the principal's office when Shane rushed out the door refusing to consider summer school to ensure his graduation from high school. *Should they have noticed the senior year decline in his academic performance? Should they have taken a more active role in his life outside the home?*

All of these questions dominated their thoughts and dinner table discussions for months. Now none of them made a difference. What mattered now was the condition of their son as he lay in the hospital suffering the agony of a brutal beating.

Danni's call shocked her parents who failed to understand how this, too, could happen. Danni's inability to provide many details about the attack, why or where it happened, only compounded her parents' confusion. Without hesitation the Stenlunds hurried as they prepared for the quick trip to the Twin Cities and Methodist Hospital.

Chapter 39

Danni met her parents in the lobby of the sprawling Methodist Hospital. Directing them to the third floor and Shane's room, she attempted to answer a string of questions about his condition. She tried to prepare them for Shane's appearance which because of the swelling and discoloration around his face tended to exaggerate his injuries.

Danni and her parents stopped at the nurses' station to seek permission to enter Shane's room. A nurse confirmed that Shane slept, but they certainly could visit him in his room. They thanked the nurse who advised them she would be checking on him in a few minutes.

Danni carefully squeezed through the partially opened door to room 335. A small light above Shane's bed offered a pale glow. A shade covered the window making up a part of one wall. A collection of monitors sat beside the bed from which extended three tubes ending in Shane's arm and wrist.

Danni and her parents quietly stepped closer to the bed. His mother cringed as she saw the damaged done to Shane's face. She reached out to place her hand gently on his free arm. He moved his arm in response to her touch. She gazed upon her son, slowly shaking her head from side to side.

As she promised, the nurse identified as Tammy by her name badge arrived to check on Shane's monitors and to administer his medication. Of course, to do that she had to wake him up. She moved next to his bed and whispered his name. Little by little his good eye opened, his damaged eye protected with a bandage.

He saw only the nurse who reminded him of her purpose simply to check his vital statistics and give him his medication which included a pain killer and an antibiotic.

Tammy smiled as she said, "Someone is here to see you."

Shane turned his head enough to view dimmed images of his sister and parents standing on the other side of the bed. His eye brightened and a weak smile crossed his swollen lips.

Martin stepped to the bed. "How you doing, son?"

Shane attempted to push himself up higher in his bed. "Not too bad, I guess." He spoke in a soft, harsh voice partially obstructed by swollen lips.

The nurse efficiently went through the routine of checking his monitors and helping him take his medication, his swollen lips complicating the procedure. With that accomplished, Tammy adjusted his pillow then asked, "Do you need anything else right now?"

Shane slowly shook his head and whispered, "I don't think so."

"I'll be back in a while to check on you. Until then you treat your guests kindly." Tammy smiled as she patted Shane on his leg before moving to the door.

Left alone with their brother and son, the Stenlunds stood in silence each in his or her own way determining what to say. Of course, the question of what happened dominated each of their thoughts. How to begin caused the silence.

Finally, Danni asked, "Can you tell us what happened?"

Shane looked off into the corner of the room then turned his head to face his sister, his voice firm but weak, "Someone beat the shit out of me."

Danni glanced first at her mother who stood at the end of the bed and then at her dad who stood just behind her. She turned to face her brother. "Could you give us any more detail?" she asked.

Shane breathed deeply, a rasping sound emitted from his throat. "Someone jumped me in the parking lot. That's all I know."

Reluctant to force him to talk any more than he had to, Shane's family still contended with a cascade of questions flowing through their minds. *What parking lot? Why was he in a parking lot at night?*

What did he have that a robber might want? How did he get to the hospital? A gentle knock on the door, for the moment, prevented his family from asking these questions and rescued Shane from having to answer.

"May I come in?" A young man, perhaps in his late thirties or early forties, pushed through the door carrying with him the familiar clipboard. "I trust I'm not interrupting anything. I'm doctor Winston." He offered his hand to each of the Stenlunds. "I will be checking on Shane's progress as he continues to recover from a nasty beating." The doctor stepped to the side of the bed to inquire of Shane's condition. "Nurse Tammy tells me your getting along okay. Do you agree?"

Shane nodded his head to emphasize a soft, "Yes."

"Good. If you don't mind, I want to take a few minutes to explain to your family the extent of you injuries."

Shane's swollen lips produced a weak smile.

The doctor directed Shane's family to the two chairs in the corner of the room. Danni and her mother sat down. Martin preferred to stand, to him much less confining. With everyone in place Dr. Winston described the nature of Shane's injury in complete detail including the concussion, the damaged ribs, the bruised kidney and, of course, the very visible damage to his face, particularly his eye and mouth.

The family listened carefully to the doctor's description. When he paused, Martin asked, "Will he suffer any long term effects?"

"Every one heals differently. Shane's age and his excellent physical condition should enable him to recover fully. It may take a while, but following doctor's orders should ensure good results." The doctor answered with a chuckle.

Iris stood up from her chair, walking over to stand by Shane's bed. "What about his eye? Is there danger of his losing sight in that eye?"

The doctor leaned back against the wall, holding his clip board against his chest. "I don't think so. What you see looks worse than it actually is. Our examination reveals no damage to the eye itself.

The area around the eye suffered most of the damage thus all the swelling."

The doctor took a quick look at his watch before reminding the Stenlunds that he needed to visit another patience. He assured them that if they still had questions about Shane's condition, they should feel free to contact him or Tammy, the nurse. With that, he thanked them and left the room.

The family stood around Shane's bed still flirting with numerous unanswered questions about the assault and why it happened. Nonetheless, they all relaxed in knowing that, physically, Shane would recover in time. Perhaps in time they also would learn the details of the brutal, senseless incident.

Chapter 40

Nick Karpin slid his fork closer to his plate. He reached for his glass of ice tea, taking another swallow. He moved restlessly in his chair by his usual table at the Eighth Street Grill where he faithfully ate his lunch virtually every day. In futility, his eyes searched the dining room looking for Shane Stenlund. Nick had not heard from him for three days. The last contact occurred when Shane received two pouches, one for the downtown drop off and one for the Wayzata drop off.

Concern accumulated when Nick failed to see Shane at the Grill or he neglected to answer his cell phone. Protecting his delicate drug enterprise occupied a high priority for Nick. The role Shane played helped to ensure some anonymity for Nick, who laundered his drug money through his apartment accounts. A report from the teller in the Wayzata bank only added to Nick's concern. That teller reported no deposit three days ago. Attempts to contact Shane proved unsuccessful.

He reached for his ice tea again, twirling it around as he stared into his empty plate, pondering what had happened to Shane and the money, a fistful of money. Nick sat back in his chair while he waited for his order. Scanning the dinning room another time his eyes caught a bus boy who, Nick believed, worked with Shane. He motioned him over to his table.

Max stood next to Nick. "Yes, can I help you?" he asked.

Nick took a breath and turned in his chair to face Max. "Don't you work with Shane Stenlund?"

Max nodded his head, "Yes, I do."

Nick looked around the dinning room. "Is he here? I don't see him. He usually works at this time doesn't he?" Nick sat up rigid in his chair.

Max clasped his hands behind his back. "He's not working today. He's in the hospital," Max announced calmly.

Nick pushed his chair away from the table, "In the hospital! What the hell happened?"

Max dropped his arms to his side. "I really don't know many details just that someone beat him up in some parking lot. His sister called in. I guess he's at Methodist Hospital."

Nick's shoulders slumped. He squeezed his hands into fists, slamming them onto the table rattling the dishes set for lunch. Staring down at his plate, he mumbled, "Thank you."

A whole series of problems drifted before Nick's eyes. *Had Shane talked with the police about the attack? What happened to the money? How would this incident jeopardize his lucrative money laundering scheme?* He needed to ensure that Shane kept his mouth shut. He needed to reinforce the need for secrecy even though Shane knew little about the real source of the money he deposited. Without delay Nick would visit Shane in the hospital.

Nick hurried through his lunch only to rush out to his car for the short drive to Methodist Hospital in suburban St. Louis Park. With little difficulty Nick convinced the receptionist at the hospital of the urgency of his speaking with Shane Stenlund. "He's one of my most important clients whose welfare is very important to me," Nick pleaded with the receptionist.

"Well," she announced as she turned to her computer. "Mr. Stenlund is in room 335. Down the hall, take the elevators to the third floor. Check in with the nurses' station there. They will direct you to the room."

Nick thanked the receptionist and headed for the elevator. At the third floor nurses' station he received directions to room 335. Standing outside the room, Nick knocked lightly on the door. Hearing no response, he eased the door open enough to peek into the room. Shane sat nearly upright in his bed with eyes directed to the TV attached to the wall across the room.

Nick opened the door wide and stepped into the room. Shane jerked his head to see who entered. His body stiffened.

Nick approached the bed. "How you doing?" He stood at the foot of the bed with arms crossed over his chest.

A tight smile concealing two missing front teeth spread Shane's swollen lips. "Okay, I guess," his short response.

"What the hell happened to you?" Nick spoke with more urgency.

Tired of the question but strengthened from three days in the hospital, Shane answered as he had in the past, "Someone beat the shit out of me."

"Where did that happen?" Nick moved around to the side of the bed.

Though the three days since the beating allowed for a reduction in the swelling around Shane's lips and eye, still dark coloration added alarm to his appearance. Very slowly Shane explained to Nick as much about the assault as he remembered, having no idea the identity of the perpetrator.

"How did you get here?" Nick inquired.

"I really don't know who called 911. Someone did. That's how I got here."

Silence filled the space between them. Nick stepped back from the bed, a stern look on his face. "Ah . . . ah, have you discussed with the police what happened?"

"No." Shane answered.

Nick released a long breath. "Good. Don't. We'll keep this to ourselves as just a bad deal. Okay?"

Shane locked eyes with Nick. "What about the rent money? Who ever attacked me got the money."

Nick moved closer to the bed again, placing his hands flat on the cover. "We don't care about the money. When you get better, we'll carry on like before. We'll have to be a bit more cautious about predators out there." Nick leaned over the bed for emphasis. "We don't need to get the police involved in this." He paused, opening his arms as if pleading his case. "Remember our discussion about secrecy. It's still very important. You understand?"

Shane straightened his position on his pillow. "I guess so."

"You guess so!" Nick snorted. "I need more than that." He leaned in bracing himself with hands planted on the bed. "Now, I repeat. Do you understand the urgency of secrecy?"

With a sense of intimidation, Shane uttered, "Yes."

Nick stepped back. "Good. Now you get better, and I'll talk with you when you get out of here." He stepped backwards a couple steps then turned and vanished out the door.

Shane stared at the partially closed door, a bit perplexed over Nick's unyielding insistence on secrecy over only rent money. *Why should that demand so much secrecy?* Shane ran his hand over his tender mouth and touched his swollen eye, prompting him to consider if Nick was using him for purposes the police would want to know about or if the lure of money had trapped him into something more than making innocent deposits of rent money. He would have to think about that.

While he did, a ragged vagrant, braced himself against a Hennepin Avenue bus shelter. With a bottle of vodka from which he took generous swallows, he celebrated his recent acquisition of several hundred dollars.

Chapter 41

Alisha stood before the small, coin operated newspaper stand outside the Target store on Hennepin Avenue. She debated spending a dollar on a current newspaper. Glimpses of TV news through the Target window revealed absolutely no information about the incident in the Wayzata parking lot.

Since the shock of discovery in Wayzata that dark night three days ago, she questioned who the young man was she found bleeding and unconscious on the black top, and what had happened to him. She did understand that the ambulance that picked him up delivered him to Methodist Hospital in St. Louis Park. She had no idea of the degree of his injuries. Still, she couldn't erase her concern for his condition.

In a reckless moment she dropped the coins into the slots in the stand. Quickly, she lifted the window and reached for the paper. Stepping back to rest against the building, she paged through the paper searching for any information about a young man found unconscious in Wayzata. She dropped the paper to her side; disappointment etched across her attractive but weary face. She turned to view the TV stationed in the Target display window. She saw only a soap opera.

Alisha dropped her head, her chin resting on her chest. She closed her eyes trying to understand her intense desire to learn more about this young man. *Why*, she asked herself, *could she not forget about him or his fate?* Over the past several months she assumed she had developed an indifference to others, what they thought or what happened to them. She had a responsibility to herself. That's all that mattered or so she thought. This recent interest in the young man puzzled her.

She folded the paper and stuffed it under her arm. She would deposit it in the first trash container she came to. Walking on Hennepin Avenue toward downtown, Alisha suddenly stopped, preoccupied with her search for information about the incident in the parking lot, at the same time inadvertently blocking the path of three women lugging shopping bags.

"Excuse us," voiced one of the women.

Surprised by the comment, Alisha turned to say, "I'm sorry," not realizing what she had done.

She stepped out of the flow of pedestrian traffic. She spotted a bench near the bus stop across the street. She made her way to the bench where she first dropped the newspaper in a trash container then sat down on the bench. Her shoulders slumped when she squeezed her hands between her knees. She questioned her sudden concern for this young man. The more she questioned it the more it pressed upon her mind.

Lifting her head, she stared at the heavy traffic even this early in the day. However, she really didn't notice specific details about the traffic. Instead she concentrated on her present state of mind and the possibility that her sudden interest in this young man had something to do with an emerging feeling of her own vulnerability derived from the dangers she faced with strangers in strange motels. *Could she end up on some blacktop parking lot, unconscious and bleeding*?

She shivered thinking about the possibility but quickly dismissed it with the reassurance she could take care of herself. After all she had succeeded in doing so for several months. Nonetheless, she could not erase from her mind questions about the young man. With sudden resolve she stood up from the bench committed to doing the only thing she could think of to quiet her concerns for this young guy. She would attempt to visit him in the hospital.

Shane lay propped up in his hospital bed. Tomorrow the hospital would release him. At this moment he grappled with just where he would go after his release. Dr. Winston cautioned him about returning too quickly to his normal routine. Though damage to his ribs and kidneys was minor, he still had to remember the concussion from which he would recover slowly. Also damage to his eye demanded careful observation though all indications suggested no permanent effects. In time Shane would need his two front teeth replaced, but before that happened, his mouth and gums needed to heal more completely.

On two different occasions during his hospital stay, his family addressed where he would spend recovery time. Alone with the TV producing only sounds which Shane ignored, his thoughts drifted to the latest discussion about where he would go after his release from the hospital.

Members of his family stood around his bed, his dad positioned at the foot. "Son, the doctor tells us that in a couple days you can leave here." He crossed his arms over his chest. "Your mother and I have talked about where you will go after your release. We decided you should return home where we can watch over your recovery."

Shane's body tensed with the suggestion he return home. He closed his eyes briefly, turning his head to the side to stare at the monitor blinking his vital signs. He said nothing.

Iris stood next to the bed, behind her son, as he studied the monitors. "Well, Shane, what do you think? Are you ready to come home? It's been a long time."

Again Shane failed to respond.

"Look son," his father spoke firmly. "We only want to do what's best for you. Home, we think, is best."

Shane turned to sit more erect in his bed. He licked his still slightly swollen lips. In a voice weak from lack of use, he countered, "Yeah, best for you but maybe not best for me."

Martin inhaled sharply. "Stop this nonsense. I think your mother and I have some idea what's best for you. We're not thinking only of ourselves."

At that point Danni had intervened to avoid any more shouting. She suggested they think about where Shane should go offering her condo as an alternative. Even that failed to appeal to Shane, who simply did not wish to live under the control of his family.

Reliving that previous discussion rattled through Shane's mind when he heard a gentle knock on his door.

Chapter 42

A nurse, a different one, peeked her head through the slightly opened door to Shane's room. "Excuse me, Mr. Stenlund. You have a guest."

The announcement dragged Shane quickly back to reality, rescuing him from his confusion over where he would go after leaving the hospital. He nudged himself up in his bed so that he sat upright. He cleared his throat. "Come on in," he offered, his voice having regained most of its strength and tone, his lips nearly normal size barely covering the glaring space left by the two missing teeth.

The nurse entered the room then moved aside to guide in a young girl Shane viewed for the first time.

The nurse placed her hand on Alisha's shoulder. "Mr. Stenlund, this is Alisha Sanders. Alisha this is Shane Stenlund." The nurse stepped away from Alisha. "Shane, Alisha wishes to talk to you if that's all right."

Alisha Sanders, now standing closer to his bed, left Shane momentarily without a response. His eyes looked into hers or more accurately her eyes captured his attention. Her generous smile accentuated finely defined cheeks that tampered to a delicate chin. Jeans and a sweatshirt gave distinct definition to her slim figure. A generous smile lightened her face.

Nearly mesmerized by the young girl's proximity, Shane instantly concluded she was the most beautiful girl he had ever seen. He opened his mouth to speak. Nothing came out. Then he stammered, "I . . . I guess it's all right."

"Fine. Then I will leave you two to visit. If you need anything, you only need to press that red button." The nurse moved to the door, turned to smile at the two young people then disappeared into the hallway.

An awkward silence filled the room. Shane pulled up the sheet that covered him. He studied Alisha, finding difficulty in looking at anything else. His rapt attention to her did not go unnoticed. She moved around to the end of the bed where for only a moment she looked down at slender hands folded in front of her.

"How are you getting along?" She looked up at Shane, her voice clear and confident.

Shane ran his hand over his lips and swallowed. An expanding sensitivity to his missing front teeth denied Shane the privilege of smiling. It even interfered with his speaking. "Okay, I guess." He managed to utter. He reached up to run his hand through his hair, stiff and stringy from his days in a hospital bed. Locking his eyes again on her beautiful face, he stated, "Thank you for coming, but how did you know about me?"

Alisha's eyes brightened, complimenting her alluring smile. She glanced down at her hands now resting on the end of the bed. She looked up at Shane. Her voice softened by a touch of modesty. "I found you in the bank parking lot and called 911."

Shane's mouth dropped open despite his concern for his missing teeth. He exhaled deeply. "You called 911?"

Alisha nodded her head, and with fading modesty said, "I sure did. You obviously needed help I couldn't give you. The only sensible thing to do was call 911."

"God, am I glad you did. Maybe you saved my life."

"Maybe, but for sure you look like you've made a good recovery. You look a whole lot better than the last time I saw you." Alisha combined that comment with another captivating smile.

Silence for the moment again took over the room. Shane tried to look away from his guest. He turned to gaze at the ubiquitous monitors that blinked constantly next to his bed. He turned to ask Alisha. "How did you find me?"

To this question she laughed. "Oh, it wasn't easy, but with a little determination I succeeded."

Certainly her gaining access to Shane's room did demand determination. After giving up on trying to find out information in the media about the young man she helped, she decided her only alternative was to go to Methodist Hospital and try her luck there. Not even knowing the young man's name certainly would pose a handicap; nonetheless, Alisha, for reasons of her own, needed to find out the status of the young man she helped rescue in that cold, dark parking lot.

Armed only with her resolve, she located a city bus that could take her close to the hospital. She dressed modestly, jeans and a sweatshirt, wishing to dispel any suggestion that she possessed ulterior motives in her desire to visit a young man in his hospital room.

She inquired of an attendant at the hospital front entrance whom she could ask about a friend's room. The attendant directed her to a receptionist located just inside and to the right. Entering the main reception area, Alisha was overwhelmed by the hospital's size. The receptionist did sit just to her right. However, to her left the corridor stretched for what seemed a block, people shrinking in size as they walked away from her.

Approaching the receptionist's desk, Alisha very humbly asked how she could find out a friend's room number.

From behind her desk seated in front of her computer, the receptionist looked up at Alisha to ask, "What is your friend's name?"

Alisha closed her eyes for a second, realizing how foolish what she was about to say would sound. "I . . . ah, I don't know."

With eyes wide and mouth open, the receptionist stared up at Alisha. "I'm sorry, but I'm afraid I can't help you if you can't give me a name."

Alisha hung her head, shoulders slumped. She had no choice but to explain to the receptionist the story of her coming across this young man in a parking lot and calling 911. That explanation prompted the receptionist to call her supervisor who eventually accepted Alisha's story and directed her to the third floor where she would find Shane Stenlund's room.

Shane nervously pulled on the edge of the sheet that covered him. "I guess I should also ask why? I mean, I'm grateful for your coming, but why?"

Alisha looked away, her eyes raised in thought. She refused to delve into her reflections of a couple days ago, thoughts about her own vulnerability, thoughts about her ending up beaten in a parking lot. However, curiosity about his condition surely offered reason enough to seek him out.

She looked back at Shane. "You looked badly hurt when I first saw you unconscious on the cold black top. Once the ambulance took you away, I assumed it would take you to Methodist. The name was printed on the side." She paused, leaning forward against the end of the bed, careful to avoid bumping Shane's feet. "I guess curiosity played some part in my being here. I don't know, really. I needed to find out how you were doing."

Their conversation gradually moved toward other subjects. "What were you doing in that parking lot? Do you live in Wayzata? Alisha asked.

Another deep breath prepared Shane to answer briefly about his innocent deposit responsibilities for a friend. "No, I don't live there. I help a friend by making deposits for him in that Wayzata bank. I don't know much more about the deposits, and I don't care. My friend pays me well for doing it," Shane confessed. "What about you? Do you live in Wayzata?"

A brief hesitation delayed her response. "I did."

"Where do you live now?" Shane inquired.

"Around," was her only answer.

"How about you, Shane? Where do you live?"

A moment's consideration of the recent, heated discussion with parents about where he would go upon leaving the hospital prompted Shane to answer, "Around."

Chapter 43

"Good afternoon, son. How you doing?" Iris rushed into the living room of Danni's condo where on the sofa Shane sat in indifference.

"I'm fine," his voice carrying a weariness from answering that question far too often.

Iris sat down next to her son. She reached her hand to turn Shane's head toward her. "How's that eye doing? Let me take a look."

Shane resisted, what he considered, his mother's overbearing concern. Her behavior represented exactly what provoked his leaving home nearly a year ago. "Mother, my eye is okay. It gets better everyday."

"Your mother is only worried about you, Shane. Come on give us a break." Shane's dad stood outlined in the large picture window overlooking the Nicollet Mall. Recent months had reduced little the tension that divided Shane and his father. Though the past few months included few occasions for Shane and his father to meet, when they did, neither moved toward any compromise.

Danni occupied herself in the kitchen preparing a vegetable, luncheon salad. The recent family gatherings featured the same clashes between her dad and her brother, confrontations she believed resolved nothing.

Hospital officials released Shane from Methodist one week ago. With reluctance Shane agreed to spend his recovery at his sister's condo, ending another intense argument in Shane's hospital room the day before his release. During his short hospital stay, that topic generated more conversation than even his recovery. With little success, Danni attempted to mediate her dad's insistence that Shane return home after his release. She also reminded her brother that their parents would pay the medical bills. Shane still remained under the umbrella of his parents' health insurance.

In defense of his staying with her in Minneapolis, she emphasized in explanation to her parents Shane's acclimation to the Twin Cities, to his job, and to his small collection of friends, as well as her acclimation to his reach for independence even from her. Despite the pain it might cause, she told her parents in private that Shane approached twenty years old. He needed his freedom from parental control. They simply needed to respect his wishes. Besides he needed to remain close to the health care provided by the staff at Methodist Hospital. In the end, with reluctance Shane agreed to spend some time at his sister's condo. With reluctance his parents agreed to allow him to do so.

In the days since his release from the hospital, Shane's condition improved quickly. Swelling around, particularly his eye, had nearly disappeared; only faint discoloration lingered. The soreness around his mouth also faded with the gradual healing of his gums left bare by two missing teeth. In a few days, Shane would receive temporary teeth. He would have to wait a few more weeks for more permanent replacements. Though he had little to smile about, replacing the missing teeth would definitely remove a formidable barrier to his smiling.

"Why don't you people come in here and get something to eat?" Danni looked into the living room where Shane and his mom sat on the sofa. His dad sat on the ledge in front of the picture window. "It's not much, but it's good," she laughed, adding a bit of humor to a tense atmosphere haunting her condo.

With their plates filled, Danni and her family returned to the living room where Shane and his mom reclaimed their places on the sofa. Her dad did the same on the window ledge, leaving Danni to settle into the sofa chair. Each concentrated briefly on the food, only the sound of silverware intruding on the silence.

Shane's mom balanced her plate on her lap. She turned to face her son seated at the other end of the sofa. "When will you be able to return to work?"

Not since the beating had Shane returned to work. The restaurant assured him that until he fully recovered, his job waited for him. Since the early morning call from the hospital announcing his assault, first Danni then Shane maintained contact with the Eighth Street Grill.

Shane chewed his salad then set the plate on the coffee table in front of him. He faced his mother. He closed his eyes in thought. "I meet with Dr. Winston at the hospital ah . . . ah, I think, in two or three days, yeah on Friday. He will tell me when I can."

"That's great. Do you have any trouble with your ribs?"

Shane shook his head in response.

Danni spoke up. "At his last check up, the doctor removed any concern for his ribs or his kidneys. Things are working okay."

Iris reached over to pat her son's knee. "We are so glad things have worked out as well as they have."

Shane's dad stood up. He stepped closer to the sofa. "Give me your plates. I'll take them into the kitchen." He collected all but Danni's.

Upon his return to the living room, he resumed his place by the window. He ran his hand through slightly thinning hair flecked with bits of grey. "Son, can you explain again this bank deposit job? I don't understand what it's all about."

Shane sat up on the edge of the sofa. With hands planted on his knees, he spoke softly. "Dad, I've tried to explain the situation as well as I can. All I know is that Nick asked me to deposit rent receipts from his apartments. He pays me fifty dollars for each deposit." Shane slumped back in the sofa.

The furrows in his dad's brow deepened. "Maybe you have already explained this. But why can't he deposit the money himself?"

Shane glanced over at his dad sitting on the window bench. "I don't know, Dad. He told me he didn't want to bother with the weekly deposits. He didn't give me any other explanation."

Martin shrugged his shoulders, punctuated with skepticism. "I don't know. Maybe he has something to hide?"

Shane took a deep breath. "Dad, I've told you all I know. I'll take the money he pays me."

"Yes, of course, Just use caution when dealing with people like this Nick." Martin stood up to look out the window. He desperately wanted to ask Shane, *What comes next*? He discreetly refrained. Instead, he suggested to his wife it was time to head home. They faced a three hour drive.

Chapter 44

The TV cast a dim glow in the living room of Danni's condo. Eight days since his release from the hospital found Shane spread out on the sofa, feet extended in front of him as he lay relaxed against the soft back cushions. He found little to do but occasionally stare at the TV or close his eyes in thought about his last year away from home.

During these private moments Shane pried into his storage of decisions made over the past few months. He acknowledged little change in his quest for independence, for freedom from control of his life by others. Still, reflecting on the past few months, he contemplated what his intransigence had gained him. A menial job earned him a few dollars. The simple deposits for Nick earned him a few more dollars but also could have cost him his life. *Where were his decisions leading him*?

He pulled his legs in and sat up straight. One glance at the TV persuaded him to shut it off. He didn't need to watch the travails of over sexed and bored house wives. He rose from the sofa, feeling only a slight twinge from his rib cage.

Standing in front of the window overlooking the Nicollet Mall, Shane observed the usual parade of people doing what they apparently did each day. Always a crowd on the Mall. Within that crowd Shane spotted a young couple walking hand in hand. The image of Lindsey Cooper flashed into his mind.

During the nearly year of his absence from home, he thought of Lindsey often. He thought of the crushing humiliation of prom night when his senseless behavior destroyed his relationship with a girl he, if not loved, admired. He reached into the fridge for a can of Sprite, the only soda permitted by his sister. Closing the fridge door, he stared at the picture of Danni and her male companion, Grayson Quinn, mounted there with a collection of pictures from her lab. *Did they love each other*? Shane really didn't understand the world of love, a world for him remote and arcane. *Would he know love if he ever fell in love*?

Shane sipped on his soda, the cold liquid passing over lips still tender. He headed back to the living room and the window to the Nicollet Mall. He looked down at the flow of people, not really noting anyone in particular. Staring out the window, he thought about Lindsey and if she liked college, The University of Minnesota, Duluth, he thought? *Did she ever think of him kindly or did their last night together linger as her only recollection of Shane Stenlund?*

He moved slowly back to the kitchen where he retrieved the last swallow of his soda before dropping the can in the recycling bin. Thoughts of Lindsey faded to thoughts of Alisha, that alluring, charming girl who played such a vital role in his receiving the critical help he needed that horrible night in the parking lot.

Shane rested again on the sofa. His hospital meeting with Alisha ended with an exchange of cell phone numbers. Since then he lacked the courage to call her. He sat on the sofa with arms resting on this knees. Inadvertently, he massaged his right knee, responding to a nonexistent itch. He shook his head, feeling regret over his cowardice. She made the effort to visit him in the hospital though she didn't even know his name. He could think of no other description of his behavior then ungrateful. He couldn't even generate enough concern to call her if for no other reason than to thank her again for what she did for him.

He ran his hand over his eye, still tender to the touch. Running his hand over his lips, he pressed gently on center of his upper lip, the area that absorbed the blow knocking out two front teeth. The temporary teeth, recently set, encouraged the return of his smile but came with lingering soreness which he vowed to tolerate rather than contend with that ugly space. Only a mild occasional headache reminded him of the concussion that could have produced much more serious consequences had not Alisha found him on the black top.

Suddenly, he stood up, paused for an instant to allow passage of a moment of dizziness, walked briskly to the den where he found his cell phone at the end of the futon which served as his bed. Grabbing the phone, he commanded his fingers to stop shaking. He entered his phone's directory where he located Alisha's number. He inhaled deeply then let out his breath. He punched the number under her name. Placing the phone next to his ear, he listened, his stomach growled, the back of his neck tingled.

After the sixth ring, Shane heard Alisha's voice mail inviting him to leave a message. He looked down at the floor, deciding what to say. He could think of nothing at the moment. He hung up. He flipped the phone closed and tossed it on the futon.

"Shit!" He exclaimed. "What the hell is the matter with me? Some damned coward!"

He left the den, but as he did, he pounded the open door with the flat of his hand. Humiliated and disgusted with himself, he walked to the living room where he virtually threw himself onto the sofa. He berated himself for being so damned stupid, for feeling intimidated by Alisha. During the hospital visit she displayed sensitivity, charm, and, above all, beauty. At least in Shane's opinion, Alisha ranked as possibly the most alluring and captivating girl he had ever met.

Buried in his regret, Shane slumped back in the sofa. From the den, he heard the distinctive sound of his cell phone. With a little less energy than earlier, he slowly rose from the sofa then hurried to the den to grasp his phone resting on the futon.

He glanced at the caller ID; Alisha's name appeared. Shane caught his breath, licked his lips, and answered. "This is Shane."

"This is Alisha. Did you call earlier?"

Shane dropped his head, resting his chin on his chest. "Ah . . . yeah I did. I'm sorry. I should have left a message."

"That's okay. I tried to get to my phone, but I didn't make it." She paused. "Did you want something?"

Shane smiled to himself. Of course, he wanted something. He wanted to sit down and have a long talk with her to thank her for what she did for him. He cleared his throat. "I . . . I, ah, wondered if we could get together sometime; maybe I could buy you lunch or something." Shane moved about the den nervously adjusting the blanket on his futon, pushing aside with his foot a pair of jeans, and bending to pick up a scrap of paper.

"I'd like that. What do you suggest? Alisha asked.

A bit more relaxed, Shane explained, "I see the doctor tomorrow, Friday. What about Saturday, would you be free?"

Alisha laughed into the phone humored by the thought that she maintained some kind of schedule. "Almost any time. You name it; I'll be there."

"Good," This time Shane smiled. "Why don't we meet in the Crystal Court on the Mall about eleven o'clock Saturday morning? Then we can decide where to go from there."

"I can hardly wait." Alisha's voice confirmed the sincerity of her comment. "By the way, how are you doing?"

"I'm doing fine, getting better every day. Thank you for asking."

"Wonderful. See you Saturday about eleven. Bye."

Shane stood staring at the silent cell phone, the burden of guilt he suffered only minutes ago miraculously vanquished by a simple phone call.

Chapter 45

A brisk March wind greeted Shane when he stepped out onto the Nicollet Mall. The Mall crowd thinned on weekends. At least it did from his observations over the past months. Maybe, he speculated absently, people coming and going to and from work or those shopping or seeking a place for breakfast or lunch accounted for the increased crowds during the week. Shane grinned at his preoccupation with the Mall crowds, a topic making very little difference to him.

Taking his time, he advanced toward the Crystal Court. He was early for the scheduled eleven o'clock meeting with Alisha. A shiver raced through his body, a reminder to zip up his jacket. He now questioned the decision to meet with Alisha Saturday morning at the Crystal Court. He simply failed to judge accurately the vagaries of March weather in downtown Minneapolis. Perhaps his nervousness and the butterflies he struggled to control adversely influenced his judgement. Reflecting on that phone conversation two days ago invoked another smile. He found difficult dismissing the disarming effect Alisha had on him.

He shook his arms to stimulate a little warmth under his jacket, too light for this time of year. With a quickened pace he continued on his way to the Crystal Court, those butterflies churning in his stomach. Thoughts of his visit yesterday with Dr. Winston served temporarily to calm his anxiety. The doctor's brief examination revealed satisfactory healing of Shane's injuries. His eye suffered no permanent damage nor did his ribs and kidneys. However, concerning the concussion, the doctor advised Shane to exercise cautiously. Any subsequent blow to the head could prove serious. Most important, the doctor gave him permission to return to work. On Monday he would do that.

He entered the Crystal Court where a few people milled around the tables, most, however, standing clear of the fountain. Shane slowed his pace searching for that captivating face he remembered from Alisha's hospital visit. With little difficulty he spotted her standing next to one of the tables, her arms crossed over her chest, her head rotating, searching for a familiar face.

Before approaching any closer, he studied from a short distance her alluring appearance, her entire being perfectly proportioned, her naturally tanned faced framed in the gray hood of the sweatshirt she worn under a pale blue, light winter jacket. Never could he remember a girl so fascinating as this one whom he hardly knew, but who had maybe saved his life. The butterflies resumed their rumbling through his stomach.

Suddenly, she recognized him when he still stood several feet away from her table. A smile enlightened her face; she raised her arm in a vigorous greeting. She walked to meet him with open arms.

With no reservation she wrapped her arms around his waist. Shane stood unnaturally rigid, not quite sure if he should return the embrace.

Alisha looked up into Shane's eyes, "How you doing? You look great, a whole lot better than the last time I saw you." She released her arms and stepped back, eyes locked on his. "Sorry, I guess I said that before."

Shane stood unmoving, for a moment a near paralysis rendering him speechless. Embarrassed by his sudden inability to respond, he couldn't find a place for his hands until finally clasping them behind his back.

Alisha detected his struggle to respond. "You okay?"

At last he broke the bonds that gripped him. Shaking his head, he confessed, "Forgive me. I'm such an idiot." He reached out to place his hands on her shoulders. "You look great so early in the morning. Thank you for coming."

"Thank you for inviting me." She looked again into Shane's face. "How are you doing? Your face looks like its back to normal."

Shane smiled showing his new temporary teeth. "I don't know if my face has ever been normal, but thank you anyway."

"Man, look at those teeth. When did you get them fixed?" Alisha asked.

"Yeah, they make a difference. I got them a few days ago. They're only temporary. Permanent ones come later after everything has healed completely." Shane reached for Alisha's arm. "Should we sit down?"

"Sure, as long as we can keep warm sitting down. It's chilly in here." Alisha engaged in an exaggerated shiver.

They sat side by side, draped in silence, on the bench attached to the table. Shane stretched his legs out in front of him rubbing his hand over his knees. He turned his head toward Alisha. "You know, there's so much I don't know about you." He blushed. "I don't know what to ask or where to begin."

Alisha laughed out loud, even her laugh a charming sound to Shane. "Oh, I suppose we both have some interesting things to say about ourselves." She paused, glancing down at her hands clasped in her lap. "Maybe many of them are better not mentioned."

Shane exhaled. "No doubt you're right about some things. I do want to say one thing for sure. Without you I might not be sitting here this morning."

Alisha smiled, moving closer to Shane and delivering a tender bump with her shoulder. "Yeah, that was kind of scary. But it doesn't take a genius or a hero to recognize that someone needs help."

Shane tapped Alisha on the knee. "Thank you just the same."

Silence returned. Shane leaned back against the table. "It may not be any of my business, but in the hospital you mentioned you lived around. What did you mean by that?"

Alisha offered another of her compelling smiles. "Just that, I guess. You said the same thing. What did you mean?"

"I meant that I don't always have a good place to stay. Right now I'm staying with my sister who owns a condo down the street a ways. Sometimes that doesn't work out."

Alisha studied Shane, her eyes narrowed in contemplation. "Shane, I think we need to make a decision about ourselves. Do we wish to surround ourselves in the mystery of our lives or do we wish to be honest? I think we can be friends. I also think that won't work without our talking about why we are here on a Saturday morning."

Shane followed that comment with a laugh. "Yeah, it's cold outside and chilly in here." He turned to face Alisha. "What you say, I think, is right. We need to level with each other if we want to be friends. And, ah . . . ah, I do." He rose from the bench. "I work at the Eighth Street Grill not very far from here. By the way I can return to work on Monday. I got the doctor's permission yesterday."

"Great," Alisha wrapped her arms around herself.

Shane stood up. "You're chilly. I'm chilly. Why don't we walk to the Grill where maybe we can talk and have a little lunch?"

"Alisha bounced up from her place on the bench. "That sounds good to me."

Shane offered his hand to Alisha. She placed her hand in his. Together they walked the short distance to the warmth of the Eighth Street Grill.

Shane received an excited welcome back from Max and the other staff with whom he worked. Shane introduced Alisha to his working partners who hurried to find them a quiet place to talk and to share lunch.

For well over an hour they did talk about themselves. Shane talked of the burden of farm life, of his rejection of the constant work, of his conflicts with parents, his failure in school, and his fateful knee injuries.

Alisha struggled to discuss details of the sexual abuse she experienced at the hands of her father. She described her relationship with her father as humiliating and degrading. Shane sensing the profound effect that relationship had on her did not seek details. She did talk candidly about the homecoming date and its disastrous conclusion. Finally she described to Shane her life on the streets over the last couple years. She refrained from mentioning her role as a prostitute, a subject left, perhaps, for a later conversation.

Their conversation revealed much in their lives they had in common: their defiance, their decision to leave home, their failure to graduate from high school, and their critical sexual experience following an important high school function.

The hour of revelation left them to some extent relieved and definitely emotionally weary. Reliving harsh and degrading moments in their lives opened emotional wounds that likely would never completely heal.

Finally, they rose to leave. Shane's boss at the Grill insisted the lunch served as a welcome back gift. They expressed their gratitude for the generosity. Shane reached for Alisha's hand and as they had entered, they left the Eighth Street Grill hand in hand.

Chapter 46

Shane assumed the position so familiar to him. Diligently he observed the luncheon crowd from the area where he and Max could notice when a table needed clearing or when a customer needed assistance. Shane's first day back to work since the attack which landed him in the hospital reminded him of Dr. Winston's advice: return to work but take it easy. Already after only three hours of his eight hour shift completed he felt a weakness in his knees, not so much from his injuries but more from his long confinement and lack of exercise.

Jacques Millet, the head waiter at the Eighth Street Grill, passed close to Shane to inquire how he was doing. "You holding up okay, Mr. Shane?" Jacques extended his long slender hand toward Shane, who reached out with his own to shake hands, the third time that happened since Shane arrived at eight o'clock that morning.

Jacques stood before Shane, his slim frame concealed in a meticulous official, waiter uniform including a royal blue long sleeved dress shirt and black trousers over which hung a short black apron. "Is so good to see you again," Jacques commented for at least the second time. "We've missed you here at the Grill. So have the customers. Some have asked what happened to you?"

Shane smiled, his two temporary front teeth a perfect white. "Thank you. It's good to be back." He could see behind Jacques a table needing attention. "Excuse me, but I think I need to get to work." Shane moved by Jacques.

"You take it easy, now," Jacques advised. "If you need help with anything, just let me know."

As Shane walked to the table he needed to clear and clean, he turned. "Thank you. I will."

The preceding Friday Shane had visited Dr. Winston, who approved his returning to work the following Monday with the precaution to take it easy for a few days. Shane intended to abide by his advice.

When he arrived at work after his short walk from Danni's condo, Max greeted him at the door as did several other employees of the Eighth Street Grill. Several asked how he was doing, a question he answered repeatedly. Most of the other employees knew about Shane's brutal attack; nonetheless, knowing about it didn't prevent them from asking about what happened, where and why? Shane did his best to offer brief explanations to those who inquired.

The morning dragged during the interval between breakfast and lunch. Standing in his bus boy station, Shane relaxed with the knowledge that his tables stood ready for customers. He discreetly leaned against the wall, hands folded over his stomach. He took a breath and nodded his head. The scene with Danni at the condo tarnished ever so little the eagerness he felt upon returning to work.

"Will you return here after work?" Danni asked.

Shane stood before the kitchen counter buttering a piece of toast. He exhaled and placed his toast and his knife abruptly on the counter. "Did you have to bring that up right a way this morning?" Turning, he faced his sister. "I don't know what I'm gonna do, but today I will likely come back here. Where else?"

"I'm sorry. I just need to know your plans." Danni reached for the coffee machine on the counter to pour herself a cup. "You know how I feel about your wandering around with no place to go. You always have a place here."

"I know, I know, I know," Shane uttered with irritation. He turned back to his toast, smoothed a lump of butter with the knife, and took a bite. Turning, he locked his eyes on his sister. "To be honest, as soon as I can make some other arrangements, I will move on. Please don't take it as an insult. I just want it that way."

Danni set down her coffee cup. "I guess you're old enough to make your own decisions. I just don't want anything else to happen to you."

Shane smiled displaying his new temporary front teeth. "I don't either. But shit happens." He reached for a glass of apple juice and took a healthy swallow, a cringe followed the passage of the cold liquid over his temporary front teeth. "I most definitely agree with you about my age. I'm old enough to make a few decisions of my own. I wish Mom and Dad thought that way too."

"Yes, I suppose, it would smooth the rough edges of our family. Please remember, though, Shane. They only wish to do what in their minds is best for you."

A smile spread Shane's lips. "Yes, yes, I know; they only want the best for me." Shane again gazed at his sister. "They only need to let me decide what is best."

Their conversation ended, Shane left for the short walk to the Grill and his first day back since the attack. The recent heated discussions with his parents about his future had only reinforced his aversion to living under someone else's control. He resisted talking about it any more. Despite the morning's reoccurrence of the topic of where he would live, he walked, eager to resume his life as a bus boy at the Eighth Street Grill. Concern for life beyond that would have to wait.

By eleven thirty luncheon customers occupied most of the dining room tables. Both Max and Shane kept busy responding to the crowd, good for them in that it accelerated the passage of time and good for the Grill for obvious reasons.

After an hour and a half of hectic activity in the dining room, the pace slowed giving both Max and Shane time to rest in between periods of cleaning and clearing. In the midst of the noon rush, Nick made his daily appearance. Jacques seated Nick in his usual place before notifying Shane that Nick wished to speak with him.

"How you doing, my friend?" Meticulously dressed in his usual blazer, polo shirt and dark trousers, Nick pushed back his chair, stood, and offered his hand to Shane, who grasped the extended hand in a warm shake.

"Pretty good now, just a bit tired. Not used to this standing so long."

Nick and Shane had not spoken since Nick's hospital visit several days before. "Look, I know you are busy. I won't take you away from your work." Nike sat down again and positioned his chair closer to the table. He looked up at Shane. "One thing, though. Could we get together after you are done here? Maybe I can meet you in the parking lot. What time are you done?"

Shane tensed, hearing the invitation remembering the conversation he had with his family about the deposits and where the money came from. "I'm done at three this afternoon. I can see you in the parking lot then."

"Good. I'll be there about three or so." Nick reached for the menu, looked up at Shane, and smiled.

Bright sunshine momentarily blinded Shane when he stepped outside to walk to the restaurant's parking lot. Shielding his eyes he studied the cars parked in the lot, searching for Nick's black BMW. As Shane searched, Nick drove into the lot and parked in a space only steps from where he stood.

"How did your day go?" Nick asked as Shane sat in the luxury of the padded leather, bucket seat.

"A long day but I'll survive." Shane settled into the bucket seat moving his hands over the soft leather. The car reminded him that owning apartment buildings must provide a lucrative living.

"Look, Shane, I won't keep you very long." Nick moved in his driver's seat to face Shane. "I just need to know if you want to continue our little deal."

Shane did not answer immediately, debating whether to ask again about the money. *Does it come from places other than rent? What about this money laundering he'd heard someplace? Should he risk another beating*? All of this tumbled rapidly through his mind.

Finally, Shane spoke softly but firmly. "I don't know just yet. Can I think about it for a while?"

Nick ran his hands around the steering wheel, evidence of his impatience with Shane's response. "You must understand that business goes on each day. I don't like to delay deposits too long."

Nick's last comment perplexed Shane, who doubted that renters paid rent more than once a month which wouldn't require so many deposits.

"I know what happened in Wayzata obviously concerns you as it does me. We simply have to plan the deposits more carefully or even change banks." Nick moved restlessly in his seat. "What do you think? You in or not?"

Shane sensed Nick's impatience. Still, he had reservations about continuing the deposits. So many questions clouded his decision. "Can you give me a few days to get back into the routine of work?

Nick pursed his lips, his hands gripped the sheering wheel. "All right, I'll give you one week; then you have to decide what you want to do. Remember, like I've told you before, you don't need to announce to the world what you're doing. Just consider it a private agreement between us that facilitates my book keeping. That's all any body has to know. Okay?"

Shane nodded his head and reached for the door handle. He stepped out of the car onto the blacktop.

With his hands on the steering wheel, Nick stretched to his right, leaning a part way out of his bucket seat. To Shane standing by the open door, Nick reiterated, "Talk to you about this in a week."

Shane nodded, closed the door, and moved away from the car. Nick backed out of the parking place to accelerate out of the lot. Shane watched with misgivings, remembering how simple it was months ago to agree to make the deposits. Things had changed since then.

Chapter 47

Shane fumbled for the key to Danni's condo. He prepared himself for another clash with his sister. Since his release from the hospital he had spent most of his time at the condo. With increasing frequency, however, the situation there included arguments with his sister about his late nights and his all nights spent at other places.

Shane slipped through the door to enter a dark hallway, an indication his sister had yet not gotten up for work. Through the living room and onto his den, he hurried. He needed to reach his bed before having to explain again where he spent the night.

Reaching for the door to the den, he heard, "Good morning, Shane." Danni stood outlined in her bedroom door, hair suffering from a night on the pillow.

Shane paused in the doorway to the den. He looked down at the floor then up at his sister. "Good morning."

She crossed her arms over her breast. "Where have . . ."

Shane raised his hand gesturing her to stop. "Don't even ask. Where I spent the night doesn't matter. It's none of your business." His words couched in anger.

Danni dropped her arms to her side. "I'm sorry but it is my business. You're my brother. You've only recently been out of the hospital. You had a concussion for God's sakes. You need to take care of yourself." She inhaled deeply, again crossing her arms over her breast.

Shane turned away to look into the dim light of the den. He shook his head and turned to look at his sister. "When are you ever going to accept the fact that I can take care of myself? I'm nearly twenty years old." He raised one arm and braced it against the door frame. "It's just like it was years ago at home. Someone is always telling me what I can or can't do. Danni, God dammit, I'm tired of it. I can take care of myself. If I want to stay out all night, that's my choice."

Danni spread her arms, hands out in supplication. "Okay, okay. I get your point. It's been only weeks since you suffered some serious injuries. You've got to consider how others feel about you. I'm concerned about your well being. Don't you see that?"

With a nod of his head, Shane acknowledged his sister's point. "Yeah, I get what you say. There's got to be a limit to this concern, this worry, this . . . this repression." Another pause, another breath. "I'm sorry but I can't live like this."

"I'm sorry too. I'm sorry you can't see the difference between compassion and repression."

In the silence of the hallway, the siblings stared at each other.

Danni broke the silence. "Have you been spending time with that girl?"

Shane stiffened. "What do you mean 'that' girl?"

"I don't right off hand remember her name, but you have talked of her often."

"That girl probably saved my life." Shane announced. "Besides I happen to enjoy her company. I think she enjoys mine. In answer to your question, yes, I have spent time with her."

Though Shane did share with his sister a few details about Alisha, he refrained from referring to her role as a street person. Nonetheless, he assumed that Danni suspected the truth. In the weeks since his release from the hospital, the relationship flourished between Alisha and him. In each other they found an identity, a commonality missing from their home and family.

Tired, dirty, and stiff, Shane, with Alisha, had spent the previous night sleeping in a bus shelter at the Wayzata Transit Center where few people would bother them as they sought escape from the late spring chill.

For Alisha, Wayzata represented the worst part of her young life. Still it also represented the part of the Twin Cities with which she was most familiar. Not many people needed bus transportation from Wayzata in the middle of the night. Shane and Alisha took advantage of the Transit Center shelter.

"What time do you work today?" Danni asked, reluctant to pursue a verbal fight that occurred far too often between them.

"Not till eleven." Shane moved into the den where he started to undress with the intention of capturing a couple hours of sleep. The night in the Transit Center did provide shelter but very little comfort.

When Shane woke up at ten thirty, he had already made an important decision. He would for the second time pack up his meager belongings and leave a note informing his sister of his intention to leave. Where he would go he would decide later. His options included, Max's car, the home of Derek Hayes, maybe one of the shelters established for young street people or on the street with Alisha, who also retained friendships offering the possibility for spending a few nights in a bed with sheets.

With his most essential belongings stuffed in his backpack, Shane walked the familiar route on the Nicollet Mall to the Eighth Street Grill where his tenure established him as a reliable, cooperative, and friendly member of the staff.

When he arrived, he found a place in the kitchen to store his backpack, removed his Twins T shirt to replace it with the one identifying him as a member of the Eighth Street Grill staff. Stepping out into the dinning room, Shane made a quick survey of the customers seated for lunch. At his usual table near the window sat Nick Karpin.

Upon seeing Shane, Nick motioned him to his table. With a mounting sense of skepticism, Shane did agree to resume his depositing duties. Influenced by the suspicion expressed by his parents regarding this Nick Karpin and money laundering as well as that expressed by Alisha, Shane attempted to secure from Nick a more accurate identification of the source of the money and why Nick couldn't make the deposits himself. Nick's response was no more enlightening than before. His intransigence about the deposits served as sufficient intimidation for Shane to stop asking questions. Besides, the money helped Shane survive a life he chose for himself.

Nick did agree to switch banks, both of which now were located in downtown Minneapolis, one of them the original and the other only a few blocks away. Nick, furthermore, made sure Shane's deposits in the two banks did not occur on the same day. Shane did miss the relaxing bus ride to Wayzata, but to make up for that, he had Alisha, who frequently suggested they bus to her home town.

After his visit to Shane in the hospital, Nick never mentioned the brutal attack Shane suffered. His consuming concern rested with secrecy. This emphasis on secrecy added to Shane's suspicion. Nonetheless, he anticipated the money Nick paid him for the simple task of depositing money in banks whose tellers apparently knew all about Nick Karpin.

"How are things going?" Nick dabbed his mouth with his napkin.

"Fine." Shane stood rigid next to the table.

"No more strangers lurking around the banks?" Nick smiled, ignoring the deep impression the attack etched in Shane's memory.

"No problems at the banks?" Nick asked even though he knew the answer. He followed the deposits closely, demanding without delay the deposit receipt.

"None so far," Shane confirmed. He glanced around at his section of the dinning room. "I'd better get to work."

"Yes, I see that. I'll have another deposit for you tomorrow. Follow the same routine." Nick returned to his lunch.

Shane attended to his duties with lingering thoughts about Nick Karpin and his deposits.

Chapter 48

"You did what?" Alisha reacted with mild alarm to Shane's announcement that he had moved out of his sister's condo.

"I decided to leave. It's that simply." Shane stretched out his legs and pushed his hands into his pants pockets.

The late afternoon sun cast distinct shadows on the grass and on the sidewalk in front of the bench on which Shane and Alisha sat. The recent bitter discussion with Danni about his living arrangement had provoked Shane into again leaving the comfort of his sister's condo. Now he joined Alisha in Loring Park for an aimless evening of sitting observing the range of people who frequented the park and to determine where he would spend the night. At the conclusion of his shift at the restaurant, he phoned Alisha requesting to meet her in the park.

Alisha rested her hand on Shane's arm. "Where do you intend to go?"

A grin spread his lips. "Maybe with you." He answered in little more than a whisper.

Her shoulders slumped. "What is that supposed to mean?"

Shane turned away to look at a couple walking a dog that refused to cooperate. He then moved to face Alisha. He exhaled. "I don't know what it's supposed to mean." He shrugged his shoulders. "I kind of like being with you. Is that okay?"

"Of course it is." She smiled, studying Shane's face. "Do you think it's worth giving up a warm bed every night?"

Shane looked away this time at nothing in particular. "My bed isn't that warm. Besides it's not a very good bed anyway."

"Stop it," Alisha reprimanded. "This is serious business. You need to have some place to go."

Shane faced Alisha, his brow furrowed, eye lids narrowed. "I know it's serious business. Wanting freedom, freedom from someone telling you what to do all the time is also serious business." He spoke with a firmness that cut his sentences short.

"I guess I know something about independence and freedom." Alisha crossed her legs, squeezing her hands between her knees. "That doesn't answer the practical question of where you will spend your nights."

In the short time since Alisha entered Shane's life, they had discussed some of each other's backgrounds, including how they arrived at the decision to leave their respective homes. None of those discussions asked specifically the very practical question about where they spent their nights. Since meeting Shane in the hospital, Alisha assumed he lived with his sister. That Alisha lived from day to day without a specific residence never occurred to him. Someone as attractive as she certainly must have arranged for day to day living. He could not place her in the same category as Max and his friends.

His curiosity now alerted, Shane asked, "Where do you spend your nights?" He paused. "Ah . . . where will you go now, tonight?"

Alisha closed her eyes as her knees pressed against her hands. In her mind raced by those nights in cheap, squalid motel rooms where some man grunted and groaned as his body pumped on top of hers. She had not disclosed her secret to Shane and for now didn't intend to. Looking up, she confessed, "I have places to stay, such as with friends, or in one of the available shelters or even on the street. I did leave home too. I told you that."

Her admission surprised and confused Shane. How could such a friendly, compassionate, beautiful girl end up on the street? Even though they talked about their brief history, he just couldn't imagine someone like her destined to wander the streets.

Shane stood up, resting his foot on one end of the bench. Darkness erased the earlier shadows. Small cones of light encircled the light posts positioned along the park's path. "Well, I guess we have more in common than I thought." He removed his foot from the bench and pushed his hands into his pockets. "I guess we should think about spending time together. I mean more than only on warm spring evenings. Any ideas?"

"I find flattering that you wish to spend time with me. Thank you. I don't think talking about spending time together addresses the real issue here. Yes, I would like to spend more time with you, too. More important, though, is where do we spend nights? Do you want to snuggle on one of these park benches?" She gestured with a wide sweep of her arm.

Shane smiled at her question. "I wouldn't mind that at all."

His facetious answer evoked a harsh response, "Shane, stop it. You need to get serious. This isn't funny."

"I'm sorry. I know it isn't funny. It's not the end of the world either." Shane returned to his place next to Alisha. "I don't know from day to day just what I will do. I do have a few friends, like you do. I also am aware of a couple shelters near the downtown area." He reached over to squeeze Alisha's arm. "Somehow, It'll work out."

He rose and, grasping her hand, urged her to do the same. "Look," he reached out placing his hands on Alisha's shoulders, "it's a great evening for a long walk. Why don't we check out a new shelter, not far from here, that my friend Max mentioned?" He gave Alisha's shoulders a gentle squeeze. "Tomorrow will have to take care of itself."

Alisha stepped into Shane's arms placing hers around his waist. She looked up into his eyes. "Okay, big guy, I'm with you for tonight."

Chapter 49

Routine dominated Shane's life. May and June passed quickly. Already the July 4 celebration approached to mark the middle of summer. Six days a week Shane worked at the Eighth Street Grill where he established himself as a reliable, dedicated employee. For his dedication he had received a raise boosting his hourly rate by two dollars and fifty cents. No longer did he scoff at jobs offering a wage of twelve, fifteen or sixteen dollars an hour. Most of the time he enjoyed what he did, serving others.

Only infrequently did he meet with Alisha. His schedule and hers often conflicted, particularly in the evenings. Never did she describe clearly what she did during her busy evenings, avoiding the topic with a dismissive reference to meeting with clients about something. Sensing her reluctance to talk about her activity, Shane simply refused to pursue the subject. Besides, his job, his contact with Max and his friends, and his nearly nightly search for a place to stay consumed his time.

Still he thought often about Alisha, the thoughts which commonly dragged Shane back to his crushing prom experience with Lindsey. That invoked questions about her life in college if for sure she did enroll at the University of Minnesota Duluth. *Would she ever forgive him for his senseless behavior that prom night?* In his moments of reverie the image of Alisha at times blended with the image of Lindsey Cooper, the only two girls with whom he had established even a tentative relationship.

Rarely did Shane contact his sister; however, he did respond when she called him on his cell phone. Contact with his parents occurred even more rarely. His parents did comply with Danni's recommendation to avoid interfering with Shane in his reach for independence, one that extended back several years to his days on the farm. He embraced adamantly his refusal to live under anybody else's rules. Spending nights in parks his head resting on his rolled up back pack failed to weaken this refusal.

In the past month, he finally received permanent front teeth which enhanced his engaging smile. Only intermittent spots floating around his eye reminded him of the damage it suffered. The concussion resulted in no after effects. His most recent visit with the doctor confirmed that his body had healed.

"Did you really go to that school?" Shane sat next to Alisha positioned in the expansive, carefully groomed playground behind the school building.

Not for several days had Shane enjoyed contact with Alisha. The July 4 holiday approached. A long work week prepared Shane for a weekend of relaxation. With delight he discovered Alisha's availability to meet with him over the weekend. A quiet stroll through Loring Park ended when Alisha suggested they take a bus to Wayzata to spend the beautiful, summer evening someplace that offered greater privacy.

The short bus ride to Wayzata briefly brought back memories of that cold, bitter night when Shane ended up unconscious in a bank parking lot. Upon their arrival at the familiar Transit Station, Shane's thoughts of the past were extinguished by the beauty of the evening. Hand in hand they walked down to the extensive Lake Minnetonka waterfront adjacent to Wayzata's main street. Looking out over the lake much as Shane remembered doing on his first visit to this picturesque suburban community, they watched the sun sink behind the trees surrounding Lake Minnetonka's Wayzata Bay, casting streaks of reds and pinks through the flimsy clouds gathered in the western sky.

From there they walked back to the spacious playground behind the middle school Alisha attended, and where now the vast playground surrounded them with privacy.

Alisha leaned gently against Shane, her eyes down cast, her memory turning out agonizing images of those days as a teenager. Weeks ago she and Shane discussed additional detail of her background as well as his, searching for reasons why they decided to leave home. Nonetheless, she avoided offering any more specifics about the abuse she suffered. Despite the passage of all these years, the pain lingered with the image seared in her mind of the salacious grin on her father's face as he groped in her underwear. Looking up at the building in the distance, she uttered a delayed response, "Yes, I really did . . . for three years."

"Did you often sit out here in the evening with boys?" Shane poked an elbow into Alisha's ribs.

At this she smiled. "No not usually." She paused, rising up on her knees and covering her face with her hands. Tears seeped through her fingers. She cursed herself, asking why the hell she came here, crushed by the power of the memories?

Shane looked with dismay at Alisha. "I'm sorry. Did I say something wrong?"

A shudder passed through her shoulders as she tried to control her emotions. With hands covering her eyes, she shook her head, "No."

"What's the matter then?" Shane reached to grasp her shoulders.

She dropped her hands to her sides. 'I'm sorry. It's nothing." She breathed deeply. "It's . . . ah . . . it's just sitting here brings back bad memories. I told you once about those bad things that happened at home." She looked away, shaking her head. "I'm sorry."

Shane moved closer enclosing Alisha in his arms. He drew her to him; her body molded to his. "I'm sorry too. Things like that should never happen to anyone."

Alisha rested her head on Shane's chest, she sobbed quietly, striving to catch her breath. She leaned back. "I've got to get over that shit. It keeps coming back. Maybe someday."

Shane sat back on his knees. "I know something about these bad memories. They are a pain in the ass. I guess we just have to learn to live with them." He grimaced with a twinge that shot through his knee. "Alisha, I know it's nothing like what you went through. Yet, hardly a day goes by when I don't see myself stumbling around second base and tearing up my knee for the second time." He shook his head. "It made one hell of a difference in my life."

"Yeah, here we are in a playground reliving horrid moments in our lives. Why can't we take advantage of this gorgeous summer evening and study the stars or something?" A smile vanquished her tears.

"I'll go along with that." Shane lay back gazing into the blackness of the night spotted with sparkling stars.

Alisha joined him on the soft grass of the playground. He raised up on an elbow and leaned down to place a kiss on her forehead. She reached up, her hand behind his head pulling him down to her lips. They kissed with a tenderness derived from a hesitance to presume too much. They moved apart, eyes locked together, smiles lightening both faces.

Shane moved, encouraging Alisha to lie back. He sat looking down at her, even in the darkness her tears left a visible twinkle in her eyes. He leaned down to kiss her again, this time pressing his lips hard against hers. For him he rarely enjoyed the taste of a girl's lips. For an instant the vision of prom night flashed before his eyes. He sat up.

"What's wrong?" Alisha asked. She too fought misgivings. Yet despite the numerous partners who lay on top of her over the past two years, she felt a sensation, a rush of adrenalin never before felt. She reached up pulling Shane back toward her.

Suddenly, all misgivings vanished in a cascade of emotions starving for release, exploding within two eager bodies. Shane's hands reached under her T shirt finding taut breasts waiting for his touch. She groaned with pleasure, reaching to unzip his trousers. At the same time he unsnapped her shorts which she helped slip over her hips.

In an instant they allowed nature to take control, oblivious of all other factors past or present. For Shane an initiation into the world of sexual glory, for Alisha an initiation into the world of sex for pleasure, not for money.

They lay side by side, clothes scattered around them. Shane grasped Alisha's hand. She squeezed his in response. They both stared into the starry night.

Finally, Shane rose up on one elbow and looked down at Alisha. "You said this was a playground."

"I sure did. Probably the first time that game was played here." She reminded him. They embraced in laughter.

Chapter 50

"How about another beer?" Derek Hayes stood up facing his two guests, Shane Stenlund and Max Hawkins. "After this you get your own." Derek made a quick study of Shane and Max. Both accepted his offer.

Since his latest revolt against living with his sister, Shane spent numerous nights on the street or in Loring Park where repeated police surveillance often disrupted his sleep. He much preferred Derek's hospitality. According to Derek, the invitation to spend the night with him at his parents' home was good any time. Nonetheless, Shane only occasionally accepted the invitation preferring to avoid taking advantage of a friend.

On this evening, a Sunday evening, the three decided to celebrate Sunday in the comfort of Derek's suburban home, the home where he grew up. The passage of time failed to erase the memory of Shane's first celebrate Sunday event. The night on the bluffs overlooking the Mississippi River often entered into the conversation when they gathered. Max maintained some contact with Ricky Brooks' mother.

For weeks she fought the sorrow of Ricky's death in the swirling waters of the Mississippi. Max reported that her grieving lingered, but she had found a degree of peace in her church. Nonetheless, for her as for them, the memory of Ricky Brooks would never fade.

On this Sunday night, though, the three friends were determined to relax, to savor a few beers, to celebrate what they had in life regardless of its limits. As evidence, perhaps, of their evolving maturity or, perhaps, because of impatience with finding comfort on the street, Shane and Max readily accepted Derek's invitation to meet at his parents' home.

Despite the conflicts that separated Derek from his parents, the lower level of the spacious home on an impressive wooded lot served as Derek's domain. Furnished more like an apartment than a lower level family room, the area included a spacious living room with a large sectional sofa, a part of which pulled out into a queen size bed, a small kitchen area against one wall including cabinets, a microwave, stove, fridge and dishwasher. One whole end of the lower lever contained the bedroom and bathroom while in the space opposite the sofa sat a large, flat screened TV.

Defiance, independence, and rebellion that marked Derek's early teen years, eventually culminating in his leaving home, had weakened during the last couple years with his gradual realization of the vulnerability of a future without much promise. Consequently, he moved back home, welcomed by his parents.

Seated next to a circular coffee table on which he carefully placed his beer can on a colorful coaster, Shane looked across the table at Derek. "How's the job going?"

Placing his beer can on the table, Derek stared off to one corner of the room then looked back at Shane. "Okay, I guess. It's work, but I'm thinking of quitting."

That statement caught Max's attention. "What the hell are you gonna do then?"

Derek reached for his beer to take another swallow. "I'm thinking of going back to school."

Silence settled over the room. The comment grasped at both Max and Shane, whose commitment to education ended when they dropped out of high school.

Finally Shane broke the silence. "When did this all happen?"

Derek leaned forward placing his hands on his knees. "I don't know. I guess for some time I've thought about where in the hell I was going in my life. Punching buttons in an assembly line doesn't give me much hope for the future."

Both Max and Shane sat rigid on the sofa, eyes wide, mouths partially open.

Derek continued. "I even talked to my dad about the wisdom of sticking with that job. I did a little research on local technical schools. They offer a bunch of programs . . . ah, two year programs, to prepare you for all kinds of technical jobs, many in the computer field." He paused, his eyes narrowed as he thought. "Probably about two weeks ago I contacted one of the tech schools not far from here. They sent me more information. Right now I'm thinking about what to do."

"I think that's great." Max responded with a broad smile.

"Yeah, I'm impressed. You sound almost like an adult." Shane sat back in the sofa while they shared a chuckle over his comment, all realizing the amount of time spent so far in their young lives resisting the guidance of adults. "When will this all begin?"

Derek relaxed in his place. "I'm not sure. Lots of things need to happen first. But I hope I can start this fall semester."

"Well, good luck to you." Max offered.

"Thank you. I appreciate that. I'll keep you informed." Derek gestured with his hands seeking information. "Look, enough about me, what about you guys? You intend to hang in there at the restaurant?"

Shane and Max exchanged glances. Max wrinkled his brow. "I don't know. It's been a good place to work so far. I really haven't given much thought to the future. Maybe I should."

"Me neither." Shane shifted his position. "Dealing with minor things like finding a place to sleep or to take a shower have kinda taken over. What you say makes sense. Though I haven't thought about it that much, I guess I can't really see myself busing dishes ten years from now."

"I'll go along with that." Max agreed.

For the first time in months, maybe years, their discussion awakened Shane to a consideration of the future. So much of his life so far centered on his obsession with independence, his absolute refusal to live under someone else's rules. At this moment, the conversation about Derek's pending decision sparked in Shane a need, maybe, to revisit some of his attitudes about himself and about his relationship to others.

"Hey guys, this is getting a bit serious. I've got some micro wave pizza. How about it?" Derek rose from his place and moved to the kitchen area.

"Sounds good to me." Max eased himself up from the soft comfort of the sofa. "Here let me give you a hand."

"Say, Shane, you still playing around with those deposits, the ones that got the shit kicked out of you?" Derek smiled while they resumed their places around the coffee table, careful to protect its surface from the pizza and the beer.

Shane chewed a mouthful of pizza. "Yeah, I am. It pays quite well."

"I know you've mentioned it before. But explain to me again the situation. Why can't this guy deposit his own damn money?" Derek asked.

Shane shrugged his shoulders and shook his head. "I don't know. Nick, that's the guy, keeps telling me about being secret. He wants to avoid doing it himself because he's busy taking care of his apartment buildings. The money, I guess, is rent money. That's what he says."

"Sounds fishy to me." Max interjected, glancing over at Shane. "You know how I feel about the whole thing."

Shane looked over at Max seated next to him. "Yeah and you're not the only one with suspicion about the deposits. My parents and my sister have questioned it too." He reached for his can of beer. Before placing it to his mouth, he stopped. "I just don't know what to think. The other day on one of my deposits I saw Nick's big black car drive by the bank. He made no effort to wave or anything. I think he was spying on me for some reason. Maybe he doesn't trust me anymore."

"I sure as hell wouldn't trust him," Max announced.

Shane shrugged his shoulders and finally took that swallow from his beer can.

Suddenly, all three seemed absorbed in their own private thoughts.

Derek brook the silence. "By the way, did the police find the guy who beat you up and took the money?" He reached for another piece of pizza.

Shane's shoulders slumped. "No. Nick insisted the police not get involved. The hospital staff was required to report it. But because I didn't wish to pursue it, nothing happened."

"You didn't wish to pursue it? Why not?" Derek asked.

"Nick made it damned clear that I was to talk to no one about the whole thing. So I didn't"

Max sat his beer can down on the coaster. "I've suggested to Shane that this Nick's interest in secrecy hints at something more serious than simply rent money."

"Like maybe drug money?" Derek looked over at Shane?

Shane breathed deeply. "I don't know. All I do know is that Nick owns some apartment buildings. If he's involved in the drug business, I don't know." He averted his eyes and pressed his lips together. "Maybe someday I should try to find out."

Max and Derek looked across the table at each other, nodding their heads in agreement.

"Let us know when you're ready. We'll join the investigation." Max reached over to bump Shane on the shoulder.

A grin replaced Shane's pinched lips.

All three joined in cleaning up after the pizza. With each holding a fresh can of beer, they resumed places on the sofa with the intention of watching a late Twins game.

During a Twins' promotion in between innings announced by an attractive blonde, Derek asked, "By the way, Shane, what happened with the young gal who found you bleeding in the parking lot?"

Shane smiled. "Not much. We see each other once in a while. Nothing terribly serious." In his mind anything to do with Alisha most certainly was serious. However, since the glorious moment in the grass on the Wayzata Middle School playground, Alisha seemed more reserved than before. Shane worried that his aggressive behavior, again, had damaged a special relationship. That she failed over the last three days to respond to his calls added to his worries. His messages went unanswered.

The Twins game captured their attention, the home team leading by one run in the bottom of the seventh inning. While he watched the game, Shane couldn't resist reflecting on the evening's discussion of the future and of his relationship with Alisha. At least tonight he did not have to search for a bed to sleep on. At this moment he sat on it.

Chapter 51

What was going on with his mind? Every where he looked he saw something that engendered reflection. That morning on the walk to the Eighth Street Grill he met a group of young guys all wearing letter jackets. The brief meeting ignited memories of years past when Shane anticipated the impending start of school and of the football season. He never played football, but he always followed the Twin Pines High School team, as well as the Gophers and the Vikings. In the months since his leaving home he'd rarely fallen victim to this nostalgia. *What was happening*?

Recently, but certainly since the conversation with Derek and Max a few days ago, Shane devoted more time to reflection, a rare activity for him. During his idle moments at work or during the time searching for a place to sleep or sitting in the Crystal Court watching people, he found himself thinking seriously about Derek's decision to return to school. Since leaving home, that thought had not even occurred to Shane. Nonetheless, their discussion that Sunday evening made an impression on him. It rekindled a concern for the future, an elusive concern.

"How you doing today Mr. Shane?" Jacques greeted him with the familiar smile and friendly bump on the shoulder.

Shane smiled. Jacques did a marvelous job of making people smile. "Okay, I guess. I'm here and ready to get busy."

"Yes, you do a good job of keeping busy. I like that." Jacques checked the large pockets of his apron before disappearing into the kitchen.

The lunch crowd, as usual, kept Shane busy for those crucial lunch hours, eleven to one o'clock. The demands of his job precluded any more drifting into considerations of his status in life. Hurrying to clear and reset tables, however, suddenly reminded him of his resistance to menial tasks on the farm. How he resented them. Now he did the menial tasks here at the restaurant, accepting them as part of his responsibility. Carrying a tray stacked high with plates, cups and silverware, Shane couldn't help but smile at his flight back to milking cows, picking eggs, and feeding voracious pigs.

Delivering the tray to the dishwasher, Shane moved to the station he and Max shared when waiting for their next table to clear and reset. Though he tried, he couldn't suppress the visions invading his mind, visions of cleaning chicken roosts and carrying pails of a mixture of silage and water to pigs that gave credibility to their names as they plunged into the trough.

Suddenly, vivid in his imagination he saw a young kid riding across the field, hair blowing in the wind, legs wrapped around the belly of a pony, hands clinging to the bridle strap. Guilt joined the image. Not in several weeks had he thought about his most valued childhood companion, First Mate. Standing observing his tables in the dining room, he recalled the hours he and First Mate spent together. He dropped his head when he thought about the announcement of First Mate's death and the indifference he displayed at the news. "How selfish," he whispered to himself.

The arrival of Nick Karpin dragged Shane out of his reverie. As usual he selected the same table each day he arrived to eat lunch. Shane watched as Jacques seated Nick, leaving him with a luncheon menu. Without the friendly wave and smile of previous visits, Nick studied the menu, one he studied nearly every day at lunch time.

Shane watched from his position in the corner of the dinning room. His conversations with his family and with his friends about the deposits he made once or twice a week floated through his mind. *Could this man be trusted? Could those deposits have something to do with money laundering*, about which Shane knew very little? Maybe it was only his perception, but Nick's behavior toward him had changed since the brutal beating Shane suffered. To Shane he exhibited an aloofness previously missing. Twice, when Shane prepared to make a deposit at one of the downtown Minneapolis banks, he saw Nick driving by in his big black car.

He simply did not know what to believe about Nick and his apartment buildings. He did know he needed the money earned with each deposit. Perhaps, a part of his future might include a closer look at Nick and his business.

Throughout the afternoon, a light late lunch and afternoon snack crowd kept Shane and Max occupied, not busy just occupied.

"Have you heard any more about Derek and his decision?" Shane moved a little closer to his partner in the dining room.

"No, I . . . ah, well, yes I should say." Max leaned against the wall. "Yeah, I talked to him the other day. Next Monday he meets with someone in the registrar's office at one of the local tech schools. I don't remember which one."

"What do you think about what he's doing?" Shane asked.

Max straightened, adjusting his busing apron. "I don't know. I don't mind working here, and I have for quite a while." He paused to look out over the dinning room. "Would I like to be doing this in ten years? I don't know."

Shane clinched his teeth in a gesture of misgiving. "I don't know either. I do know, in the last few days, I sure as hell have thought about what I'll be doing in ten years."

The departure of two groups of customers prompted Max and Shane to rush to their respective tables. The topic of the future didn't surface again before the conclusion of Shane's shift. He then disappeared into the employee restroom where he changed his shirt, folding carefully his Eighth Street Grill golf type shirt and placing it in his small locker.

He stepped out into the bright sunshine of a perfect late summer afternoon. Walking back to the Nicollet Mall, Shane joined a river of humanity taking advantage of the splendid day. He stopped by the Crystal Court for a soda. Almost as if under its own control, his mind returned to the farm, to his final days of school, his demand for independence, his rejection of his family. He sipped his soda, asking again why? *Was the farm really all that bad? Was he the problem, not the farm or all the tedious jobs he claimed his dad forced him to do? Just where would he wish to be in ten years?*

He rose up from the bench, searched for a container for his empty soda can, and headed for the Mall. Butter flies invaded his stomach. Tomorrow evening he would have the chance to meet with Alisha, another mystery. In several days his calls to her met only her voice mail. Her failure to answer her phone awakened for Shane lingering thoughts of the shattered relationship with Lindsey Cooper? Since the moment of rapture in the Wayzata Middle School play ground, she had changed. At least her relationship with him had changed. He didn't know if what he felt for her was love. He did know just sitting next to her gave him a feeling he found difficult to define. Even her scent intrigued him.

Earlier in the day, his persistence paid off. Alisha answered her phone. She apologized for not responding to his many calls. She stumbled attempting to describe an accident resulting in bruises to her arms and face. She explained her reluctance for Shane to see her in that condition. The conversation ended with an agreement to meet the next day in Loring Park after Shane's shift at the restaurant.

So, to all the other thoughts swirling through his mind, he now added Alisha.

Chapter 52

"You don't feel well today, Mr. Shane?" Jacques reached out to touch Shane on the shoulder, his voice soft and gentle.

Making eye contact with the head waiter, Shane lips spread in a weak smile. "I'm fine." He looked away and wetted his lips. "The day drags a little," he admitted.

Jacques nodded his head. "Some days just do that, don't they." He glanced at his watch. "Only a couple hours left and you're free." He patted Shane on the shoulder and walked away.

Since making the arrangement yesterday to meet Alisha in Loring Park after work today, the anticipation of that meeting shadowed Shane. He found Alisha strangely elusive and ambiguous after their succumbing to the force of nature in a Wayzata playground. He could only think of Lindsey Cooper and the dreadful night following the prom. He shook his head, perplexed over the repetition, the tenacity of these thoughts.

The demands of his job interrupted his thoughts. He hurried to clear and reset one of the tables in his area of the dining room. His stomach gurgled; butterflies fluttered. A quick look at the clock above the cashier confirmed less than a half hour before freedom.

Their conversation yesterday included more than agreeing to meet. It also included Alisha's feeble attempt to explain why she failed to return his calls, something about a stupid fall near a downtown bus stop. Seeking details about the accident produced for Shane only vague responses about bruises to a part of her face. He assumed female vanity played a part in her reluctance to meet him because of her bruises.

With Alisha dominating his thoughts, Shane skipped over Max's suggestion of his interest in securing an apartment. Normally that announcement would have evoked from Shane mild consternation. Shane saw Max as one content with the freedom living in his car afforded him. Besides, for as long as Shane knew him, Max considered his car home.

Along with his announcement, Max intimated that Shane might consider joining him in renting an apartment. Perhaps, he suggested, the two of them could afford the rent. That conversation likely would not have happened without the discussion Shane and his friends had only days before, one that awakened serious considerations of their lives now and in the future. Nonetheless, right now Shane's attention focused on the impending meeting with Alisha.

At the conclusion of his shift, Shane headed for Loring Park. He plunged into the human flow on the Nicollet Mall, picturing in his mind Alisha seated at their favorite bench waiting for him. Often, without provocation, the mystery of how she occupied her time each day grabbed Shane's attention. In a day mixed with conflicting thoughts about his relationship with Alisha, he wished to avoid that subject. He had enough to think about. Besides, Alisha's reluctance to talk about what she did encouraged Shane to respect her wishes.

His path to Loring Park took him passed his sister's condo complex. How many times he walked by the condo where he lived for part of his stay in the Twin Cities he couldn't calculate. However, recently he did think about his sister and his parents more often than he did since his escape from the tedium of the farm. He questioned this renewed interest in family, hastening his pace in his anticipation of meeting Alisha.

Shane's eyes surveyed the extent of the small park seeking to locate Alisha. Their favorite bench sat empty. He stopped after a few steps into the park. He turned his head from left to right, eyes wide; he did not see her. With hands stuffed into his pants pockets he walked deliberately to that favorite bench. He sat down extending his legs and leaning on the bench's back rest. His eyes continued their search of the park.

Ten minutes past, then fifteen. Shane glanced at his watch. Several people walked by, none of them Alisha. Suddenly, he thought he saw her entering the park from the opposite end. He shot up only to discover the girl was not Alisha. With time passing, he sat slumped down on the bench, wondering if she forgot or simply decided not to come. Restless, he stood up from the bench and walked a few steps down the path. The sun now slipped behind the trees lining the western end of the park. He worried, his worries feeding those butterflies in his stomach.

Reaching into his pocket, he pulled out his cell phone. He debated about calling her. His tension demanded it. With nervous fingers he punched her special number. He held the phone to his ear, listening to the rings, one, two, three, four. Her message stopped the rings but only increased his apprehension.

He shoved the phone back in his pocket. The wait eating away at his patience, he walked to the center of the park, each step accompanied by a search for Alisha. About ready to give up waiting, he caught a glimpse of her approaching the park from another entrance. He stopped to make sure this time his eyes weren't deceiving him.

Even from a distance he could identify her, hair bouncing with her every step, her attractive figure outlined in the fading sunlight. Dressed in jeans and a bright red, long sleeve top, Alisha approached, her eyes searching for Shane. She stopped several feet in front of him. They stood staring at each other, neither moving any closer. At last, Shane could resist no longer. He rushed to greet her. Rather than welcoming his out stretched arms, Alisha held her arms up, hands spread in a halting signal.

Shane obeyed her signal, shocked by what he saw when he stared at her face. "My God, what happened!" he declared.

Alisha stood, unmoving, her eyes focused on the ground beneath her. "I told you I fell."

Shane studied her face. A slit divided swelling around her upper lip. Pinkish purple encircled the bottom of her left eye. Even her tight necked top failed to conceal the bruises around her throat. Shaking his head in disbelief, he uttered, "What kind of fall did you have?" With that he moved closer to her. She offered no more resistance. He studied her face. With a tentative reach he touched her swollen lip and moved his hand gently over the marks on her throat.

Alisha winced. "Why don't we sit down over there." she suggested. With her hand she nudged Shane toward the closest bench. They sat down in silence. She folded her hands in her lap, staring out in the twilight now punctuated with the spread of park lighting. She took a deep breathe. "Ah . . . Ah, well, ah, it's a long, stupid story." She attempted to reconstruct what had happened several days ago, trying to explain the damage to her face.

Shane studied her beautiful face now cut and bruised, listening intently to her description. "Could your fall cause the marks on your neck?

Alisha looked away. "I don't know. It all happened so fast."

Suddenly her body started to tremble, shaken by audible sobs. She leaned forward her head falling into her open hands, tears flooding through her fingers and onto her jeans.

Shane sat stunned while Alisha gave in to cascading emotion. After a moment, he jumped off the bench to kneel in front of her. Tenderly he reached up to push her hair away from her face.

She shook her head.

"Is there something I can do?" he whispered.

Without comment she slide off the bench, collapsing into Shane's arms. Her emotions burst producing another rush of tears this time falling on his chest as she crushed her body against his.

For several minutes they clung to each other, Shane running his hand through her soft hair, rubbing her back with his right hand.

Alisha slowly gained control of her emotions. She leaned back on her knees, reached for a tissue to dab her eyes, careful about her left eye. Taking a deep, deep breathe, she relaxed. She reached up to touch Shane's face. In a soft but firm voice she confessed, "I'm so sorry. I'm a prostitute." Gently she ran her fingers over her swollen lips. With eyes closed she whispered, "An unhappy customer did this."

Chapter 53

"I can't believe we're doing this." Shane ran his hands through his hair and looked over at Max whose eyes followed west I-94.

Max laughed. "What do ya mean? You're giving me a lesson in rural Minnesota."

Shane pulled on this seat belt loosening its grip on his shoulder. "Yeah, but I'm not sure it's worth the time. It's just country."

Max repositioned his hands on the steering wheel. "Country I've never seen in all my life. You, at least, can say you've seen the big city after growing up on the farm. I can't claim anything but the big city." He paused, cocking his head to the side. "Do you realize I've never gone outside the limits of the Twin Cities? Now, that's stupid."

"I'm not sure it's stupid, just a bit unusual. Didn't ya ever go to one of the county parks at the edge of Hennepin County?" Shane asked.

"No!" Max blurted. "I didn't go any place. My parents were always too busy for that shit."

Only light traffic dotted the usual busy west I-94. The road stretched ahead toward St. Cloud. Silence filled the space in the small car. Shane's mind reached back to last weekend's spontaneous conversation with Max in between hurried clearing and resetting tables in the Eighth Street Grill's dining room where Shane and Max reigned most days.

Inspired by the presence of a customer dressed in bibbed overalls, a large straw hat, and clumsy working boots, Max asked Shane if the man looked like a farmer? Shane laughed at the obvious stereotyping but at the same time had to agree the man did look like a farmer. The conversation extended sporadically throughout the day.

"Say, Shane, was that guy here earlier really like real farmers?" Max asked in all sincerity.

Shane pinched his lip between his thumb and forefinger. "Some of them maybe." He looked over at Max standing next to him. "But not many."

"Did you wear overalls like that?" Max asked.

"No, except maybe to a Halloween party," Shane quipped.

More demands for clearing tables interrupted their conversation. In only minutes they returned to their station next to the kitchen entrance.

"When were you last at the farm?" Max inquired.

Shane inhaled then slowly released his breath. "I guess, about a year and a half ago."

"Do you plan to go back sometime?" Max refused to let the subject drop.

Shane bumped back against the wall. "Oh, I suppose sometime." He closed his eyes and shrugged his shoulders. "I don't know when."

"When ya do, will ya take me along?" Max asked.

The conversation eventually ended with the decision to drive to Twin Pines the next time they shared a day off. That time had arrived. Now they skirted St. Cloud on their drive west to Twin Pines.

The long ride on the freeway with little traffic made Shane drowsy. Max absorbed the scenery that spread out on both sides of the freeway. "Hey, farm boy, you still with me?"

"Yeah." Shane mumbled.

"Ya know. This is a pretty drive. I like the rolling hills and clumps of trees around all these farms. I thought you said the land was so flat you could see for miles."

Shane straightened his legs as much as the front seat would allow. "You just wait and see."

Through Alexandria and heading for Fergus Falls, Shane's mind drifted back to the meeting with Alisha in Loring Park. For an instant he relived the shock of her confession about prostitution. In his mind he recaptured the scene. She sat before him on her knees, her eyes fixed on his, tears streaming down her slender cheeks.

Never did he imagine someone as beautiful, as charming as Alisha could fall victim to the ravages of prostitution. Never could he imagine anyone so desperate to succumb to the squalor of selling your body for sex. Indeed, he had led a sheltered life.

His mind would not let go of that traumatic moment. The two of them balancing on their knees, straining to control emotions threatening to engulf them, left a vivid image not easily erased. He remembered feeling insulted by her admission. *Was he just another sexual client?*

The answer to that question came in her detailed explanation of the sexual abuse at home, the rape in high school and her grasping for revenge against men; the most important one in her life had abused her. She explained her sense of control over these slobbering, grunting men who writhed in an ecstasy she never shared with these beasts. She also admitted to the practical part of her decision. She needed to earn some money.

He will forever hear her words as she finished the tearful but complete explanation for her decision to turn to prostitution.

She had cradled her hands around Shane's face. "What we did on the playground was the most beautiful thing I've ever experienced. Don't you forget that." She leaned forward to place on Shane's lips a very tender kiss despite soreness of her own. "Shane, I love you," she whispered, leaning back on her legs, a smile spreading her swollen lips.

"Buddy, ya with me?" Max reached across the front seat to nudge Shane's shoulder.

Shane's body jerked. "Ah . . . ah, yeah, I am."

"We just passed around Fergus Falls. You said something about getting off the freeway after Fergus Falls." Max advised.

"Yeah, up here a ways we'll turn off and head north and west toward Twin Pines." Shane yawned and rubbed his eyes.

"Just tell me when."

"It'll be Highway 59 toward Detroit Lakes." Shane reassured Max.

"You mean we're goin through Detroit Lakes? I've heard of that town. Quite a summer playground, I guess." Max's voice exposed his increased anticipation to visit a part of the state he had never before visited.

"Twin Pines is a few miles beyond Detroit Lakes on Highway 59." Shane confirmed.

As their route took them through Detroit Lakes, Max again questioned Shane about the terrain. "Where's all the flat land you told me about? Nothing but trees, hills and lakes around here."

Shane smiled. "Just wait."

In a few miles Shane's promise came true. Almost as if a line marked the end of rolling hills and lakes, the road ahead stretched flat and straight. Fields of corn, grain, and beans, as identified by Shane, spread out on both sides of the highway. Max gazed with wonder at land so flat you could see to the horizon.

Soon a "Welcome to Twin Pines" sign greeted them. Shane insisted they not stop for fear someone would recognize him.

"Are ya some kind of fugitive from the law or something?" Max kidded.

"No, I just don't want to get into an explanation about the last year or so." Shane explained.

"Oh, I understand. Just kidding." Max admitted.

Driving a few blocks toward downtown Twin Pines, Max commented. "Say, this is a nifty little town. Not all that traffic. Not all those people hanging around on the sidewalks." He craned his neck out the window. "Look at the colorful flower pots hanging from the street lights. Neat."

"Yes, life's a bit simpler here, slower and quieter too." Shane, for an instant, relived the dozens of times he had ridden and driven these streets of Twin Pines. "The high school is just to the right a few blocks, at the next light."

"Do ya really want to visit the school?" Max asked with a grin.

"Probably not but we can drive by it."

As they did drive by the high school, Shane pointed out the baseball field where a stumble around second base shattered his knee again and ended his baseball career. He and Max had previously discussed the saga of Shane's knee.

"Do you think you would still be living at home if that hadn't happened? Max asked.

Shane hung his head in thought. "God, I don't know. All I do know is that it fucked up one of things I enjoyed most besides maybe riding my pony."

"Didn't you say your pony died not long ago?" Max brought the car to a stop at a traffic light.

Shane looked out his side window. "Yes, a few months ago, just something else I fucked up."

They drove around Twin Pines for a half hour, taking the chance a stop at a MacDonald's would not include someone recognizing Shane.

"What else do ya want to see?" Shane asked.

"How about your farm?" Max looked over at Shane for his response.

Shane stared out the windshield in front of him. "Okay but we're not stopping, not now anyway. I haven't been back since I left that morning."

The route to the road leading to Shane's home took them by the area where he and Lindsey stopped after the prom. As they drove by, he said nothing about the spot and what happened there that fateful, prom night.

The area around Shane's home also impressed Max with its wide open spaces. "My God, you can almost see forever around here. Doesn't it give ya a feeling of freedom? He asked surveying the vast expanses of grain ready for harvest and corn standing tall, covering acre after acre.

Ironically, the lack of freedom served as a basis for Shane's discontent with life on the farm. The burden of numerous responsibilities draped over the potential freedom. "Maybe it looks that way," Shane interjected, "but life on the farm doesn't give much time to think about freedom."

"Still, it's a hell of a lot better looking than the Nicollet Mall." Max commented.

"Two very different styles of living, I guess." Shane confessed.

Passing by a couple neighboring farms followed by a quick return to Twin Pines where they connected with Highway 59 back to Detroit Lakes and eventually the freeway concluded Max's brief geography lesson.

On the long ride back to the Twin Cities, a strange feeling of nostalgia distracted Shane from paying attention to their route. They almost missed the passage around Detroit Lakes. Resuming the drive toward the freeway, Shane relaxed his resistance to the nostalgia, letting the dimming memories of his youth drift through his mind.

Chapter 54

Rays of a warm, late summer sun peaked around buildings, casting strange shadows across the Nicollet Mall. A bench positioned on the Mall looked awfully inviting to Shane after a long, busy day at the Eighth Street Grill. The back on the bench made it even more inviting.

Shane plopped down leaning against the hard wooden surface. His long day of clearing dishes and resetting tables reminded him of the recent discussion with Alisha of her getting some kind of job. Since the moment in Loring Park when she confessed to him her plunge into prostitution, they had discussed the need for her to search for some kind of job. Thinking about jobs directed Shane to remember his dad's comments about jobs and a high school diploma. Like him, Alisha didn't have one either. However, he did get a job, not a career but at least a job. Certainly she could too.

Suddenly his concentration shifted to his day at work. During their busy shifts Max commented about the recent drive to Twin Pines. The area impressed him. Another mention of an apartment produced little discussion, mainly due to the volume of customers most of the day. Shane stared blankly at the coffee shop across the Mall from where he sat. Maybe he should walk over to grab a cup of some kind of coffee. People who did appeared very happy with their choices as they walked out of the small shop. However, he really didn't like coffee, even some mixtures that contained much more than just coffee.

He shifted on the bench crossing his legs. He found simply relaxing satisfaction enough for right now. Later in the evening he would meet Alisha at one of the newly opened shelters for teens and young adults. Only blocks away on Washington Ave., the shelter gave young people a chance to gather in a large recreation room and if registered early enough in the evening, a place to sleep. Alisha discovered the shelter and urged Shane to met her there. He would.

Suddenly the vibration and ring of his cell phone interrupted his quiet relaxation. Fumbling to release the phone from its case attached to his belt, he quickly glanced at the caller, his sister.

"Hello," he answered in a voice colored by his surprise at hearing from Danni.

"Hi, Shane, can you talk now or should I call back?" Danni asked.

Only rarely since his hospital stay, release, and the latest futile attempt at his sister's condo to unify the family did he speak with Danni, never his parents. Shane clutched his small phone to his ear, a nervous twinge grasped the back of his neck. "No, I can talk. What do you want?"

The hint of antagonism in Shane's voice delayed Danni's response. A deep breath preceded her answer. "Would you consider stopping by the condo Saturday night if you don't work?"

Weeks had elapsed since his last visit to her condo. That one only intensified the familial hostility that, in Shane's mind, made future family gatherings ill advised. "I don't know. What's going on?"

Another pause, "Now please listen to all of what I have to say before you make up your mind, okay?" Danni searched for the most diplomatic approach to her invitation.

"Yeah, go ahead," Shane agreed.

"On Saturday Mom and Dad plan to drive down here for a brief visit." She paused waiting for some response despite her precaution. Shane said nothing. "We haven't seen you for so long. We're eager to find out how you're doing."

Shane's shoulders slumped as he listened to his sister explain the invitation. "I'm fine, no problems."

"Would you be willing to come? Danni implored.

This time Shane hesitated before answering. In the seconds before he did, recent events, the conversation with his friends about the future, the drive north to Twin Pines with Max, flashed through his mind. "Ah, I don't know. I don't want to go through another battle with Dad about how I've screwed up my life, my future."

Danni smiled; not hearing a blunt rejection from her brother, she spoke with a bit more confidence. "I think, maybe, we have gone beyond the emotions of the past. We simply want to see you, to get reacquainted, to act like a family again."

"I don't know if I want to face Dad right now. Also I'll have to check my work schedule." Shane cleared his throat, took a deep breath then exhaled. "How about I think about it. I can let you know in a day or so. You did say this Saturday, right?"

"Yes, that's right." Danni confirmed.

"Okay. Maybe, I'll call you back tomorrow or the next day. I will let you know." Shane assured his sister.

"Thank you, Shane. Give me a call. I know Mom and Dad are looking forward to seeing you. Bye for now."

"Good bye," Shane repeated before shutting his cell phone and replacing it in its belt case. He leaned back, pushing his legs out before him. He did feel some guilt over his lack of contact particularly with his parents. Nonetheless, a persistent resentment lingered over too many demands placed upon him by his parents, particularly his dad, and too little appreciation for his independence.

He glimpsed his watch to note time had arrived for him to make his way to the shelter located on Washington Avenue in an abandoned and remodeled former car dealership. Alisha assured him she would register both of them upon her arrival. She also advised him to check in with the receptionist near the front door. She would direct him to the large recreation room.

Shane stood in the entrance to the recreation room, scanning the area in search of Alisha. What he saw as he scanned impressed him. The large room contained several fabric sofas positioned strategically in front of a large screen TV and where several young people relaxed. Certainly far from luxurious, the sofas provided a soft pillowy comfort for people who often found themselves on hard cement. In addition, separate lounge chairs intermingled with the sofas separated from them with small end tables on which sat decorative lamps. On one wall, enlarged photographs depicting familiar Twin Cities scenes added to the appeal of the room.

"You found it," Alisha approached Shane from the side laughing at his undivided attention to the room itself.

Her sudden comment startled Shane. "Yeah, I did. Sorry I didn't see you. Where were you sitting?" He asked warping his arm around her shoulders.

"No place. I went to the restroom. How long you been standing here?"

Shane shrugged his shoulders. "I just got here." He looked into Alisha' eyes than around the room again. "This is quite a place. Do ya know any of these people?"

Alisha snuggled closer to Shane, urged by the pressure of his arm around her shoulders. Her eyes made a quick survey of the room. "I think I've seen some of them around, but I don't think I really know any of them." She slipped out from under Shane's arm. "Why don't we find a seat before they're all gone?"

Together they moved toward a vacant sofa off to one side of the room. On the way Alisha literally skipped around the furniture pulling Shane behind her. Standing next to an empty sofa, she turned to face Shane, her lips spread wide in a smile. "Guess what?" Her eyes latched onto Shane's, who stood puzzled by her sudden excitement.

"Okay, I give up." He opened his arms in a sign of surrender.

"I got a job!" Alisha declared.

Shane reached out to enclose her in his arms. "That's fantastic! Where?"

"At the downtown Target working the late shift." She returned Shane's embrace. "Not my favorite shift," she grinned. "I don't think I ever mentioned this before, but I did work that shift a long time ago at the Target in the Ridgedale area. It didn't last long," she bit her lip. "For reasons you already know."

"When do you start?" Shane asked.

"On Monday of next week."

They settled into the soft, floating surface of the sofa. Shane grasped her hand, giving it a tender squeeze. "I'm proud of you. Now we'll have to get used to your late shift."

Alisha clinched her teeth as if suffering a moment of pain. "Not the best schedule but it's a job."

"Yeah, it's a start or maybe a restart." Shane smiled.

Comfortable in their places, they allowed silence to settle over them. "Does this place fill up each night?" Shane ended the silence, straining his neck to view the entirety of the room.

Alisha wiggled her body into the cushion. "I don't know. The place is new. I'll bet it won't take long for it to fill up."

"We could use more places like this. That's for sure." Shane sat back to look up at the TV some distance away but large enough for anyone in the recreation room to see and hear.

For a few moments they sat staring at the TV. "By the way, how was your drive to the north country?" Alisha asked.

Shane shrugged his shoulders with a slight jerk of his head. "Interesting, I guess, for Max."

"Did you stop any place in town?" Alisha asked.

"Only at a MacDonald's for a snack."

"Did you drive by your farm?" Alisha pushed for more information.

Shane only nodded his head.

"You didn't stop, right?" Alisha turned her attention to the TV, sensitive to Shane's feelings about his home on the farm.

They sat absorbed in watching other young people in the room, more all the time casually finding places to sit, some alone, others in small groups of two or three.

Shane brook the silence. He reached over to tap Alisha's knee. "I need your advice about something."

"If it's about finding a nice place to stay for a little bit, you've come to the right person." She smiled and squeezed Shane's hand resting on her leg.

"Well, I'm glad you found this place, but that's not my question," Shane admitted.

"Your question is?" Her response came packaged in a bit of humor.

Shane turned slightly to face Alisha. "This afternoon while I waited to come over here, my sister called. I hadn't heard from her in a hell of a long time."

"What did she want?" Alisha asked in a tone a bit more serious.

"To invite me over to her condo this Saturday for a kind of family powwow or something." Shane studied Alisha's face. "Do you think I should go?"

"Did she explain in more detail? How about your parents?" Alisha inquired.

"Not really. My parents will be there. I haven't seen them since my hospital days."

Alisha stared over Shane's shoulder, concentrating not on what she saw, but on what she was thinking for an answer. Finally, she reached for Shane's hand and gripped it firmly. "I don't pretend to know what's best for people like us. I do know that maybe someday something like that will happen to me too. What I would do I don't know. All I can say right now, Shane, is that since meeting you, some things have changed in my life, changed for the better. If you feel the same way, maybe you should forget for a while all that shit from the past."

Shane reached over to grasp Alisha's chin, positioning her head for his light kiss on her lips, only a faint line on her upper lip the last vestige of the brutal assault. "Thank you. I think you're right."

That night in separate dormitory type rooms during those quiet moments before the arrival of sleep, both Shane and Alisha glimpsed a world where families got along and every night included a soft bed on which to sleep.

Chapter 55

As usual for a Saturday evening, people crowded the Nicollet Mall, some in pursuit of dinner, some staring up at the tall buildings and some simply enjoying the freshness of early autumn. Shane walked, hands in pockets, contemplating what would occur when meeting with his family for the first time in several weeks. Since Danni's call inviting him to spend Saturday evening with his family in her condo, he attempted to visualize the scene particularly with his dad. He much more than his mom showed little tolerance for the choices Shane made during the past few years including his refusal to accept the chance to graduate by taking a short, summer school session.

A smile spread Shane's lips as he remembered sitting with Alisha in the shelter discussing Danni's invitation. The moment before his lips touched hers he lost himself in her eyes, captured by their magnetic beauty. So far in his young life he had not thought much about love or what it meant to fall in love. However, at that instant of innocent intimacy he believed, at least for him, he had discovered the meaning of love. He would forever remember the surge of affection that marked that discovery.

Approaching Danni's condo complex, Shane whispered a thank you to Alisha for her helping him decide about this evening. Since confirming his acceptance of his sister's invitation, Shane faced moments of apprehension about the decision. His stomach reminded him of the stress generated thinking about his family. Why it had to be that way he didn't know but it saddened him. He reached into his pocket for another Tums. With his hand on the entrance to the building's lobby, he quickly realized he no longer could find the key allowing him entry to the building. A call to his sister from the lobby phone resulted in the release of the door and access to the elevators.

Stepping out of the elevator gave Shane a chill. He found elusive anticipating what he would face in Danni's condo. Nonetheless, he considered Danni's invitation a start toward some reconciliation in the family. Approaching the condo, he saw Danni standing in the open door. Dressed in white shorts and flowered top that helped define her attractive figure, Danni moved into the hall with open arms waiting for the chance to give her brother a hug.

"Damn, it's good to see you little brother." She laughed as she looked up, stretching to give him a kiss on the cheek.

Shane stiffened before relaxing in his sister's hug. "I'm fine." He stepped back. "You look great."

"Thank you. So do you in your Twins T shirt." She pinched a bit of the T shirt hanging over his belt. "Clean too," she laughed.

Tucking the loose shirt into his jeans, Shane joined his sister with a chuckle.

Together they walked into the condo through the small kitchen and into the living room. On the sofa sat their mom; by the large window overlooking the Mall stood their dad, and getting up from the lounge chair Grayson Quinn walked briskly with hand extended to greet Shane.

Though Shane had met Greyson months ago, it was only a brief introduction. Since then he had paid little attention to him, particularly after that dreadful night when he discovered him sleeping on his futon. Seeing him for the first time in months, Shane was impressed with his obvious, excellent physical condition, tall and slim with broad shoulders. Straight, white teeth enhanced his smile which involved his eyes as well as his lips. A prominent nose helped draw attention to his dark brown eyes. Thick blonde hair trimmed neatly around his ears and neck, nonetheless, hinted at an expanding forehead. Dressed casually in trousers and a Polo golf shirt, he made an attractive partner for Shane's sister.

"Good to see you again, Shane. It's been a long time." Grayson gripped Shane's hand in a firm shake. "You obviously have completely recovered from the assault?"

Though he wished to avoid the subject, he realized it would come up. Perhaps responding to it now would put an end to it. "Yeah, I've no problem with that. Thanks to the doctors and therapists at Methodist Hospital."

"Also to that young girl who called 911." Danni quickly added.

"That's for sure," their mom confirmed. Dressed in a dark colored skirt and plain white blouse, something she typically would wear to church, Iris stood up from her place on the sofa, waiting for a chance to give her son a hug.

Seeing his mother waiting suddenly ignited a feeling of regret, of guilt over the agony he had caused his mom and his dad, too, over the years. Combined with the guilt came a rush of compassion. He turned with open arms to welcome his mother with a firm hug. "I'm sorry, Mom."

"You don't have to be sorry for anything. I'm just happy. You look great." She patted him on the cheek.

Martin moved little from his spot by the window, choosing to observe, from a distance, the reunions taking place in front of him. Now all eyes looked in his direction.

Shane squeezed his mother's arm before turning to his dad. A twinge trickled through his stomach. "How's the Twin Pines' farmer of the year?" Levity masked his disquiet.

Martin Stenlund stepped forward to grasp his son's extended hand. In a controlling voice all too familiar to Shane, his dad said, "I'm all right. How about you?" They shook hands.

Shane had never felt really comfortable talking with his dad. He always felt so inferior to his dominating father. The passage of time and the occurrence of unexpected events did little to alter that feeling. "Well, I guess you heard my answer to the question a few minutes ago. I'm doing okay."

"That's good." His dad smiled. "Are you still working in that restaurant?"

Shane gritted his teeth and stuffed his hands into his pants pockets. He hoped that his present circumstances would not surface as a topic of conversation. He didn't need any more reminders of his future. "Yeah, almost everyday." He looked up at his dad standing directly in front of him. "Maybe, sometime you and Mom could stop in for lunch . . . a free lunch?" This time his mild humor chipped away at the emerging tension in the living room.

Observing the interaction from near the kitchen counter, Danni finally stepped into the living room to encourage everyone to find a seat. Dad returned to his perch in front of the window. Mom sat back in the sofa. Shane sat next to his mom.

Danni grabbed Grayson by the hand, leading him to stand with her at the center of the living room. She looked at each member of her family then at Grayson, a smile accompanying each turn of her head. "Thank all of you family members for taking the time to spend a Saturday evening here." Before continuing, She turned to face Grayson. "Grayson and I have an announcement to make, and we wanted my family to hear it first." All eyes concentrated on Danni.

She took a deep breath, exhaled slowly, then said, "Grayson and I are getting married."

Mouths dropped open; eyes widened. Mom jumped up from her place on the sofa, rushing to embrace her daughter and future son in law. "That's wonderful sweetheart! Congratulations!"

Shane followed his mom in offering congratulations. Even Martin moved away from the window to offer his congratulations with a hug, a gesture untypical for him.

"When is the big day?" asked Mom.

Danni looked up at her fiance. "Sometime next spring or summer, we think. We plan to have the wedding in Twin Pines."

"That's fantastic!" shouted her mom.

The excitement of the announcement produced a few minutes of explaining wedding details, most of the conversation between mother and daughter. Finally all returned to their places where for the next half hour or so conversation ranged from the weather, to the harvest, to Danni's job as well as Grayson's, and to more wedding details.

With the intensity of the conversation waning, Shane's dad, still sitting on the large window sill, moved with a restlessness derived from usually controlling the conversation. "Say, Shane, when do you think you'll come home again?" The question plunged the room into silence. Danni looked from her dad to her brother. Iris sat up straight on the sofa glaring at her husband.

Shane slumped back on the sofa, ran his hands through his hair, closed his eyes for a second, then folded his arms across his chest. "Ah . . . I ah . . . I just don't know."

In a sharpened tone of voice, Martin asked, "When will you know? You don't have forever."

Shane stood up in a gradual motion, his eyes narrowed, his lips squeezed tight. "Look, Dad, you will be the first to know when I know."

Even more agitated, Martin countered, "I don't need your smart ass comments. I asked a reasonable question and expect a reasonable answer."

Danni turned to her dad. "Drop it!" Her voice cut through the thickening tension created by her dad's questions. Silence settled over the living room. She looked down at the floor then up at her dad. "You promised me you wouldn't bring up anything about Shane's future. Now just stop it." She breathed heavily. "I've made lasagna for dinner. Let's enjoy the rest of the evening with some food. Okay? Mom, you go first."

Conversation was guarded while they are their dinner. Shane helped his sister clean up, a job he did well from considerable experience. By ten o'clock Shane heard the call again of freedom from dominance. Though the topic of his future did not arise again, still that it did earlier only strengthened the wall that separated father from son.

Shane thanked his sister and offered further congratulations to her and to Grayson. He bid a brief good bye to his parents who, with Danni and Grayson, stood in the condo entry as Shane departed.

Back on the street on a warm, early autumn night, he tried to dismiss his father's comments. Though they reverberated in his mind, they didn't generate the anger and resentment of former occasions when his dad pressed him for a commitment. He shrugged his shoulders, shook his head, and expected to meet Alisha at the new shelter where he assumed she waited for him.

Chapter 56

A cool breeze greeted Shane as he walked out onto the Nicollet Mall. During the time spent with his family, Mall activity had altered little. Dozens of people seeking entertainment on a Saturday night found it on the Mall. Some stood in the pools of light beneath the ornate street lights; others made their way to a late dinner reservation or sought a conclusion to a Saturday evening in a downtown bar. A few just wasted time with a walk on the mall.

In the past, comments like those of his dad earlier in the evening would have rendered Shane seething with anger. His dad refused to allow his son to grow up, to assume command of his own life without returning to the farm. Now, however, his dad's unrelenting dominance merely annoyed Shane. Walking briskly away from the condo complex, he gritted his teeth and mumbled, "Fuck it." He had more important considerations; one of them, he supposed, he shared with his dad, his future.

The shelter would require about a fifteen minute walk along the Mall all the way to Washington Ave. where he assumed Alisha waited for him in the shelter's large recreation room. Leaving behind the condo and the events of the evening, his mind turned to Alisha and their relationship which hinted at a future of searching, nearly every night, for a place to sleep?

As he walked, he suddenly noticed his shadow dancing in front of him. Considering the hours he spent walking the Mall, he simply hadn't paid much attention to shadows. Decorative lights along the Mall, with their concentrated rays, produced few shadows. He turned around to look, amazed, into the fabulous harvest moon suspended in the southern sky. Shane stopped to gaze up at this autumnal spectacle. Not often did he have the chance to witness the glory of an autumn night or any night. The lights of downtown Minneapolis precluded seeing the night sky with any clarity. Tonight, however, the enormous moon, almost close enough to touch, afforded a rare opportunity to experience what Shane found common place on the farm, the harvest moon.

He turned back in the direction of the shelter, his shadow bouncing along in front of him in the darker spaces between street lights. That harvest moon awakened memories again. In weeks since his assault, thoughts of the past occurred more often all the time as did his curiosity about them. Shane questioned what provoked those memories. Right now the harvest moon served that function as his mind drifted to those clear, sparkling nights during harvest. He ran his hands through his hair, surprised at the nostalgia that swept over him, surprised also at the extent of his introspection, his questions about the direction of his life, his relationship with his family and with Alisha.

He could almost feel the chill of an autumn morning. An early sun ushered in a hot afternoon of harvesting in a dusty grain field or of desultory hours on the seat of a tractor rolling on gigantic tires, pulling a massive cultivator turning over the rich black soil in preparation for winter and for the next spring's planting.

Maybe life on the farm wasn't all that bad? Shane grinned at the thought. Still, his memory persisted in its reach into the past. He always remembered with affection his pony First Mate. Probably at no other time in his young life did he feel more content, more happy than when he clung to the broad back of First Mate. He could almost feel the breeze in his face and through his hair when First Mate raced across an open field. *Maybe life on the farm wasn't all that bad*? Again the question circled through his mind.

Feeding chickens, dragging five gallon pails of feed for voracious pigs, milking cows nearly every morning before school, cleaning roosts in the chicken coop were all jobs Shane despised while he had to do them. Now that he didn't have to do them anymore, he viewed them as interesting and in some ways entertaining. He laughed to himself at his conclusion. *Would he ever have to do them again? What would he think if he did*? He shrugged his shoulders and shook his head, dismissing such needless speculation.

He stopped before crossing Third Avenue, leaving only three more blocks to the shelter. His brief evening with his family nudged thoughts of the farm from his mind. His sister's wedding received so little attention during the evening's conversation. At least he thought it did. He started across the street, thinking with renewed interest of the first wedding in his small family. He remembered Danni's mention of the wedding taking place in Twin Pines. However, he remembered nothing about who would take part in the wedding party. At this moment he declared to himself that if asked, he mostly certainly would. Suddenly the question of whether his dad would ever get off his back popped into his mind. He shook his head, eyes closed for an instant in temporary surrender to his dad's intransigence.

Standing in the entrance to the recreation room, Shane surveyed the sprawling area for any sign of Alisha, who promised to meet him after his evening with family. He spotted her sitting by herself in a center, sofa chair directly in front of the large screen TV. She paged through a magazine.

Shane walked around and between three rows of end tables, colorful, fabric sofas, and stuffed chairs before he stood behind Alisha. Peaking over her shoulder, he saw she studied pictures in a *People* magazine. He cleared his throat. She jumped, dropping the magazine onto her lap.

"Finding anything interesting?" Shane asked, reaching over the back of her chair and squeezing her shoulders.

Her body twitched. "You scared me." Alisha strained her neck to look back at Shane.

"I'm sorry. I didn't mean to," Shane apologized. He stepped around to find a place next to Alisha on another of the large colorful sofas.

Alisha looked over at Shane, fixing her enchanting eyes on his. "Well, tell me how it went."

Shane bit his lower lip, furrows in his brow narrowed. "All right, I guess." He paused. "My sister's getting married."

Alisha jerked forward in her chair, reaching over to grip Shane's hand. "That's great, isn't it?"

Shane nodded his head. "Yeah, I suppose it is. We haven't had one in our family yet."

Alisha laughed. "Well, I can understand that with only two kids in the family." She sat back in her chair. "What about your dad? How was he?"

The question gave Shane reason to consider his response. He ran his thumb and forefinger around his lips and exhaled. "Better than last time. He really didn't have too much to say about anything, not even the wedding. Oh, he did finally slip in his question about when I'm coming home?"

"What did you say?" Alisha's eyes opened wide.

"Well, I said I didn't know, which is true; I don't. He then asked me when I would know. I said he would be the first to know after I did. I think he called that a smart ass comment."

"Oops," Alisha uttered.

"Well, Danni politely told him to lay off. That thankfully was the end of it." Shane rested back against the sofa.

They both sneaked a look at the TV where ironically the gang on *Saturday Night Live* portrayed a family deep in conflict. They laughed along with a few others scattered around the room at the scene on TV which to many of them reflected far too accurately on their own short history.

Shane tapped Alisha's hand. "Say, have you seen the moon tonight?"

She turned to face him, a puzzled look narrowed the space between her well defined eyebrows. "Really? I didn't know you were a moon gazer." She pinched his cheek to punctuate her sarcasm.

"Ha, ha," Shane quipped. "No, I'm serious. It's amazing how big and bright it is. Why don't we go out and take a look?"

Alisha rolled her eyes. "And miss out on this great TV?" she laughed.

"Ah, come on. It won't take long to have a look," Shane urged.

Easing herself up from her deep cushioned chair, she conceded, "Okay, Mr. Romantic, let's go see the moon."

Stepping outside the shelter they walked around the building away from the nearby street lights. Downtown buildings blocked their view momentarily. Finally, they stood in a position where downtown lights offered the least interference. Though the moon had traveled farther toward its destination at the western horizon, it still hung suspended in the dark night sky, a combination of blue shaded with a reddish hew making it spectacular.

"My God, it's gorgeous," Alisha pronounced.

Shane placed his arm around her shoulder. "I told ya so. It's called a harvest moon." He paused, breathed in, then continued. "I saw many of them on the farm. They're much easier to see there. Not so many things in the way like street lights and big buildings."

"Do moons like this only happen during harvest?" Alisha asked.

"It only happens in the fall, I think is more true. It just so happens that's harvest time, and somebody gave it that name. It doesn't really matter, I guess. Wherever the name came from it's still a great sight."

Alisha snuggled closer to Shane. "It sure is. Kind of romantic too."

"Yeah, I never thought much about that when we looked at the moon back then. Now it's a little different."

They stood staring up at the moon, Shane reaching for Alisha's hand. He squeezed it tight; she returned the squeeze. In the silence of the next few moments, Shane's thoughts drifted again back to those days of harvest when that magnificent moon lighted up the country side. Unlike now, however, his lying in bed thinking about the start of another school year, or his resenting the obligations he shared with his father in completing the lengthy harvest replaced the thrill of a harvest moon.

Soon they turned to face each other. Shane leaned down to kiss Alisha's tender lips which not so long ago suffered the revenge of a violent sexual client.

"Thank you for giving me this moon lesson," Alisha bumped against Shane's hip. "You know, ah . . . ah, you know, life on the farm couldn't have been all that bad." Her voice now carried a serious tone.

"Maybe not, but the harvest moon came only once a year and lasted only a few nights. The year had a hell of a lot more nights when looking at the moon meant just another day's end with more work in the morning." Shane swung Alisha's arm. "It's just . . . it's just kind of interesting that the harvest moon should occur on a night when my family tried to get together without some anger screwing things up." He swung her arm again. "Enough about the moon. We've seen it together, and now you know what a harvest moon is."

Walking back to the shelter entrance, Shane pulled Alisha to a halt outside the door. "By the way I meant to tell you that Max made the strangest comment the other day."

"On really. What did he say?" Alisha asked.

"Well, he asked me if I had ever thought about renting an apartment."

"Coming from him that does sound a bit strange. At least what you've told me about him, he seems rather content with his life." Alisha pushed against the entrance door. They walked by the receptionist, who recognized them from earlier in the evening, then headed for a place in the recreation room.

When seated, Alisha asked, "Well, have you thought about renting an apartment?"

Shane scratched his head then cleared his throat. "I don't think so, not until he mentioned it."

"So, what do you think now?"

Shane shrugged his shoulders and tilted his head to the side. "I really don't know. Maybe we should talk about it sometime, but not now."

They sat back in their places on a sofa and turned their attention to the large screened TV.

Chapter 57

Surrounded by the opulence of his den and office, Nick Karpin studied his latest bank statements. No one paid more attention to bank statements than did Nick. Since childhood when his family struggled financially, money provided a lure for Nick which over the years made him a very rich man. He did not reach that level without sacrifice, intelligence, and sound judgement of events and of people.

Several years ago with the passing of his father and the sale of his father's small pharmacy in St. Paul, Nick had the opportunity to buy two deteriorating apartment buildings only a block off Lake Street in south Minneapolis. In foreclosure, the two buildings occupying one side of an entire block stood abandoned and crumbling in neglect. On the outside, screens hung over cracked and broken windows. Weeds dominated the small patches of ground that extended from the front of the buildings to the sidewalk. Inside, Nick at first held his breath to avoid the pungent odor of decay. He shook his head ducking down under fallen ceiling tile and stepping over ripped carpets. Soiled walls and rusty water pipes appalled him.

Already Nick's adventure in the drug trade established him as a shrewd business man who insisted on loyalty and secrecy from those who worked for him. Despite the degradation he witnessed standing in the filth of the main floor of the one, three story building, he sensed a marvelous economic opportunity in the two apartment buildings and soon decided to make an offer for the purchase of both. The bank holding the mortgages stood ready to negotiate an agreement. In only days of discussion with Nick, the bank and its real estate company agreed to his offer.

Necessary to accommodate his burgeoning drug business, he plunged into the renovation of the two over forty year old buildings. He secured an architectural firm to assist him in the renovation which entailed, for some of the apartments, stripping out everything down to the studs. Following months of resurrecting the buildings at a cost in the hundreds of thousands of dollars, Nick prepared to advertise the availability of his apartment buildings, one, a three story, eighteen unit building occupying nearly an entire block and another, a two story, four unit building which along with the parking areas took up most of another block.

The first tenant to move in was Nick himself. He wished to stay close to what he owned; therefore he designed a special apartment for himself. On the day he moved in he paused at the front entrance to the three story building which now boasted a completely restored brick exterior, new windows and screens. Flowers lined the front of the building with grass stretching out to meet the public sidewalk. Beyond the sidewalk sprawling maple trees shaded both the street and the sidewalk. The four unit building received the same attention and likewise stood proud awaiting tenants.

Nick's special apartment represented living conditions he always dreamed of. On the third floor of the larger building, he carved out a two bedroom apartment covering the entire end of the third floor and eliminating a portion of the third floor hallway. His apartment included the two bedrooms, a living room, kitchen with oak cabinets and a cooking island, two baths decorated in a pale green marble, Nick's favorite color, the color of money.

The designation as the most important room in his apartment went to his den or his office as he preferred to call it. Enjoying dimensions exceeding either of the two bedrooms, the office contained oak bookcases lining two walls of the nearly square room with windows looking north to Lake Street with a glimpse through the trees of the Lake Street Light Rail Station. On the floor, a plush, pale green carpet, again Nick's favorite color, produced a calm, warm atmosphere where he could command his expanding business interests.

Nick relished the time he spent in his office because he enjoyed the ambience he found there and because there he could monitor the money flowing into his various bank accounts. He studied the bank statement spread out across the screen of his computer positioned on corner of the heavy, oak, executive desk behind which he sat. He ran his finger down the list of deposits, most made by Shane Stenlund, then compared them to the deposit record from the bank. They all corresponded. He sat back in his regal leather chair, a smile softening the contours of his face.

Obviously, his business suffered no adverse consequences from the assault on Shane some months before. Ultimately, Nick concluded that someone got an undeserved present of several hundred dollars. He also concluded that Shane was only the victim of the assault and the theft of the money. He believed Shane worked well in his job depositing what Shane assumed were receipts from tenants living in Nick's apartments. Some of those deposits did included rent money. However, most of the money came from Nick's drug enterprise.

Nick controlled a network of area captains and street workers, most of whom never met in person. Once the territory was established with sellers and managers, no longer would business require personal contact with those within one area. Of course, never would contact occur between or among other areas in the Twin Cities. Nick would tolerate no exceptions.

Following establishment of an area, technology provided the only means of all subsequent contact. Of course, Shane's position defied the restrictions imposed on the rest of Nick's empire. However, to remove Nick from direct contact with the banks where he laundered the drug money required the depositing arrangement he made with Shane. Except for the one scare in the parking lot of a Wayzata bank, the system worked very efficiently.

Nick liked Shane who in Nick's mind displayed intelligence, loyalty, and a serious regard for secrecy, all qualities Nick admired. He would have to offer some gratulations to Shane some time when he saw him again, probably at the Eighth Street Grill. He preferred to keep personal affairs out of the regularly scheduled deliveries of deposits to Shane which took place usually when Paul, Nick's immediate assistant, would contact Shane by cell phone.

Nick stood up behind his desk, quickly surveying his private domain. He turned off his computer, satisfied with the world and his place in it.

Chapter 58

A light lunch crowd induced a bit of day dreaming for Shane. His weekend exposed him to his tarnished family relationships that recently had taken on added importance. He braced himself against the wall where he and Max positioned themselves for instance response to tables requiring clearing and resetting. Shane's part of the dining room attracted fewer luncheon customers than usual.

Echoed in his ears, his dad's question when he would return home assumed more significance than at any time since he left home over a year and a half ago. Thoughts of home and future stole into his mind with increased frequency.

Visualizing standing with Alisha on the street outside the shelter gazing up at the harvest moon brought a smile to Shane's face. What a romantic moment for him and he assumed for Alisha, for whom seeing a harvest moon proved a first time experience. Never one to succumb to sentimentality, Shane now questioned his reaction to the family meeting and to the power of a harvest moon to take him back so many years to life on the farm.

"Sure hell's slow today," Max interrupted Shane's day dreaming.

"Yeah. What's going on?" Shane stepped away from the wall to rub his eyes in a gesture helping to bring him back to reality.

"People aren't hungry, I guess." Max moved toward one of his tables sensing the four customers were preparing to leave.

Shane relaxed, his arms crossed over his stomach. Nick occupied his usual table near one of the dining room windows. Of course, Nick's presence nearly every day commanded Shane's attention. He watched for any indication he might need something, though his waiter should assume that responsibility. Still, Shane observed Nick just in case he would need something. So far he apparently didn't.

Max returned to stand next to Shane. "Say, by the way, how did your family thing go . . . ah . . . Saturday, wasn't it?"

Shane grinned realizing the significance in the minds of others of his actually meeting with his family. "Okay," he replied with a shrug of his shoulders. "My dad still can't accept my leaving home when I did."

Max turned to face Shane. "Oh yeah, what did he do?"

Shane explained briefly the potential disruption of the family gathering by his dad's question about coming home. He also pointed out his sister's quick reaction to the comments reminding her dad to lay off the subject. Beyond that he announced his sister's marriage to Grayson and his general satisfaction with seeing his family again for the first time in several weeks. Shane glanced down at the floor while he shuffled his feet.

"Hey, I think your buddy over there needs something." Max nudged Shane.

What he needed Shane discovered was a brief meeting in the usual spot at the far corner of the grill's parking lot.

His shift completed, Shane stepped outside the restaurant to bright sunshine even though the days grew noticeably shorter, another hint of impending winter. Shielding his eyes from the sun's glare, he spotted Nick standing next to his car parked at the very end of the parking lot. Heading toward Nick, Shane noticed he wore his usual attire: blue blazer, a light green Polo shirt, khaki trousers, slightly touching black, tasseled loafers. An immaculate dresser, Nick favored the outfit he now wore. Flecks of gray sprinkled through heavy, curly black hair added to Nick's physical appearance. Usually, Shane saw Nick sitting down, paying little attention to what he wore or to his physical features. Now, however, Nick stood against the backdrop of his luxury, black BMW, waiting for Shane's arrival.

When Nick asked for a meeting, the question gave Shane a moment of concern. The two had not met except in the confines of the Eighth Street Grill since Shane's subjection to assault and robbery. After their brief visit in the hospital, Nick said nothing more about the unfortunate incident. Nor did Shane mention it even though he still wished to see some justice done. After all, he suffered for weeks with the injuries he sustained that night in a Wayzata parking lot. Nonetheless, he abided by Nick's insistence to avoid any police involvement.

Nick stepped forward hand extended when Shane approached. They shook hands.

"Thank you for taking the time to meet." Nick rarely needed to thank anyone, except maybe Shane, who nearly every day cleared Nick's lunch table. "Did you have a good day at work?"

"Yes, a bit slower than usual but the day went by really fast." Shane stood before Nick, hands locked behind his back, his mind speculating about the purpose of the meeting.

"Look, Shane, I won't take much of your time. I know you've put in a long day already. I just wanted to congratulate you on the great job you've done helping me with the deposits."

Shane moved from one foot to another, a hint of embarrassment in response to Nick's kind words, words not often coming from his mouth. Shane hung his head for an instant then looked up at Nick. "Thank you. I appreciate that." A sudden urge to ask about the source of the money he deposited at least once a week threatened to invade the conversation. Shane resisted the urge.

"I appreciate reliable employees who do their job without blabbing all over what their job is." Nick turned to open the door to his black BMW then paused. "By the way, I've meant to ask you. Do you still live with your sister?"

The question created a mild impact on Shane. It kind of forced him to straightened up. "No. not now," he answered.

"Where do you live?" Nick asked.

Shane hesitated before answering. "Sometimes with friends."

"And other times?" Nick persisted.

"Just around, wherever." Shane felt uneasy about the questions. What made the difference where he lived. He did his job.

Nick eased himself onto the soft leather driver's seat. He looked up at Shane standing next to the car. "Look, I don't know what your plans are, but I have a suggestion about where you could live. Only a few days ago one of my small, one bedroom apartments became vacant. Maybe you might be interested in renting it."

Shane's eyes opened wide; with his foot he kicked a small piece of debris that ended up under Nick's car. "I don't know. I haven't thought much about that. Money's a problem."

Nick turned to grasp the steering wheel, closed the door and lowered the window. "It's nothing urgent. Think about it. It's mostly furnished with nothing elegant but still it has most of the necessary things. The rent is cheap, I think, about $300.00 per month with a little extra for utilities like phone and electricity." He paused as he turned the switch which brought the powerful engine to life. "I'll talk with you again. Just think about it. See you later." He put the car in gear and drove out of the parking lot.

Shane stood perplexed, questioning if he could afford $300.00 a month. After deductions his bimonthly check didn't allow him much latitude. *Did he really want to tie himself to an apartment?* Maybe he could talk to Max about sharing it. With winter around the corner, having a place to spend each night had definite appeal. Yes, he would think about it.

Chapter 59

Alice Sanders slumped in her chair, hands folded on the table before her. Rarely did she spend time in one of Wayzata's popular coffee shops located on the main street. However, rarely had she faced the deeply troubling circumstances that now gripped her heart.

A petite woman in her early sixties, time had rounded her earlier attractive curves. Nonetheless, at five feet four and one hundred fifteen pounds, she retained an attractive figure for a woman her age. Thick, dark hair accentuated the refined lines of her checks and chin. Anxiety clinched her full lips and dulled the sparkle of her eyes.

Recently diagnosed with breast cancer, she shifted in her chair trying to calm her nerves as she waited for the arrival of Alisha, the daughter she had not seen for countless weeks. She rested back in her chair, pulling her sweater around her shoulders. Dressed in a black skirt and grey cardigan sweater over a white silk blouse, she appeared more ready for dinner at one of Wayzata's fine restaurants than at a coffee shop on Wayzata's main street.

In the months since Alisha left her home in Wayzata, Alice labored over the question of why? She and her husband, a successful real estate agent, had provided a secure home, at least secure materialistically for their only child, Alisha. Hints that her husband sexually abused their daughter she simply could not accept. She loved her husband and following forty years of marriage, she believed she knew and understood him thoroughly. He would never endanger the emotional stability of their daughter. Why Alisha resorted to such malicious charges Alice could never understand.

Still she loved her daughter; even her baseless charges could not alter that love. Each day she worried about where her daughter spent her time and what she intended to do with her life. During the many months of Alisha's absence, time gradually reduced the debate between Alice and her husband over what drove her away from their home to an occasional comment at the dinner table about her status.

Edward Sanders, Alisha's dad, had from the beginning vehemently denied Alisha's crazy accusations about his sexual abuse. However, no amount of discussion could remove the stain on their marriage. They simply narrowed their attention each day to their own private worlds with only intermittent moments of interchange.

The breast cancer diagnosis awakened Alice to the fragility of life. Until the diagnosis only days before, she enjoyed a life free of serious illness. Like everyone else she suffered an infrequent cold and more recently depended on an antacid to calm her rumbling stomach. The cancer discovery altered the confidence in her health she had cherished for so many years.

Alice needed to talk to Alisha. She needed to take her in her arms to try to absorb the pain that compelled her to leave home more than three years ago. She needed to talk about her cancer and about the future treatment. Though she maintained cell phone contact with Alisha, her calls often met with a sullen and indifferent daughter. This response discouraged making contact.

Two days ago Alice resolved to overlook the past; nothing could change that. The future now included more doubt and apprehension, doubt about the cancer and increased apprehension about her daughter and the life she led. She called Alisha, asking if she would meet with her mother, giving no hint of the cancer diagnosis. Alisha expressed reluctance but ultimately agreed to meet her mother at the Wayzata coffee shop.

Dressed in jeans and a hooded sweatshirt, Alisha pushed open the door to the coffee shop. She paused as she stepped inside to gaze over the several tables around which sat customers, young and old, savoring their favorite coffee. At first she failed to locate her mother. She moved over to the serving counter when she saw her mother standing up by her table in the corner of the room.

Alisha hesitated. Her mother looked more pale and weary than usual. Alice stepped from behind her table, moving to meet her daughter. Alisha stood watching her slow approach. With arms open wide, Alice reached for her daughter. She wrapped her arms around Alisha's back, pressing her head against her chest. Her body trembled as Alice tried to suppress her sobs. Alisha's body stiffened, her arms rising in a tentative embrace.

Alice breathed deeply, looked up with tears sliding down her pale cheeks, and whispered, "I'm sorry. Thank you for coming."

Alisha's shoulders drooped; she relaxed. "Don't be sorry." She stepped back to ask. "Is something wrong?" To Alisha, a question with an obvious answer; something definitely was wrong.

Alice reached for her daughter's hand. "Come. Let's sit down at the table over there. Do you want a coffee?"

Alisha shook her head. "No, I don't think so." She followed her mother's lead, a familiar tingle trickled through her stomach, a sensation common even with only rare contact with her mother.

They positioned themselves across the table from each other. Alice moved her coffee cup closer, then brought it to her lips to take a small sip. She secured a tissue from her sweater pocket, dabbed her eyes and wiped her mouth. Reaching across the table to placed her hand on top of Alisha's, she asked, "How have you been, sweetheart?"

Alisha squeezed her mother's hand then reached down to nudge her chair closer to the table. "I'm fine." A discussion of exactly what she did both discreetly avoided. Also avoided was any reference to her dad. Noting her mother's pale complexion combined with her emotional greeting, Alisha asked, "How are you?"

Alice now sat back in her chair. She looked down at the table, reaching again for her cup of coffee. She stared at the cup, rotating it with her well manicured fingers. Glancing up to meet her daughter's eyes, in a weak but clear voice, she confessed, "I have breast cancer."

Alisha's mouth dropped open and her eyes widened. She caught her breath. "My God!" She raised her hand to her mouth. "When did you find this out?"

"A few days ago. I, ah, I felt a suspicious lump in my left breast the last few weeks. I went for a check up. The doctor confirmed the cancer."

The initial shock fading, Alisha asked, "What happens now?"

Alice took another sip of her coffee, dabbing her lips with the tissue. "Well, I'm not sure at the moment. I think I will face surgery to remove the suspicious lump. The result of that procedure will probably determine what's next."

Silence invaded the table where they sat. Alice broke the silence. "I'm sorry to have to tell you this. I know you have your own life to deal with."

Alisha sat up straight. "Oh, Mother, please don't be sorry about telling me. I'm still your daughter, and despite all that has happened, I do love you." She paused to meet her mother's eyes. "If there is something I can do to help in all this, please let me know." She inhaled then released her breathe. "I'm sorry but that does not include my moving home."

A faint smile crossed her mother's lips. "I know, sweetheart. We won't get into that. Just promise me you'll take care of yourself. I will let you know what develops with me."

Across the table their eyes met in a silent understanding that each had her separate life but beneath that lay a natural bond neither could deny.

Chapter 60

Max stretched back against the bench's hard surface, his legs extending out onto the sidewalk. He looked up into the early evening sky, a sliver of a moon peeking around the top of the IDS Tower. "Damn it's a beautiful night, even here on the Mall."

"Yeah, I guess so." Shane joined Max in observing the evening sky. "Not much to see with all these buildings." Shane folded his arms across his chest. "It is a nice evening anyway."

Max reached over to give Shane a gentle punch on his arm. "Come on, cheer up. You gotta like a Saturday night under the stars and moon." Max laughed. "Maybe it's not like evenings on the farm but it's all we have right now."

"Yeah, I know." Shane offered a smile and dropped his hands to his lap.

Saturday night, oddly, was not one of the busier nights at the Eighth Street Grill. Max and Shane didn't bother to question why. They simply concentrated on their function at the Grill, adhering to the schedule given them by their boss. Consequently, Max and Shane enjoyed an early night off with essentially nothing to do. Alisha's recently acquired job working nights at the downtown Target store drastically reduced her availability, particularly in the evenings.

For several minutes Max and Shane silently watched the people walking the Nicollet Mall, a popular place almost anytime but particularly on a Saturday night.

Shane broke the silence. Turning to face Max, he offered, "Remember I told about my talk with Nick and his apartment."

"Yeah, I remember." Max pulled his legs in and sat up straighter. "What about it?"

"Oh, nothing, I guess." Shane stared at the sidewalk below him. "I was just thinking about your comment a few days ago, the apartment one. Were you serious?"

Max breathed in and exhaled. "I really am not sure." He shook his head. "I don't know if I could afford it. What do ya think?"

"I don't know either." Shane paused. "Maybe we should take a look at the apartment Nick told me about." Shane's eyes narrowed in thought. "I think he said something about $300.00 a month for this one bedroom with some basic furniture, whatever that means."

Max smiled. "You know, I've gotten so used to living in my car I've not given an apartment a whole lot of thought. Maybe it's time to give it some thought."

Shane eased himself up from the bench. He stretched his back then placed his foot up on the bench. "Do ya think we could work together then live together too?" He laughed.

"As long as you remember to raise the toilet lid when you pee." Max returned the laugh.

"I think I can do that," Shane promised. He removed his foot from the bench and in a more serious tone suggested, "Maybe next week sometime we should take a look at the place."

"Sounds good to me," Max agreed.

Shane turned to face the sidewalk when a tall young man with a head crowded with thick black curls, dressed in jeans, a blue blazer and a dress shirt open at the neck stopped next to the bench now occupied only by Max.

"Do you mind if I sit down. It's been a long day."

Shane moved toward Max. "Sure, be our guest. We were about to leave anyway."

"Thank you." The young man sat down pushing his long legs toward the sidewalk, displaying expensive, highly polished loafers. He reached into his sport coat pocket to bring out a pack of cigarettes. "Either of you care for a smoke?"

Both Max and Shane declined. The young man lighted his cigarette, inhaled then released a stream of smoke. "My name is Meeker, Charles Meeker. I hope I'm not intruding."

Still standing, Shane replied, "No, not at all."

Meeker took another hit from his cigarette. "Beautiful evening. You guys got plans for a Saturday night?"

Shane looked down at Max seated before him, shrugged his shoulders and confessed, "No, nothing special, just relaxing after a long day."

"You live around here?" Meeker asked.

Reluctant to extend the conversation, Max replied, "No, we work at the Eighth Street Grill near here."

"Oh yeah, I know where that is." Meeker dragged again on his cigarette. "You guys want to have some fun tonight?"

Max and Shane locked eyes. Max answered, "I don't know. What did you have in mind?"

Meeker smiled then pulled down on his blazer uncovering an intricate tattoo on the right side of his neck. "Friend of mine who lives in Plymouth, just a short drive from downtown, is having a small party tonight. He's a friendly guy who has this thing about entertaining guests. If you're interested, I can give you directions."

Max got up to stand next to Shane. They made eye contact with each other again. Max shrugged his shoulders. "Why not?"

Meeker stood up, reaching into his blazer pocket to withdraw this time a business card containing directions to his friend's house in Plymouth. Handing the card to Max, he explained, "The directions are on my business card. My friend's name is Hector Vincent. Simply tell him Chuck Meeker sent you. Okay?"

Max and Shane nodded they understood.

Chuck Meeker smiled, reaching out to shake hands with his newly acquired friends. "Have a good time."

"Do ya know where we're going?" Shane sat in the front passenger seat of Max's car staring out the window in search of their destination.

"No, I haven't spent much time in this part of town. It's kind of a ritzy area, I think." Max drove slow enough to allow them to check out the street signs.

After a few missed turns and flirting with a decision to give it up, they found the street printed on Meeker's card. Lined with impressive homes featuring three stall garages and boulevards graced by towering maple trees whose emerging fall colors even the evening twilight failed to conceal, the street curved around to one particular home with front lights blazing and several cars parked in the driveway.

"This must be the place," Max chuckled. "I wonder what this guy does for a living?" He pulled into the driveway to join the cars already parked there.

They stepped out of the car to stand before an elaborate entry way crowned by a huge window lighted from inside by a vast collection of small lights working together to create an extravagant chandelier. Max and Shane looked at each other with skepticism.

Shane asked, "What do ya think? Is it worth it?"

"I guess we won't know unless we try it. If nothing else we can look at how the rich live." Max opened his arms as if to welcome a friend from the past. "Let's go."

Standing before the ornate wooden front door, Shane rang the door bell. In seconds a man opened the door. Of medium height with thinning hair, a goatee, an ingratiating smile, and immaculately dressed in a dark suit complemented by a bright red bow tie, he stated, "Welcome gentlemen. May I help you?"

Max removed the card given him by Charles Meeker. "Charles Meeker sent us," he announced.

The man nearly exploded in smiles. "Well, by all means come right in." He held open the heavy door. "My name is Hector Vincent and welcome to my humble home." He offered his hand to both Shane and Max. Soft and pliant, the hand suggested Mr. Vincent worked little with his hands. "Come right in and join the others."

Max and Shane stood amazed at the hallway extending into the interior of the house. In the distance they could see people mingling in a spacious room beyond a graceful arch. A strange aroma pervaded the hallway. It grew more pungent the closer they walked toward the large room. Standing at the entrance to the room, Max and Shane could see it contained several conversational settings, one directly in front of a glowing fireplace. Furnished with opulent looking, leather sofas and sofa chairs, the room contained several coffee tables lighted by elegant floor lamps. Rich carpet throughout except for the area directly in front of the fireplace helped transform the room into a perfect party room.

Scattered around the room, small groups of people both men and women, most dressed casually in jeans, slacks and sweaters or sweatshirts, engaged in conversation, each clinging to a drink of some kind. In addition that aroma evident upon entering the house filled the room with a faint haze ceiling fans struggled to dissipate.

"Help yourself to the hors d'oeuvres and a beverage." Mr. Vincent then moved away toward one of the small groups near the fireplace. Max and Shane headed for the hors d'oeuvres and each grabbed a beer. The people in the room paid little attention to them. With a small plate of food and a beer, they turned to locate someplace to sit or at least to set down their plates. A group standing in the far corner, on the other side of the fireplace motioned for Max and Shane to join them. A simple exchange of names proved sufficient for them to join in with more idle conversation.

In only minutes Shane and Max could tell people in that room did not restrict themselves to beer and liquor. Mr. Vincent hovered around the small groups of people, offering them samples of his "goodies." Some of the goodies came in small packages while others came as cigarettes.

In a short time the suspicions that followed Max and Shane all the way from downtown Minneapolis proved valid. This was not some happy home owner opening his house to anyone looking for a good time. Instead it was a place to acquire and consume an apparent assortment of illegal drugs.

Mr. Vincent approached the group Max and Shane joined. "How you doing? You got something to eat? Now, how about a little dessert?" A smile spread his lips and partially closed his eyes. He reached into his inside suit pocket to bring out a small packet of a white substance and several cigarettes obviously rolled by hand. "Take you pick gentlemen. There's more where this came from."

Shane looked around at the others standing near him. At that moment none of them partook of any goodies. Never having succumb to the temptation of illegal drugs, never having even succumb to regular cigarettes, and restricting his alcohol to beer, the goodies offered by Mr. Vincent failed to tempt him. "Maybe later," was his response to the generosity of the host. Max followed Shane's lead. Vincent frowned then turned away without a comment.

Recognizing the reality of the party to which Mr. Meeker invited them, Max and Shane stayed only a short time before inconspicuously heading for the front door. As they approached the front entrance, Mr. Vincent's casual glance carried with it none of the flowing hospitality he displayed upon their arrival.

Driving back to downtown Minneapolis where they would decide the night's lodging, Max commented, "That was some party."

"I wonder how many people they snag with that shit they push?" Shane pulled on his seat belt. "Should we say something about it?"

"Who would we tell? Max shrugged his shoulders. "I think we should just forget about it and let the bastards do their dirty thing. We have enough to worry about right now in finding a place to sleep." Max looked over at Shane, a grin punctuating his comment.

"Yeah, you're right." Shane gazed out his side window as they entered I-394. "How many people do you think that Meeker guy gets to attend his parties?"

"I don't know, but I do know we're not among them." He paused. "Ah, let's forget . . . forget about tonight. That place was a damned pit for stupid people to get high. Why don't we think about looking at the apartment Nick told you about?"

"Yeah, sometime next week." Shane agreed.

Chapter 61

"You have the directions, right?" Max turned onto Lyndale Avenue heading south.

"Yeah, Nick wrote them down. I don't think they're that complicated for someone like you who's been around this big city for a long time." Shane unfolded the half sheet of paper on which Nick had written the directions.

"Maybe, but I don't spend much time around Lake Street." Max checked his rear view mirror before changing lanes. "Didn't you say the building is on Chicago Ave. about two blocks off Lake Street?"

"That's what Nick told me." Shane folded the piece of paper, straining against the seat belt in an attempt to stuff it into his pants pocket.

Turning onto Chicago Avenue gave them an introduction to an area with a combination of single family homes and multiple unit dwellings. Located on the west side of the street, Nick's apartment buildings dominated nearly two blocks.

Max slowed easing his car to the curb. "Not bad looking." He peeked over the steering wheel then faced Shane. "Where're we supposed to meet Nick?"

"At the entrance to the smaller building. That's the one next to this one." Shane pointed to the much larger apartment building in front of which they parked.

They climbed out of the car to walk the half block to the smaller building. Before they turned onto the sidewalk leading to the front entrance, Nick emerged from inside the building. He stood waiting for Shane and Max to reach the entrance.

"Right on time, guys." Dressed in his usual blazer, pale green polo, and highly polished tassel loafers, Nick greeted them, reaching out to shake hands. "Obviously, you had no problem finding the place."

"No, none at all. Max always knows where he's going," Shane said in jest.

"Well, that's good. We can always find a place for someone who knows where he's going." Nick added to the jest.

Nick reached back to open the entrance door. "Come on, follow me. Let's take a look at the apartment."

Max and Shane stepped into the apartment building noting immediately the clean carpet and the fresh paint on the corridor walls. They exchanged brief glances accented with a smile. They followed Nick up one flight of stairs to the one bedroom apartment on the second floor. The building contained only four apartments, two on each floor.

"Guys, there is an elevator in the building, but I didn't think we needed it just now." Nick reached the top of the stairs and pointed to the door at the end of another short hallway. "The apartment is the one at the end of the hall on your left over looking the street." Again Max and Shane noted the obvious care given the second floor hallway.

Standing in front of apartment 204, Nick reached into his pocket for the key. He nudged the door open. With a noble gesture he welcomed his guests into the apartment. Shane and Max entered a very short hallway, similar in Shane's mind to that in his sister's condo, only shorter. Nick explained to them the simple layout of the apartment. The kitchen and living room occupied one room separated by an island around which were positioned three stools. As Nick promised, the apartment contained essential furniture which translated into a sofa which they could convert into a double bed, three common chairs, a coffee table, and a TV placed on a sturdy stand. Though equipped with only minimal dishes and cookware, the kitchen contained a microwave, a fridge, a gas stove, and even a small dish washer.

"What do you think, guys?" Nick leaned against the island dividing the kitchen from the living room.

"I'm impressed." Shane looked across the room. "I suppose that door over there by the sofa is the bedroom?"

Nick chuckled. "Oh, you need a bedroom, too?" He walked to open the door Shane pointed to. Inside stood a large bed and a small chest of drawers. A tiny closet occupied one corner of the room supplemented by a free standing clothes rack next to the closet door.

"What do you think?" Nick addressed Max.

"Looks good to me. I think you mentioned rent to Shane."

"Yes, I did, $300.00 a month including water, heat, and air conditioning. You'll have to pay for your own phone, cable, and electricity. Of course, you likely each have cell phones anyway. Incidentally, washing facilities are located on the lower lever, free to residents." Nick again leaned against the island, crossing his arms over his chest. "Why don't you guys give the place some thought? I think you'll find living here quiet and comfortable."

"Thank you for taking the time to show us the apartment. We appreciate it." Shane folded his hands behind his back, not knowing what else to say.

Nick guided them back to the first floor, explaining the location of the washing facilities. Back to the front entrance, they stood for a moment, Nick again urging them to give the apartment some thought.

"We certainly will do that," Shane acknowledged looking to Max for a gesture of confirmation. "We'll see you probably tomorrow at the Grill."

"You can count on that. Maybe in a few days you can give me your decision," Nick suggested.

"Sure, we can do that," Shane answered for the two of them. "Thank you again and see you tomorrow."

Back in the car they rode in silence winding their way to Lake Street and the drive back down town. Finally, Max spoke, "What do you think?"

"Can we afford $300.00 a month rent?" Shane asked.

"Between the two of us? Shit yes, no problem. I guess the question is do we want to tie ourselves down to such conventional living?" Max chuckled with his question.

"I think I can get used to that again." The rest of the drive found both in a quiet, contemplative mood.

Chapter 62

"Awesome, huh?" Shane grinned and waved his arm in a half circle, directing Alisha's attention to the apartment.

Alisha, sitting on the sofa bed dressed in her Target uniform of red shirt and black slacks, rolled her eyes while following the summons of Shane's arm. "Well, ah, it's a place to sleep." Her head moved from side to side. "It has a certain intimacy to it. I know you and Max like intimacy." Her hand helped muffle her laughter. What about sleeping arrangements with only one bedroom?"

"You're sitting on my bed. The thing unfolds into a real bed, not bad either. Wanna see?" Shane asked.

"No, that's fine, just curious. I like the kitchen area."

"It serves our purposes. We're not much into cooking. Thank god for the microwave." Shane crossed his legs, leaning back into his chair.

Alisha's eyes made one more tour of the small living, dining, sleeping area. She asked, "How much did you say this place cost a month?"

"Three hundred dollars plus some utilities."

Alisha shrugged her shoulders. "You can't beat that, a generous landlord." She looked over at Shane seated in the chair positioned at the end of the sofa bed. "This is the same guy you deposit money for, right?"

"Yeah, that's right. His name is Nick Karpin. He owns this building and the bigger one next to it." Shane shifted in his chair, making a sudden shift in the conversation. "Can I get you anything, soda, water, champagne?" He chuckled.

"No, nothing right now. Remember I need to get to work in about two hours," she reminded Shane.

"I know. Max should be here in time to take you." Shane leaned forward resting his elbows on his knees. By the way how's the job going?"

Alisha cast her eyes on the carpet beneath her, rubbing her foot over a small dark spot in front of the sofa. "All right so far. Hours are not very good, but the pay isn't bad."

"You still spend most of your time stocking shelves? Shane asked.

"Oh, yeah, for hours several of us toil away dragging boxes out from the shipping and receiving area which nobody else sees."

"Kind of tedious, I'm sure, but better than before." Shane's allusion to Alisha's prostitution he quickly realized was a time in her life Alisha would like to forget. As Alisha stiffened, he apologized. "I'm sorry. It was a stupid comment."

For a moment they sat in silence each reliving past transgressions. Shane got up from his chair to sit next to Alisha on the sofa. Placing his arm around her shoulder, he leaned closer to place a tender kiss on her cheek. "I'm sorry."

She reached for his hand and closed her eyes. "I know you are. Thank you."

Another silence surrounded them. Again Shane broke the silence. "How's your mom getting along?"

In the days following Alisha's meeting with her mother when she learned of her mom's breast cancer, she turned to Shane for a source of comfort and strength. Despite her absence from home for over two years, she retained an attachment to her mother. Since that meeting and the revelation it produced, contact with her mother occurred on a more regular basis. "Okay for now. She started chemo already. I spoke with her only two days ago. She's had no serious reactions to the chemo, I guess. At least she didn't say anything about that." Alisha ran her fingers through her dark hair bunching it behind her head.

"Does she know any more about what to expect?" Shane asked.

"Not really. Oh yeah, her doctor has tried to give her some confidence in the future." Alisha shook her head. "I'm not a pessimist, but I doubt if anybody can predict what the cancer will do." She ran her finger under her eye chasing a tiny tear. "We just have to take things one day at a time."

"Have you considered moving home again? Shane introduced a topic of conversation they had discussed before, more than once.

Without hesitation, Alisha responded. "No. That's not going to happen." She inhaled then released her breath. "I regret that it won't."

"I understand." Shane did understand the role Dads played in their decisions to leave home when they did. "How has your dad reacted to your mom's cancer?"

Alisha locked her hands between her knees. Shaking her head, she declared, "I don't give a damn what he thinks or does. My only wish is to forget about him." Her eyes closed as her head dropped.

The conversation had almost inadvertently drifted toward topics neither Shane nor Alisha found comfortable to discuss. They had talked about their respective Fathers in the past. An agreement to avoid the topic didn't always work, however. Shane sensed they had stumbled into tender territory. He rose from the sofa to take the few steps to the fridge where he grabbed a can of Sprite.

He turned to the sofa. "Here take a drink of this." He handed her the can.

Alisha reached for the can; placing it to her lips, she took a generous drink. She released her breath. "Thank you."

After Shane returned to his place next to her on the sofa, he took a couple swallows from the can before handing it back to Alisha, who declined.

She crossed her legs, folded her hands on her lap and looked over at Shane. "Have you talked with your sister lately?"

Shane scratched his chin. "No, not for quite awhile." He stared off into a corner of the room. "She did call . . . ah, I don't know, about two, three weeks ago asking about what I was doing. I told her I was doing about the same. Oh, I did mention this apartment thing. She thought it a great idea."

"Have you talked at all to your parents?" Alisha asked.

"No. I think Danni keeps them informed about me and my troubled life. At least my parents call it troubled, I guess." He paused, again his eyes looking off into nothing. "You know, maybe I haven't been all that fair about my parents. I've done a little thinking about them and about me. I don't feel the resentment that I used to feel. Maybe it's just my imagination, but I do feel a little different about the whole thing. What I'll do about it, who knows?"

Alisha straightened up prepared to answer when Max burst through the door to the apartment. He advanced to the island separating the kitchen from the living area. "Hey guys, what's going on?"

"We've just decided that Alisha gets the bedroom. I get this thing we're sitting on. You get the floor." Shane laughed, relieved at the timely appearance of Max to rescue them from a discussion of home and parents.

"Thank you. That's very thoughtful of you." He leaned his elbows on the island. "How are you doing Alisha? How's that job at Target?"

"Keeps me out of trouble at night." Alisha replied. "It's going okay. It takes a while to get used to a different schedule."

"You work nights, right?" Max asked.

"Yeah, five nights a week."

Max pushed himself away from the island. "Say, Shane, you know who, I think, I just saw going into the other apartment building?"

"No, who?"

"This guy, ah, Mr. Glitter or Sleeker or whatever his name, the guy who invited us to that party the other night"

"No shit? What the hell, does he live here?" Shane got up from his place next to Alisha on the sofa. "I think his name was Meeker, Chuck Meeker."

"Yeah, that's it. I've not seen him around here before, but then we've only been here a short time. Do you suppose he does his job around here too?"

Shane looked at his friend. "Are you thinking what I'm thinking?"

Chapter 63

Shane settled into the soft cushion seat in the light rail car taking him from downtown to his apartment in south Minneapolis. Its proximity to the light rail station on Lake Street proved an important benefit of the apartment's location. During their deliberations regarding accepting Nick's generous offer of $300.00 for the small one bedroom apartment, neither Max nor Shane considered the value of the light rail for their transportation needs. Of course, Max retained his aging car; nonetheless, walking the three blocks to the station to ride the train downtown appealed to Max as well as Shane. Economic considerations favored the train. Besides traffic proved an annoyance for most of their scheduled shifts at the Eighth Street Grill.

This time Shane rode alone. Max worked a later schedule and had driven his car to work. Completing a long eight hour shift dominated by a flood of football fans in town for Sunday's Viking game against the Bears, Shane leaned back in his seat and closed his eyes. The short ride to Lake Street afforded the chance for moments of reflection, moments increasingly more often grabbing Shane's attention. The status of his life, the events of the over two years since leaving the farm, his job at the Grill, his apartment, his relationship to Alisha, Max, and the enigmatic Nick, and most all his own ambiguous future all filtered through his mind vying for his consideration.

The two weeks living in the apartment with Max he considered a definite improvement in his life, especially now with the approach of winter. Sharing the apartment with Max and potentially with

Alisha lacked any threat to his insistence on independence. A smile spread his lips when he remembered those days when any hint of subjection to someone else's rules incensed him. Now he realized how little difference that made in his life. Everybody had to live by some rules. He tapped his knees. That's the way it was.

His future had acquired more importance, particularly since the brutal attack in the Wayzata bank parking lot. A bit philosophical, he found himself thinking about the meaning of life, about where his life headed, thoughts that only a few years ago completely evaded him. Maybe his experiences over the last couple years had awakened an entirely different perspective of his future.

He again closed his eyes and squeezed his lips in a tight smile. *Where would Alisha fit into his future? Did they have a future together, two wayward people who spent so much time alone on the streets of the big city?* So far his life included only brief relationships with girls until the arrival of Alisha. His fragile relationship with her had endured for months. He expected, he wanted it to continue. Yet, he wasn't even convinced of that. Though they had engaged in serious conversations about their previous lives, so much of hers remained shrouded in mystery. He assumed she felt the same about his.

Shane glanced out the window next to his seat. The Lake Street Station drew near. Suddenly, Lindsey Cooper flashed through his mind. Thoughts of her made him shake his head. No contact had nearly erased her from his memory. Still at this moment she rekindled the anger and shame of that prom night so long ago, the night which culminated a period of unrest and bitterness about his life on the farm. That night marked the end of his life on the farm and prompted his leaving home.

The train slowed as it approached the Lake Street station and Shane's time to exit. As the train stopped, he rose from his seat with a grimace, even his young legs rebelled against his standing on his feet most of the day at the Grill. His damaged knee probably played a role in that rebellion.

He stepped off the train onto the deck of the station and walked to the stairway that would take him down to Lake

Street and the short walk to the apartment building. With some perplexity he considered his serious contemplation on the short ride from downtown. He dismissed the brief venture into the vagaries of his life and pushed his hands into the pockets of his light jacket. He walked with a renewed sense of confidence that maybe he was at the threshold of a new phase in his life.

Turning at Chicago Avenue, Shane visualized the evening giving him time to relax his weary body and maybe meeting with Alisha somewhere. Though she received an invitation to move in with Max and him, she had not made up her mind. Her job at Target and her luck in finding space at the youth shelter entered into her consideration. Her presence in the apartment would create a bit more crowding than any of them desired. Nonetheless, Shane anticipated with eagerness her decision to join them.

In the distance loud voices attracted Shane's attention. He made a quick visual search for the source of the voices. The closer to the apartment building the louder the noise. Nearing the larger apartment building, the one containing Nick's elegant office, Shane saw two men standing at the front entrance apparently engaged in some dispute. As he approached on the sidewalk, he could clearly see one of the men was Nick. The other he did not immediately recognize. Whatever the basis for the dispute, Nick displayed a violence that surprised Shane.

With his left hand, Nick grabbed the other guy's shirt and pushed him solidly against the front door of the apartment building, yelling something about doing his job and keeping his mouth shut. Reluctant to get involved where he didn't belong, Shane only slowed as he walked by the larger apartment building. A closer look suggested to him that he had seen this other guy before. His size, his distinct hair style, and his sport coat and jeans all pointed to Mr. Meeker, who offered Max and him an invitation to a party replete with an assortment of mood altering drugs. Only a few days ago Max spotted Mr. Meeker entering the other apartment building. Quickly Shane remembered comments by others about the source of the money he deposited for Nick. The mystery of that source intensified.

Meeker struggled to free himself from Nick's grasp. The two of them stumbled, nearly falling off the slightly elevated front door step. Nick regained his balance. He stepped back away from Meeker. With a finger pointed in Meeker's face, Nick shouted, "You damn better know who the hell is the boss around here. One more word about your job and your ass is out of here. Do you understand?"

Meeker nodded his head, shoulders slumped, arms hanging loosely at his sides.

"Now get the fuck out of here. I don't want you hanging around the apartment. I'm not telling you again." Nick turned to notice Shane walking passed on the sidewalk. A sinister stare encouraged Shane to walk faster.

Entering his apartment, Shane hung his jacket on a hook just inside the door. A dark cloud followed him into the living room. Plopping down on the sofa, he reached for the TV remote. Late afternoon TV offered nothing of interest except a distraction from the intrusion of thoughts about Nick, about Meeker, his presence at the apartment complex, and about suspicions Max and Shane already discussed. In his hand Shane juggled the remote, flipping through the channels to discover what he already knew, nothing worth watching.

He could not escape the concerns created by this Meeker guy, his presence at the apartment and his possible connection to Nick. Suddenly Shane caught his breath, held it for a few seconds then exhaled. If his suspicions about Nick's involvement in illegal drugs proved correct, then his depositing the money each week made him a part of the whole scheme.

With furrowed brow, eyes squinting, Shane stared into empty space, thinking about Max, the apartment, and Nick's explosive behavior. Shane sank back in the sofa, his hand still clutching the TV remote. He dozed. The remote slipped from his fingers.

The rattle of the key in the door jerked Shane back to consciousness. He sat up straight, rubbed his eyes and yawned. He glanced at his watch. How long had he dozed off?

"Hey, buddy, what's up?" Max opened the fridge, reaching for a can of beer. "The action at the Grill never let up after you left. What a day."

"Yeah, I even dozed off here on the sofa. Must be getting old," Shane joked. He rose from the sofa and stepped to the island where Max stood sipping his beer. "You know, something interesting happened on my way here this afternoon." Shane grasped the edges of the island, pushed with his arms and arched his back.

Max set his beer can on the island and waited for the explanation. "Well, what was it?"

"On my walk from the station when I got close to the apartment, I heard these shouts. Someone sure as hell wasn't happy about something." Shane went on to describe in detail the scene he saw upon reaching the apartment. He included his identification of this Meeker guy, the physical violence displayed by Nick as well as the threatening language.

"What finally happened?" Max asked eager to find out how it all ended.

"I'm not sure. I didn't hang around long enough to see what finally happened," Shane admitted. "Nick saw me watching them. He didn't look happy about it either. I got my ass out of there."

Max clinched his lips. He took another swallow of beer. "I don't know, but I think something's going on here, something probably not so good." He moved to one of the chairs positioned next to the sofa. "It's kind of obvious, isn't it? This Meeker guy is up to his ass in the drug business, and here he is hanging around Nick, who treats him like shit."

Shane leaned his elbows on the island. Staring at Max, he agreed. "You're probably right. So much of it smells bad."

"And you could be part of it," Max noted.

"Yeah, I know. I've thought about that."

Shane took his turn in the fridge retrieving a can of soda. He snapped it open. "So, what the hell are we gonna do?"

Max stared at the beer can he held in his hand. "I sure as hell don't know." He paused. "I think we should just be watchful and not jump into something we can't handle. Maybe these drug monkeys will screw themselves."

Shane nodded his head. "I think you're right. What about my making those deposits?"

"You'd better not say anything to Nick about that right now. Don't ya think it would only make him suspicious of what we know about his little world?"

"Maybe we're all wrong about him?" Shane cautioned.

"Could be. Anything on TV this evening?" Max asked, trying to end for now the speculation about Nick and his private world.

Chapter 64

The incident between Nick and Chuck Meeker served as a topic of conversation the next day during the hours Shane and Max worked at the Grill. The short periods between demands of dirty tables and dishes, dragged them back to consider their suspicions of Nick's connection to the drug world. With only speculation to guide them, they wavered in what they should do about their suspicions.

During one of the few quiet moments following lunch, while Max and Shane assumed their places near the kitchen entrance, Max, mentioned to Shane, "I haven't seen anything of our strange landlord."

"I haven't either. He doesn't miss lunch very often. Maybe the thing last night . . . ah, I don't know. Maybe he doesn't want to see us." Shane shrugged his shoulders.

"Could be. I can't see the big Nick." Max looked to Shane for help. "What's his last name again?"

"Karpin."

"I can't see the big Nick Karpin hiding from anyone."

"Well, he hasn't showed up yet, and at this time I doubt he will." Shane bounced back against the wall, his eyes surveying the dining room in front of him. "Damn slow right now."

"Yeah. What time are you done today?" Max asked.

"Four o'clock. How about you?"

"Not until six." Max shoved his hands into the pockets of his apron.

They stood side by side in silence. Then Max poked Shane with the back of his hand and blurted out, "We should have a party to celebrate our new apartment."

Shane looked over at his friend and grinned. "Sure, we have so much room for a party."

"We wouldn't need much. I was thinking of inviting Derek Hayes over for a couple beers. We haven't seen him for quite a while."

Shane titled his head. "Good idea." He paused. "Could I invite Alisha?"

"No, no, absolutely not. This is a man thing." Max laughed out loud. "Of course, you can invite her. You don't have to ask my permission, that's for sure."

"Good. That sounds like a good idea. Maybe this Friday?"

"Sure, I'll go for that. I don't think we work, do we?" Max asked.

"No, I don't think so. I know I don't." Shane acknowledged. "You better check your schedule." Shane started to move to a recently vacated table. When he returned, Max confirmed he did not work on Friday evening.

"Good," Shane answered. "Why don't you give Derek a call? I'll talk with Alisha. She doesn't work this Friday night."

Staggered schedules found Shane off work a couple hours before Max. His shift completed, Shane reminded Max that he would take the light rail back to Lake Street. Max would follow at the completion of his shift.

The short train ride gave Shane another chance to relax. Last night's incident he could not erase from his mind. Thoughts of a possible small party on Friday did help in diverting his attention. The Lake Street station arrived to interrupt his reverie. He descended the station stairs to make his way back to the apartment.

He turned onto Chicago Avenue, alert to anything unusual happening in the neighborhood. He exhaled, relieved to see nobody, no unfamiliar cars, no people walking dogs. He approached the first apartment building, the site of last evening's incident between Nick and this Meeker guy. Shane quickened his pace even though he noticed nothing out of the ordinary.

Suddenly someone burst out of the front entrance to the larger apartment building, the one where Nick maintained his impressive domain. It was Nick. He hurried toward the sidewalk. Shane recognized him and slowed down, not particularly interested in talking with him at this time.

"Hey, hold on a bit." Nick shouted at Shane. Buttoning up his jacket, Nick took his time reaching the sidewalk where Shane waited. Without a hello or any kind of greeting, Nick announced, "If you know what's good for you, you will forget you ever saw what happened here last evening." He grasped the front of Shane's jacket. "Do I make myself clear?" Leaning so close his breath invaded Shane's sense of smell, Nick spit out his words in rage.

Alarmed by Nick's pugnacity, Shane winced; his stomach tightened. He tried to step back away from the intimidating sneer spread across Nick's face. He uttered a barely audible, "Yes."

Nick leaned even closer to Shane's face. "I didn't hear you." Spindle sprinkled Shane's face.

"Yes!" Shane declared.

Nick dropped his hold on Shane's jacket, turned and hurried back to the building's front door. Shane stood transfixed, nerves flickering from his neck down his back. He watched Nick vanish into the building. Shaken but in control, Shane adjusted his jacket then hurried to his apartment building.

When Max returned from work, Shane described his encounter with Nick.

"Obviously, this shit head has something to hide," Max commented. "Did he say anything about the deposits?"

"No, not a mention since his compliments some time ago."

"Screw it. He isn't worth all this attention we've given him." Max studied the TV tuned to an evening sitcom. He turned to Shane sitting on the other end of the sofa. "Say, I talked with Derek. He's available for Friday evening. I'll pick up a little beer if you'll get maybe a frozen pizza or something."

"Sounds good. Alisha's available too." Shane smiled. "I mean available to show up Friday evening."

"Come in, welcome." Max greeted Derek at the door of the apartment. "Good to see ya again. How's it goin?"

Derek unzipped his jacket. "Thanks. Good to be here." He shrugged. "Everything's about as good as can be expected."

Hanging Derek's jacket on the hallway hook, Max guided him into the apartment. "I heard you're going to classes at the Hennepin County Technical College. Is that true?"

"It sure is"

Max and Derek entered the living room where Shane rose from the sofa to shake Derek's hand.

"Derek's attending the Hennepin County Technical College," Max announced.

"Really? That's great. What are you taking?" Shane asked.

"Right now courses dealing with computer programming." He ran his hands through his hair. "That may change, but so far it goes well."

Shane and Max exchanged glances of approval, expressing the same to Derek.

Alisha's arrival, for a moment, diverted attention away from Derek. Shane met her at the apartment door to welcome her and to admire her light blue winter jacket accented by a fluffy scarf loosely tied around her neck. Her jacket and scarf secured on another hallway hook, Shane paused to admire Alisha's firm fitting jeans and light gray sweater over a white turtle neck. As usual her hair framed a face which Shane found irresistible. He leaned to give her a brief kiss on a cold cheek.

Their guests seated comfortably in the crowded living room, Shane and Max made certain they each had a beverage and a chance at snacks. Shane introduced Alisha to Derek, who at an earlier gathering had met her but expressed his delight having the chance to meet her again. Shane and Alisha sat on the sofa while

Max hovered around the island. Derek slumped in one of the chairs next to the sofa.

"Derek has started back to school," Shane addressed Alisha.

Her response echoed that of both Shane and Max. "That's great."

Derek repeated the explanation of the computer program he was enrolled in.

"I think I know the answer to this, but do you need a high school diploma to enroll at a technical college?" Shane sat forward on the sofa.

"Yes, I think you do." Derek answered.

"I'm not sure I'm going to jump into a technical college, but what if ya don't have a diploma? Some people don't, like me." Shane rested his elbows on his knees.

"I think you can get a GED which a technical school or maybe even a four year college will accept." Derek suggested.

For only a moment Shane thought about what Derek said. "I think I've heard of that. Exactly what does GED stand for?"

Derek scratched his cheek. "I think it's something like General Educational Development. I'm not sure. Not long ago, I saw a poster about it in the registration office. If I remember right, that's what it stands for."

Shane wrinkled his brow, looked away from Derek, rubbed his hands against his knees, then abruptly changed the subject, "Alisha has a job," he interjected, "at the downtown Target store."

"That's good news." Derek nodded his head.

Max moved around the island resting his elbows on the counter top. "By the way, Shane tells me your mother has some health problems."

Alisha bit her lip then explained. "Yes, she has breast cancer."

"I'm so sorry to hear that," Derek looked at Alisha seated near him on the sofa. "How's she getting along?"

"So far, I guess, okay. I haven't talked to her in a few days. The last time I did she described her chemo."

"Do you see her often?" Derek asked.

Alisha closed her eyes and lowered her head. Looking up, she confessed, "No I don't. I haven't lived at home for a long time. But I do keep in touch."

Max asked if anyone needed more to drink or more snacks.

"I think we're doing fine," Shane confirmed. "You really take your job as host seriously." He smiled.

The conversation continued addressing a range of subjects including the incident with Nick a few days before. They talked about the apartment deal that impressed Derek, who asked Shane, "Are you still making those deposits?"

Shane nodded his head. "Yes, I am, but don't know how much longer. This mess with Nick kind of complicates things." He explained the intimidating clash of a couple days ago. "We just don't know exactly what to do. We suspect he's involved in something less than honest. We just don't have much evidence of what it is. Besides what would we do if we did?"

"If it's what you and Max suspect, where does that put you for making the deposits?"

"Yeah, a good question." Shane reached for his beer, his first in days, with obviously no answer to the question.

"Anybody want a little pizza?" Two sharp pops followed Max's question. His eyes opened wide, searching in the faces of others in the room for an explanation of what he heard. "What the hell was that? Did you guys hear it? It sounded like gun shots."

Three more sharp reports obviously came from outside the apartment building. Max dashed out the door followed by Shane and their two guests. They bounded down the stairway to the front door. Derek had gained the lead and pushed the door open. The others immediately followed. What they saw stunned them. A man stood in the middle of the sidewalk aiming a hand gun at the front of the large apartment building. Lying on the ground only a few feet in front of him, a man struggled to get up. Two more shots knocked him to the ground.

Sensing the danger standing at the entrance to their apartment building, Max urged all of them to get back inside. Shane rushed for the door, holding it open for the others. The last in line to reenter the building, Derek made one step when another shot rang out striking him in the upper back. He cried out, "Ahhh, dammit." Then he slumped to his knees.

It took a moment before the others realized what had happened. When they did, Max shouted, "Call 911!"

Alisha rushed into the building, grabbing her phone.

Max then eased his way out the door to tend to Derek as best he could. As he did, the gunman dashed to his car parked at the curb, jumped in and tore away, smoke billowing from screeching tires. Despite the confusion of the moment, Max thought he recognized something familiar about the assailant, his hair.

Max and Shane reached for Derek, quickly but gently pulling him into the building and away from the door. Blood soaked his shirt, his face already pale.

"They're coming," Alisha declared.

"Somebody run up and get a jacket or blanket. We need to keep him warm." Max directed.

Awake but struggling to breath, Derek attempted to sit up. Shane forced him to stay down. A bloody foam seeped from his mouth. The bullet likely had penetrated a lung. He needed help fast. Alisha returned with a jacket which Max draped over Derek. In the distance sirens screamed, bringing closer the police as well as the ambulance and emergency medical technicians.

Shane ventured outside to offer directions to the police and emergency medical help. He noticed people gathered around someone lying on the sideway near the entrance to the larger apartment building. He stepped close enough to see the man lying on the sidewalk was Nick Karpin.

Four squad cars and two ambulances screamed to a halt on Chicago Avenue in front of Nick's apartment buildings, their strobe lights flickering through the branches of naked trees and reflecting off apartment building windows. Police and paramedics emerged from their respective vehicles; three officers stood guard near the street.

Shane approached one of the officers in his attempt to get help for Derek. The officer cautioned him to stand back while they made sure to secure the area against any more gun fire. Minutes passed before two paramedics made their way to Derek barely conscious on the entry floor. Two others headed to Nick sprawled on the sidewalk of the adjacent apartment building.

Only minutes after the paramedics reached the two victims, they were briefly examined then transferred to separate ambulances headed for the Hennepin County Medical Center, lights flashing, sirens blaring. For the next hour police questioned Shane and Max regarding Derek as well as those who witnessed the bloody assault on Nick.

Close to midnight, Shane, Max and Alisha sat in the apartment attempting to reconstruct the drastic, dramatic events of the evening, one they would not soon forget.

Chapter 65

Four months had elapsed since the traumatic shooting at the Chicago Avenue apartment buildings. The passage of those four months produced significant changes in the life of Shane, his family, his friends, and his acquaintances. Never will he forget the violence, the blood, the sounds of the shots echoing through the neighborhood on that crisp, winter evening.

Shot in the back, Derek Haynes survived his wounds, left with a damaged lung which doctors speculated would require careful observation. Released from the hospital after nearly two weeks of treatment, Derek returned to classes at the Hennepin County Technical college where he specialized in computer programming. Derek continued to live at home with his parents.

Nick Karpin suffered a debilitating head wound besides a gun shot wound in his right shoulder. His head injury left him with permanent brain damage. Sequestered in a special medical treatment facility, he was indicted for trafficking and distribution of controlled substances. The question of his mental capacity delayed the start of his trial. Regardless of conclusions of the trial, Nick Karpin would never again visit the Eighth Street Grill for lunch or exercise rigid, authoritarian control over a network of servile drug pushers. With both parents deceased and no evidence of other relatives, all Nick's assets, especially his apartment buildings, fell under the control of the court.

Chuck Meeker surrendered only days after the shooting. Charged with attempted murder and assault with a deadly weapon, he cooperated with authorities enabling them eventually to arrest nine members of Nick Karpin's intricate and highly secret drug network. Meeker remained in custody awaiting trail on his charges.

Shane confessed to his role in depositing money collected by the Karpin drug network. No prior association with drugs and no previous violations of any kind, Shane faced two years' probation combined with fifty hours of community service.

Max still retained the apartment along with Shane and Alisha. He recently received a promotion to assistant manager of the Eighth Street Grill. He considered enrolling in one of the community colleges around the Twin Cities to seek a degree in business. That plan remained undecided.

Danni and Grayson enjoyed impressive success in their separate careers, Danni in biological research and Grayson in computer sales. They anticipated their wedding, planned for several months, and now to take place in a few weeks at the Twin Pine's Lutheran Church where both Danni and Shane were baptized and confirmed, and where Martin and Iris Stenlund enjoyed years of faithful membership.

Alisha met Danni for the first time following the shooting at the apartment complex. Danni expressed her long delayed gratitude for Alisha's role in, perhaps, saving Shane's life the night of the beating he took in the bank parking lot. Something served to weld the two. Shane noticed how easily they communicated despite their different backgrounds. He suspected Alisha admired Danni's success in her profession as well as her kind, gracious manner. Danni, he suspected, admired the tenacity and determination that enabled Alisha to rise above the domestic problems which caused her to leave home at such a young age. Whatever the reason for their attachment, they found friendship without difficulty.

The last four months saw a strengthening of Shane and Alisha's relationship. Shortly after the tragic events the night of the shooting, she moved in with Max and Shane. Her mother's fight against breast cancer proved, at least temporarily, successful. Her last test revealed no evidence of cancer. Alisha still refused to meet with her dad. With reluctance, she and Shane addressed that issue without reaching any solution. For the next few months she would continue working at the downtown Target store.

Shane squinted into the bright spring sunshine, his hands gripping the cushioned steering wheel of the Green Monster. On two different weekends during the spring, Shane worked with his dad preparing fields for spring planting. This marked the first time in more than two years he had returned to his home on the farm. Those two weekends found Shane and his father arguing only about the faltering start to the Twins' baseball season.

On this weekend, Shane asked for time off from the Eighth Street Grill to further assist his dad in spring seeding. How quickly he recaptured his skill in driving the Green Monster surprised him. He settled back in the spacious driver's seat. He looked around to check on the huge cultivator the Green Monster pulled, churning the rich, black Red River Valley soil. Turning back, he gazed into the sparkling blue sky that blended with the soil at the horizon.

For a moment Shane closed his eyes to see galloping across the field a small pony. A young boy, hair blowing in the breeze, grasped the pony's neck. His eyes open again, a smile spread his lips as in his gaze he now saw his future, a much more appealing future. Leaving home had helped define that future as did a beautiful girl whose quick thinking may have saved his life.

Printed in the United States
By Bookmasters